# WHITE SNAKE

## LEON WHITESON

**MOSAIC PRESS**
Oakville-New York-London

CANADIAN CATALOGUING IN PUBLICATION DATA

Whiteson, Leon, 1930-
  White snake

Originally published: Toronto : General Publishing,
1982.
ISBN 0-88962-402-X

I.Title.

PS8595.H57W55 1988      C813'.54      C88-094815-9
PR9199.3.W55W55 1988



Published by MOSAIC PRESS, P.O. Box 1032, Oakville, Ontario, L6J 5E9, Canada. Offices and warehouse at 1252 Speers Road, Units# 1&2, Oakville, Ontario, L6L 5N9, Canada.

Mosaic Press acknowledges the assistance of the Canada Council and the Ontario Arts Council in support of its publishing programme.



ISBN 0-88962-402-X   PAPER

MOSAIC PRESS:
In Canada:
        MOSAIC PRESS, 1252 Speers Road, Units# 1&2, Oakville, Ontario L6J 5N9, Canada.  P.O. Box 1032, Oakville, Ontario L6J 5E9

In the United States:
        Riverrun Press Inc., 1170 Broadway, Suite 807, New York, N.Y., 10001, U.S.A., distributed by Kampmann & Co., 9 East 40th Street, New York, N.Y., 10016

In the U.K.:
        John Calder (Publishers) Ltd., 18 Brewer Street, London, W1R 4A5, England.

# CONTENTS

# 1

# EVEN STONES HAVE EARS

*White Snake is the spirit of Inkulunkulu, First Ancestor of the Ndebele people. The Creator gave the Earth to him in the beginning, before male and female were split in two. It was said that this Bleached Serpent would return at the death of the last king in Matabeleland, to restore the Ndebele race to the realm of pure spirit.*

*But if White Snake appeared before its true time, it would bring disaster. It would destroy the kingdom and the people. For many Ndebele this disastrous apparition of the Pale Serpent occurred when the British arrived at the court of Lobengula, their last king, in the late nineteenth century.*

*Lobengula lived to see his regiments destroyed. Matabeleland was stolen by the whites. The old king died in disgrace and despair, despised by his own people. The last Ndebele monarch was ground to dust by this untimely apparition of White Snake.*

''Nyogamhlope,'' Nkabi jeered.

The black pastor twisted in the front seat of the speeding taxi to cackle in my face. The clerical collar sliced his jowls. His big body bounced with derision so that the gilt image of Christ on his lapel seemed to dance on the Cross.

"You, Mr. Kahn," he crowed. "You." He jabbed a chunky finger at me. "White Snake."

He sobered abruptly. Elijah Nkabi recalled his dignity as a minister of the American Methodist Church, and as a district secretary of that "banned subversive organization," the Zimbabwe African People's Union.

"Your pale face is your disguise, Mr. Kahn," he muttered. "Remember that, if the security forces stop us. No Rhodesian policeman would ever believe you were a terrorist — or trying to become one!

"And remember," he ran on before I could respond, "you have hired this car to visit the tomb of Cecil John Rhodes, the Founder of Rhodesia, in the Matopos Hills. And I am a reverend father taking a lift back to his home mission."

"I'll remember, father."

Nkabi turned his broad back on me. I watched the bush fly past as the old yellow taxi scooted up the dusty side road. The driver was a midget under his wide check cap. In the rearview mirror his anxious eyes squinted for pursuit, but the bush was empty, stunned into vacancy by the midday sun.

Bulawayo was twenty miles behind us in the flat Matabeleland scrub; a sleepy suburban sprawl on that hot spring morning. Bulawayo, the town where I was born, means "Place of Slaughter" in Ndebele. In September 1973, the second year of the African nationalist guerrilla war against the white Rhodesian government, the killing went on, though distantly, out in the lowland bush.

"And remember, Mr. Kahn," the parson's voice rumbled, "when you meet The Leader, do not use his name. Even stones have ears."

The dirt road faded into a rutted track snaking around boulders piled like tombstones. In the distance a naked granite slope tilted to the sky. Nkabi's skull was a black stone balanced on a starched white collar.

"Mr. Kahn," he accused, "you are a famous architect?"

"Was," I said curtly.

His solemn gaze locked mine. "You are a Christian?"

"A Jew."

Nkabi beamed. "Excellent!"

"What's so damn excellent about it?"

"A Hebrew funded my education. He sent me to the Methodist U. in Wisconsin. I owe a very great debt to that generous white man."

"Honorary white man," I amended. "A Jew."

Nkabi scowled. "You are an awkward sort of person."

"Yes."

"Yet you wish to aid us in our struggle for the liberation of Zimbabwe? Why?"

"I was born here."

"But you've been absent for many years, I believe?"

"Twenty-two."

"Then why — "

"Are we far from the rendezvous?" I cut in.

"I truly believe," Nkabi began in a preachy tone, "that we can make a great Zimbabwe here, when we win our freedom from Mr. Smith and his kind. We must! If not, all the killing that has happened and will happen has no purpose."

"Killing is killing."

His head jerked. "Cynic!"

"Are we far from the rendezvous?"

The minister turned his back on me again. His cropped head was rigid with offense. I had not meant to antagonize him. Nkabi was clearly a most righteous man, of a rather antique variety. The Nonconformists had poured his mind into a late Victorian moral mould that was almost quaint in its simplicity. This stiff-necked puritanism was a colonial legacy to many Africans of Nkabi's generation.

"Look, reverend," I said. "I am a Rhodesian and a Jew, and a would-be terrorist, as you say. You are an Ndebele and a Christian, and a would-be Zimbabwean. May we not respect one another's ambitions?"

He did not reply. The taxi seemed lost among slopes and boulders. Three decades before, as a Boy Scout, I'd often camped in the Matopos. From this old memory I reckoned we were in the Tribal Trust Lands, the African reserve that bordered the plateau where Rhodes was buried. The Founder's Methodist bones were set in a slot in the granite on a hilltop sacred to Mlimu, the Ndebele Creator.

Nkabi was peering through the dusty windscreen in search of our meeting place with The Leader. "Here!" he barked suddenly. The car jolted to a halt under an acacia tree vivid with crows. The birds exploded from the bare branches in a burst of inkblots.

We all got out. My legs were locked with tension and I tried to shake them loose. Excitement prickled my nape.

The taxi was filmed in dust. A collison had left an old dent, but in the bone-dry air the cracks were unrusted. All four hubcaps were lost. The midget driver found a cloth and tenderly dusted off the yellow Vauxhall's narrow nose.

"Come," Nkabi snapped.

We climbed a narrow track. Nkabi trudged implacably up the stone slope. I tried to keep close behind that broad back, but my tennis shoes slipped on the smooth rock. The sun scalded my scalp and my open cotton shirt was a wet rag. Just as I was about to melt into my socks, the pastor stopped. He gestured at me to wait, then vanished round a corner.

My temples throbbed with heat. To make a cap, I tied four knots in my hankie. Granite cliffs shut me in, under an arch of hot white heaven. It was an amphitheatre fit for gods, or demons.

When I sat down the dust about my shoes came alive. Ants, spiders, beetles, crickets and centipedes animated the dirt. My smell drew them, the odours of my perspiration, that rose up in my own nose earthy as baked bread. Every insect for yards around seemed eager to sniff me out.

A scorpion touched its foreclaw to my toe. The compact body was a squash of amber beads in the dust. Scorpions are night hunters, but this one was nosy. I shifted my shoe a fraction; the arachnid arched its stinger. I jerked my foot; the scorpion backed off under a stone.

I'd collected insects when I was young. My sleeping porch stank with the smell of formaldehyde embalming countless specimens in bottles. *"Goggas,"* my mother had called them, in the Afrikaans of her native Orange Free State. "Bloody *goggas*!" Every variety of carapace and claw had floated round my iron cot. My boyhood dreams had been charged with their menace. It had been my way of trying to domesticate this weird Africa in which I — a grandchild of Ukranian Jews — had chanced to be born.

But Africa is not gentled all that easily.

"Come!"

Nkabi commanded me from the neck of the gorge. I ran towards him. The reverend looked me up and down. I was dusty, damp and smelly. His glare rested on my head. "Remove that silly cap," he ordered. I obeyed. Nkabi turned away. I followed. In a moment I was in the presence of The Leader.

Josiah Nkunzi, President of the Zimbabwe African People's Union (ZAPU), was a huge man. *Nkunzi* means *a bull* — and that he was.

The President's bulk was bound by a dark Whitehall pinstripe complete with waistcoat, starched collar and regimental tie. The 300-pound body perched on a shooting stick in the shade of a flame tree in full flower. Carmine blossoms crowned Nkunzi's massive skull. Round his blunt neck hung a chunky golden crucifix.

Two goons were at his back, rooks in black leather, ravens haughty behind silvered shades. Snub-nosed pistols were welded to their fists. Beyond was the snout of a dark Mercedes saloon, chrome grinning in the sun.

Nkabi halted me several paces short of the old nationalist. "This is Paul Kahn, sir," he said, keeping tight grip of my wrist.

The Leader looked me over. Iron-grey bristle capped his huge face. His eyes were opaque, black and rubbery as a pair of squash balls. I fidgeted in the dust, feeling grubby and gauche. Sweat trickled down the backs of my knees.

As I waited to be acknowledged, there flashed into my head the description Rhodes's agent Rudd had given of old King Lobengula: "A very fine man, only very fat, but with a beautiful skin, and well proportioned. He has a curious face; he is partly worried, partly good-natured, and partly cruel. He has a very pleasant smile."

"Mr. Kahn." Nkunzi's teeth flashed charmingly. "Welcome." He flicked a finger; gold rings glittered. One of his guards snapped open a camp stool and set it at his feet. Nkunzi gestured at me to sit.

Seated, my gaze was on a level with The Leader's navel. His great globe of a stomach stretched the pinstripe. The white lines on his worsted thighs were arrows at my heart.

The guards withdrew. Nkabi stayed close, watchful as a nanny.

"Paul Kahn." The voice was a rockfall. "What may I do for you?"

"Sir." I wobbled on my tiny platform. "The question is, what may I do for you?" In my parched throat, my words were croaks.

A silence. The big man was so close I sensed the heat of his body in the burning air. It was an oven of energy.

"Why?"

One word, but it was dense with questioning. I considered my reply very carefully.

"I was born here. In Bulawayo. Grew up here. At sixteen I fled." I paused, to calm my breath. "I left because I couldn't stand it, for very personal reasons. It frightened me. Africa scared me stiff."

Nkunzi grunted. I looked up at his face. It was patient.

"I went to England, to study architecture. I never wanted to see Rhodesia again, not ever. I stayed away for twenty-two years. Now I'm back."

"Why?"

Again that word. I took time to light a cigarette, gesturing for his consent, which was gracefully granted.

The bush was locked in midday silence. Even the crickets were stunned. The air around us was a block of white heat.

My eyes were on Nkunzi's navel. He heard me speak with the globe of his belly. My voice bounded back at me, as from a drumskin.

"Full circle," I said. "Back to square one."

"Ah." The grunt came from his gut.

I had a flash of irritation. "What do my motives matter? So long as you find me useful?"

"Motives always matter. So much so that, if I'm not satisfied here, a body will be found in the bush."

"Oh."

"Officially, I am under restriction. I am not supposed to move from my farm ten miles from here, nor am I permitted to see anyone not vetted by the Special Branch. So if I don't trust you ... "

I bowed my head and kept mute. At my back Nkabi cleared his throat warningly.

"I need to understand you, Mr. Kahn," Nkunzi said.

"You manoeuvred this interview. Insisted upon it. Here it is. There's no turning back."

"I've no intention of turning back."

"Well, then, speak to me. I'm all ears."

"Well, I am a white man. Jews are honorary whites in Africa. The white man owes the black a debt of misery. I'd like to pay some of it off."

"Commendable."

"That's part of it." I smiled, acknowledging his irony. "When I was a toddler I had my own picanin, like all small baases here. His name was Sixpence. He followed me everywhere, washed my face, picked up my dirty socks, saw me safely across the street, comforted me when I fell over. I had a favourite game with Sixpence. He had to lie down on his back in the dust and open his mouth wide. The little white master pulled up the leg of his khaki shorts and pissed in the picanin's mouth."

Nkunzi sighed. "A very Rhodesian story. What's the other part? The part that really matters."

"I've been all over. Lived and worked in many places: France, Spain, Greece, America, Cuba, Venezuela, and India. I was successful, even a little famous. It was fun. But it was — complicated. Gradually, in my life and my profession, I began to feel the need for something very simple. A growing need, a lust, for that one simple, unambiguous act. It came to me: Rhodesia is the place. Things are black and white here. So here I am."

My speech ended lamely. The words sounded hollow in my own ears. Phony. At that moment I fully expected to end up a "body in the bush."

In that same report to Rhodes, his agent wrote that King Lobengula was "sharp as a needle at his own style of palaver." If he caught the white man in a contradiction, he'd rap out: "You have two words. You lie!" Nkunzi had not cut me down, yet. I rushed on.

"My grandfather caught the wrong boat. In his village in the Ukraine, he bought tickets for Manhattan. At Liverpool he and his family were waved up the wrong gangplank. Three weeks later they landed in Cape Town. He didn't know it wasn't America. Sure, there was no Statue of Liberty in Table Bay, but the place was jammed with *schwartzes* he took for the Negroes of the New World.

"Grandpa Kahn was an international failure. He failed to make a living in the Ukraine. He failed in Vienna. Failed in Prague. Failed in London. Failed in Cape Town. He had a dairy there, till one of his two cows, irritated by his clumsy milking, hooked him in the groin. Rhodesia was his very last throw. So he forded the Limpopo with a mule cart laden with pots, pans and kids, in 1897. He survived the river's crocodiles and reached Bulawayo. He sold his pots and pans. There was a desperate need for kitchenware in the new tent-town in the bush. Even he could prosper. Best of all, he was accorded status as an Honorary White Man. 'Boo-la-vayer' was Paradise for a failed Ukrainian Jew. That he'd ended up in the middle of Africa was a fact he never could quite concede. The gentiles must've hidden the Statue of Liberty some place for diabolical goyish reasons of their own."

Nkunzi's belly surged with silent laughter. "What a tale! My grandfather was a Karanga Chief."

"Yes?"

"A splendid man, bigger even than me. He wore skirts of *rijobo* skin and carried his manhood in a white *ilala* sheath. Around his neck was an antelope horn stuffed with *muti* against the evil eye. His many wives never addressed him but on their knees. Men crouched on their haunches in his presence. He was wise. No judgement of his ever antagonized the *midzimu*, our ancestral ghosts. He was a rock. Yet he lived to see the red-coated soldiers cross the river and claim his best grazing land. The shame of it killed him."

I nodded in sympathy at his passion and the golden crucifix caught my eye.

"Yet now you are a Christian? A disciple of Jesus, the whitest snake of all?"

"Yes," he agreed. "I am a Christian by faith and a democrat by conviction."

"How very European," I murmured.

Nkunzi nodded. "I read you, sir. The true question is, even when we rid ourselves of the European's rule, how will we cleanse our souls of his nihilism? His barren whiteness?"

Nkabi spoke up, breaching his silence hoarsely. "We will eat the nut and chuck away the husk!"

"Not so simple, Elijah," Nkunzi said. "Ask our friend here."

"But he is white!" Nkabi cried. "The colour of death!"

Nkunzi winked at me. "Elijah has a pure heart. You and I, we must struggle for simplicity, eh?" He shrugged. "Elijah fought tooth and nail that I shouldn't meet with you, Mr. Kahn. 'This one is a snake!' he said. 'Snakes can be turned,' I told him. Am I right?"

"I'm already turned," I said, and smiled.

"So it seems," The Leader murmured. "So it would seem."

Another silence. Behind Nkunzi's bulk I could see the goons leaning against the snout of the Mercedes, smoking. Their pistols were alert.

"I like your splendid motor," I said.

Nkunzi's eyes lit up like a boy's. "Mercedes 450SE. Computerized fuel injection. Power steering. Air conditioned. A gift from the Prime Minister of Sweden!"

"Bravo Olof Palme!" I laughed.

"So," he said. "What do you offer us, Mr. Kahn?"

"Sabotage."

"Pardon?"

"My white skin is my disguise. It can get me places no black would ever get within a mile of. Urban sabotage, in the city, where the white man lives. Something your guerrillas have never managed to pull off."

"True."

I leant forward. "Out there, on the border, in the bush, you can only attack a few isolated farmers. But most Europeans — ninety per cent — live in the towns: Salisbury, Bulawayo, Umtali, Gwelo. Bring the fight home to them, hard."

"Yes!"

"My cousin is chief electronics engineer at the Post Office Telecommunications Centre in Bulawayo. He's very keen to show off his toys. Been begging me to visit there for weeks. A lump of plastic explosive in that place would destroy all military and civilian coordination in the whole of Matabeleland. More than that, it would kick the European where it hurts. Where he lives."

"Excellent!" Nkunzi exclaimed. "You hear, Elijah? This white snake is sharp!"

Nkabi released a grudging grunt. The Leader dropped his large palm upon my shoulder. "You're a real pro, Paul Kahn," he murmured. "I like that." He squeezed my bones. "I, too, am a professional. I had you thoroughly checked out. So far as I can verify, you're no police spy. Still, you could be a *provocateur*. The Special Branch is sly. There's no certain way of knowing who you really are, in your heart. But this is the kind of messy war where a man must risk his instinct. My instinct tells me you are straight."

"Why so?" I asked, betrayed by curiosity.

Nkunzi's smile sagged. "You're a displaced person."

"Like you?" I shot back.

He shrugged. From his jacket pocket he pulled a folded copy of the local newspaper, the *Chronicle*. He thrust the front page under my nose. "This is our country today. Look!"

There were two photos, side by side. One was a snapshot of the winner of the "National Flame Lily Contest" — a juicy blonde in a bikini, bosom drowned in blossoms. Beside it was a shot of an African whose lips, nose and eyelids had been ripped off. The caption under this read: "African Constable Victim of Terrs".

*"Terrs!"* Nkunzi snorted. "Terrorists!" He shook the paper in my face. "How can the whites live with this schizophrenia? How can they contemplate such a front page and not think?"

"You don't know your masters too well," I said drily. "They have swimming pools on their minds, not terror."

He glared at me. All at once I was the enemy. A growl rumbled in his gut. He muttered, softly at first, "Hell and damnation."

His outrage swelled. "Hell," he grumbled. "Hell!" Then all his ferocity burst forth, blasting through bafflement. "Hell! Hell! Hell!"

The bellow buffeted me on my seat. Nkunzi stood abruptly. The shooting stick dropped to the dust. His face was stone. He stared down at my white face with harsh loathing. *"Hamba, wena,"* he grunted. "Go!" He turned his back on me as the guards ran up to retrieve his stick and escort The Leader to the Mercedes.

"Power to the *Chimurenga!*" Nkabi shouted. He jerked me from the stool. *"Hamba,"* he snapped. As he pulled me away I heard the door of the dark saloon slam like a fist on flesh.

**2**

# THE MODERN MUD HUT

Nkabi's taxi dropped me at the edge of the White Zone, in the gap between Bulawayo's European core and the surrounding African townships. The pastor had not said a word to me on the long drive back from the Matopos. His eyes swept across me as I got out, as if I were blank space. The yellow Vauxhall scurried off, anxious to lose me.

Another taxi took me to Main Street, at the intersection with Eighth Avenue. I paid the driver off under the statue of Cecil Rhodes. The Founder's bronze body gestured north, up the length of Africa. The inscription on the granite base declared: "Your hinterland lies there."

The Pioneers had made the streets of Bulawayo wide enough to turn an ox wagon and full team. The tarmac glittered in the noon haze. A few cars rolled by, shiny as beetles in the sun. White faces and black drifted along the pavement.

Crossing Main Street, I was almost run down by a gaggle of white schoolboys on bikes. Blue blazers unbuttoned, bare knees pumping under khaki shorts, they tossed back bright blond heads and shouted with glee at my fright.

Down the road from The Founder, in a redbrick Victorian colonial building, an old schoolfriend of mine, Shaun Connaughton, ran an architect's office. The main doors were etched with the Rhodesian coat of arms: a soapstone bird's head mounted on a shield sporting a pickaxe flanked by rampant horned kudu.

Cool air fanned my face as I entered. After the sun-struck street the dark lobby was ice on my eyes. A mahogany staircase led to the top floor where Shaun had his drawing office.

"Paul!" Shaun cried, soon as he saw me. "My favourite genius!" He laughed in my face, relishing the boyhood jibe. But his bright green eyes were solemn. My "genius" was no joke to Shaun.

We went through the busy drawing office to his private cubicle. His diploma was on the wall, from the Architectural Association in London, like mine. We had gone together to England to study; then he had returned to take over his father's practice.

Shaun sat at his desk and plunked his grubby tennis shoes on the papers there. He was kitted up in camouflage battledress with a major's crown on each shoulder. A service revolver in a webbing holster sagged on his hip.

"Been on a tour of duty up the Sharp End," he said, meaning the war zone on Rhodesia's northeastern frontier. "Tracking terrs. Just got back this morning. Bloody bind. Interrupts work, but has to be done."

"How's it going up there?"

Shaun's fair Irish face darkened. "A bloody massacre. Kids, that's all the terrorists are. Raw lads from the tribal lands with Russian rifles. Blow their own brains out, often as not."

"Wars are always fought by children."

"But these are —" he broke off, voice clogged with baffled shame — "kids."

"So it's all under control, then?"

"Militarily, yes, we dominate. But they keep on coming. No shortage of cannon fodder, it seems." He dropped his feet abruptly. "These boys are pawns for fat politicoes like Josiah Nkunzi. Pitiful. I weep for them."

There were real tears smudging his eyes. "Weep?" I queried.

"Weep!" He slammed his fist down on the desk edge. "For their incompetence, their foolishness, their hopeless dedication! And for their blind idealism, that I admire and loathe." He grinned at me with sudden impishness. "Not so odd for a good Catholic like myself to be ambivalent about such dedication, is it?"

"Not odd. Just confused?"

Shaun grunted. His gingery coils were darkened dull red by the sun. He rubbed his bristled cheeks wearily.

"It's a new struggle now, this *Chimurenga,* as they call it. We crushed the first assault. This second wave is an endless tide of martyrs. Yes, martyrs. Misplaced. Fervour belongs in the Mass, not the masses."

"Neat phrase."

He scowled at my dryness. "These young idealists will make a rich compost for a ruthless fascism some day. Hell, I don't much favour Ian Smith and his gang, you know. 'The Simple Farmer,' as the twit calls himself, is a menace. I'd vote for black rule tomorrow, if we could find an African of stature who could forgive us for being white."

"That is some forgiveness."

"True. True." He shrugged. "Still, I do my duty."

I indicated the patch of medal ribbons over his tunic breast pocket. "And do it thoroughly, it seems."

Shaun shrugged. "Bronze Cross. For rescuing an African NCO from an ambush, in a contact near Mount Darwin. Listen, you want to be some help?"

I was startled. "Help?"

"I'm planning adviser at Tshabalala, the new African township on the Khami Road. I'm on my way there now. Want to come along for the ride? We could use a genius."

I bowed. "Always glad to be of service, major."

Shaun gripped my arm. "That's what I love about you, Paul," he said.

In the gutter outside Shaun's office was an African woman suckling her baby. The infant was tied to her back, and she had swung one drooping black breast under her armpit into its greedy, fly-covered mouth. As the baby suckled, the mother smoked a cigarette made of tobacco rolled in a tube of newspaper and idly dug at the corns on her horny feet with a nail.

"Ay, *umfaaz*," Shaun chided her gently. "Don't feed your baby in the street," he told her, in Ndebele. "The police will bother you. Go inside this building. Tell them the baas said it's okay. Please?"

The woman rose obediently, humping the infant up on her spine. A passing white matron in a floral frock flashed the suckling mother a salmon-pink scowl. "Bloody *munts!* No decency!" The African woman scuttled off the sidewalk and loped away down the street.

Shaun's eyes blazed green fire, but he clamped his jaw shut and led me to his Citroen.

We drove west along the Khami Road for a few miles. South Africa, the Fortress of Apartheid, was to the left of us, an hour or so away. Ahead was Botswana, now an independent desert kingdom. We were on the southern edge of the four-thousand-foot high Rhodesian spine. From this relatively temperate ridge, on which most of the Europeans had settled, the country dropped away east and west into sweltering lowland bush.

"Why did you come back?" Shaun asked suddenly. "Even when we were students in London, twenty years ago, you said you hated Africa."

"Oh, I'm a great hater."

"And now you're famous. An architect and planner of international reputation. Hell, you've done large projects in India, Venezuela, Cuba — you name it. One entire issue of *International Planning* was devoted to your work. Why come back?"

"I'm a Rhodesian."

"Bullshit." But he smiled, and laid a bony hand on my knee. "You know, I've had a secret instinct about you, ever since school days. I knew one day you'd want to convert."

I burst out laughing. "Me? Become a Papist?!"

"If any man I've ever known needs grace, it is you, Paul."

"You make me blush."

"Blush away. But one thing's plain to see. Whatever's happened to you these past twenty years has ripened you for redemption."

"But I'm a Jew, damnit."

"Look, Judaism is a superb creed, but such hard work! It leaves a man to pull himself up out of sin by his own honour. Catholics are gentler. We know we need grace." He squinted round at me. "What do you believe in, Paul, here and now?"

"Nothing but survival. The ultimate virtue."

"Survival of what?"

"Simplicity."

"I don't get it."

"Is this the time and place for metaphysics, on the Khami Road?"

"Sure. Why not? Saint Paul's Damascus Road was not even paved. What 'simplicity'?"

"The simplicity of one unambiguous act."

"No such thing."

"Perhaps not. But I'm still looking."

"You always were a searcher. Remember those hot afternoon chats we used to have in your sleeping porch, with all those smelly insects in bottles all around? Because of you, theology for me will always stink of formaldehyde."

"Its natural stench."

"Lord, we were innocent, then. Pig ignorant. A couple of kids in khaki shorts deciding the nature of existence. Yet there never was another soul who grasped the contradictions more lucidly than you. Not in my life, anyway."

"Innocent. Ignorant. Is there a difference?"

"You know there is," he said, rather shocked.

"I've forgotten. Remind me."

"Ignorance is not-knowing. Innocence is un-knowing."

"Well, let's say I know and I know. And know nothing. Okay?"

"No. Not okay. Your problem is, you know too much. It has muddied you. You've taken one bite too many at the 'big apple'. You should have stayed here, where things are black and white. Africa is always black and white."

"Soon it may be all black and black."

"Never. Oh, Africans may rule the continent, from the Cape to Cairo, but this landscape" — he gestured at the passing bush running to the far, flat horizon — "will always be crystal in its contrasts. That's why I love it. Why I'd die for it."

"And kill for it?"

"Yes. If necessary. To preserve it from ideology." He shrugged. "There's always been blood spilled in the 'Place of Slaughter'. Ndebele killing Shona, white man killing black. It's the natural order. Hell, the Ndebele only conquered this country forty years or so before we did.

And those Zulu cousins were ruthless warriors. Slaughter was their delight."

"True."

"Listen, you must come visit my ranch near the Botswana border. Eighty thousand acres of grazing. I'm establishing a herd of prize Brahmins, flown in from Texas. My best bull stands seven feet tall. Weighs in at a thousand kilos! I've named him Cecil John Rhodes the Second." He grinned. "He has the same solemn face as The Founder."

"You're into ranching, too?"

"I'm searching for a source of cheap meat for the African market. The tribes are protein-starved. My Brahmins are walking flesh factories. And they can graze in the noon heat that wilts a lesser breed. They feed all day, adding kilos by the hour. They're bloody marvellous!"

"And so are you, Shaun," I said. "So are you."

The township of Tshabalala was a neat diagram of tin-roofed semi-detacheds on squared lots in the virgin bush. Each concrete block bungalow was a cheap parody of suburban coziness, complete with tiny veranda and stunted palms in dusty gardens. Proud housewives in checked aprons came out to greet us as we drove by. Children scampered in the dust, dwarfed by the endless brown scrub.

David Llewellyn, the Township Superintendent, showed us round. His narrow jaw was sardonically Welsh under the floppy bush hat. He led us into homes that were painfully bright and clean. Their red cement floors were polished to a brilliance. The floral three-piece Chesterfield suites, bought on credit, were solemn as household gods. Pottery Canada geese honked mutely across whitewashed walls. Kerchiefed matrons beamed at our compliments, jerking aprons to their mouths to stifle giggles of embarrassed delight.

"And every dwelling has indoor soil!" Llewellyn exclaimed. "Well, almost all," he qualified, with a pinch of fact.

I was conducted round the new school, the clinic, the community centre, the public pool.

"Well, Mr. Kahn, what do you think?" the superintendent asked, as we rested on a bench in the shade of an acacia.

"Yes, Paul," Shaun said. "How does it measure up?"

"Impressive," I murmured politely.

"Of course, it's a showplace," Shaun cut in quickly. "Houses only a fraction of our urban blacks. We couldn't afford —"

"Don't be so damn honest, Shaun," the superintendent said. "Hell, you know the battle we had to get even this much out of the red-tape merchants."

"What do you say, Paul?"

"It lacks imagination."

The two faces gaped at me. Llewellyn blinked. "That's blunt."

"Go on," Shaun urged.

"This is a parody of white suburbia. Costly and vulgar. And insensitive. This is Africa. Look around."

Shaun frowned. "It doesn't match the landscape?"

"What 'landscape'?" Llewellyn snorted.

"Rhodesian towns are like tandem bikes," I said. "The front wheel's white suburbia — the bush spoked into bungalows and swimming pools. The back wheel's black and punctured. The crossbar is their common fate — that of refugees."

"What's the man on about?" Llewellyn asked.

"The whites are refugees from bad old crowded Europe. The blacks've escaped the kraals where they scratched at the dry dust for shrivelled maize, or tended scrawny cattle."

"So what?"

I tried another tack. "The other day I was in Mzilikazi, the old location. For all its hovels and shanties, it is a town. A vibrant, bubbling slum. This, here, is nothing and nowhere. It's a few lines scraped in the bush and dotted with dolls' houses. It's a condescension and a vulgarity."

"This chap doesn't mince words, eh?" Llewellyn scowled.

"But we can't build new Mzilikazis," Shaun objected. "They just happen."

"But there's another model for a black town. An old one. The kraal."

"But those places are made of mud and straw," the Welshman protested. "Their huts are paved with dung! No urban black would be seen dead in a kraal hut."

"You know why, don't you?"

"They stink. They're primitive. They're —"

"Cheap. And sensitive to the landscape. And to the African's life. But the Europeans have told the blacks so often that they are savages, they equate their own traditions with barbarism. For the bemused African, the kraal is everything that keeps them from the good life the white man glories in. No black boy or girl can hope to share in it while remaining tribal. To house them in these shrunken parodies of suburbia only hardens that crippling schizophrenia."

"Right," Shaun muttered, looking troubled. "But what can we do?"

"We can't build kraals," Llewellyn said. "The authorities would never wear it. The blacks would hate it. They want to get shed of all that kraal stuff, just as my grandpa fled his slate hovel in the Valleys."

"Our grandpas did too much running altogether," I retorted. "Time the grandchildren started looking at where we've all run to."

Shaun said again: "But what can we do?"

"Look at your resources. Consider traditional wisdom. Stop being arrogant. Imagine you don't know what's right just because you're white." I paused and lit a cigarette. "The natives have been building here for hundreds of years. Perhaps they've learnt something about the landscape?"

"Yes. Fear," Llewellyn said.

"Fear is a positive force. It can energize. Rhodesians should learn to fear, a little. Might make them think."

"But what can we do?!" Shaun cried out.

"First off, throw out your blocks and mortar. Factory-made blockwork is expensive and looks cheap."

"And use what?" Llewellyn demanded. "Mud?"

"Mud. Rhodesia's greatest natural resource. Mud walls, stiffened by tough thorn slats, also plentiful hereabouts. And, to add permanence, a gloss of progress, face the walls with one of the new gun-sprayed, filament-bonded cements. Result? An enclosure with all the porosity and coolness of dried earth, combined with the structural rigidity of cement."

"Holy Mary," Shaun muttered. "Why not?" His eyes lit up. "Didn't I say the man was a bloody genius!"

"But the roof," Llewellyn queried. "Tin?"

"Too hot. Too costly. Use thatch. Cheap and cool."

"The women wouldn't like that. All those spiders —"

"Not if you creosote the straw. Stiffens the reeds, too."

Shaun clapped his hands delightedly. "The Modern Mud Hut!"

"And," I ran on, in full flood now, "shape your community like a sort of collection of compounds. Circles of housing, each centred round its urban village square. A natural place to meet and chat. Give people a link between the old life and the new, the kraal and the city. Give the township a comprehensible social and visual shape. Don't just plunk down bumpkins in a shabby toytown."

"G.C.M.," Llewellyn grunted. "The man's a bloody poet." He grinned. "Makes us colonials look a right bunch of nits." He squinted at me. "If you're so damn clever, what're you doing here?"

"I'm a Rhodesian."

He looked me over shrewdly. "You could've fooled me."

"We must draw up a scheme along those lines," Shaun cut in. "Build a prototype house. Paul? Will you advise? On a consultancy basis?"

"Me?" I said, startled.

"Who else?" He smiled. "You're a real professional, you know that?"

"I'll advise. Without a fee. Okay?"

"I can offer you a drawing board in my office."

"Done."

"The marvellous thing about your scheme, it uses largely unskilled labour — another Rhodesian resource," Shaun enthused. He gestured round. "Fact is, I never was too happy with this."

"I was," the superintendent grumbled. "Until he made me think."

Shaun chuckled. "Painful, eh?"

"Very," the Welshman agreed, and walked off.

# 3

# MY SISTER'S POOL

$M$y sister's pool was egg-shaped and bright blue. A giant flame tree shed red flowers into the water. An acre of lawn surrounded the low white bungalow. Sprinklers hissed. The garden-boy raked the driveway. Go-away birds gave out clockwork croaks. Ndebele voices rattled, the consonants clicking like gravel on a tin roof.

Beside the pool, on a canvas recliner, I lay offered up to the heat. The sky grilled my flesh. In the darkness behind shut lids I listened to the generic sounds of a hot afternoon in the suburb of Kumalo.

4,000 miles to the north — Europe.

4,000 miles to the south — Antarctica.

4,000 miles to the west — Brazil.

6,000 miles to the east — Australia.

"Tea, baas?"

The smiling face of Grace, my sister's housegirl, hovered over me with a laden tray. I sat up as she drew back the teacloth to reveal two large cream cakes among the crockery.

"The baas wants me to pour?"

"Thanks, I think I can manage that much, Grace."

The woman giggled, as if I'd been witty. Her pale yellow face was framed by a blue headscarf wrapped round an Afro wig. Grace was from Botswana, a "foreign native," one of thousands who trekked to Rhodesia from the neighbouring black-ruled states in search of work. The whites preferred them to the locals, who were "lazy."

I rolled off the recliner and flopped into the cool pool. From under the surface the sky seemed to come down and put its blue cheek to the water. I came out dripping and poured myself a cup of tea and lit a cigarette.

Ray, my sister's houseboy, was traversing the lawn on his knees. He was shovelling up dogshit with a pan and brush. Snuggums, my sister's pudgy golden retriever, trotted up to me to beg a piece of cake. The bitch's eyes were weepy with food-lust. I pushed the cake plate at her and she buried her snout in cream with a joyous fart.

"Tenja!"

The bellow shattered the stillness. Lovey, my sister's thirteen-year-old boy, was racing up the driveway on his bike, shouting for the garden-boy.

At the steps he wobbled off his bike and let it fall. The schoolbag jumped loose from the carrier and spewed books over the gravel. "Tenja!" he screeched again, red in the face. "Where is that effing *munt?*"

The garden-boy hurried up to collect the books and the bike. Lovey aimed a kick at his slim behind. "Lazy kaffir! Put my books in my room, you hear?"

"Yes, baas."

"Put my bike in the garage."

"Yes, baas."

"Bloody *munt.*"

Lovey saw me at the poolside. His plump face switched from scowl to beam. "Hi, Uncle Paul!"

"Hi, Nephew Lovey."

Lovey wandered up and slumped on the grass beside me. He was a fat boy in straining khaki shorts with pockets that bulged out from under. A soiled school hat was tipped back on a mop of wild hair. Grey socks dangled about sausage ankles. Marooned in all this flab was a pair of fine grey eyes.

The family claimed Lovey was the spitting image of me, at thirteen.

"You say such funny things," he giggled. " 'Nephew Lovey'!"

"Yeah. I'm a real wag."

The boy's face darkened. "I don't like 'Lovey' — a baby name. My name is Louie."

"Hi, Nephew Louie."

He giggled again. "You say such funny things."

Lovey tore off his socks and shoes and dangled his swollen feet in the pool. Snuggums waddled up and nuzzled his groin. In the background Tenja was gathering up the bike and books.

"Have a dip," I suggested.

"Can't. Get my ears wet. My plastic tubes'll fall out."

"How long will you have to go on wearing them?"

"The doc says till I mature." Lovey jiggled the water with his toes. "Why did you leave Bulawayo, Uncle Paul?" he asked.

I considered my answer carefully. This was a very serious question.

"It frightened me."

Lovey flung back his head and bellowed: "Grace! Bring us a cool drink!"

Grace appeared instantly in the french windows of the bungalow. She bobbed her head, vanished, and returned a moment later with a bottle of Fanta orange.

Lovey suckled the bottle greedily. He smacked his lips. "Why?"

"I woke up one day and found I was helpless."

Lovey's eyes jerked round at me. They were wide with fright. "Huh?" His school hat fell off on the grass.

I stroked the boy's hair to soothe him. "Yes. I woke up one day, suddenly. Happened in a funny way. You want to hear, Lou?"

"Yeah." The syllable was reluctant.

"I was about your age. Thirteen. One hot afternoon I wanted to pedal my bike to the Princess Bioscope to see a movie. Jimmy Cagney and George Raft in *Each Dawn I Die*. I was crazy about movies."

"Me too," Lovey exclaimed.

"But there was a problem. The back tire of my bike was flat. I screamed for the garden-boy — 'Tickey!' No answer. 'Tickey! Tickey! Where is that bloody *munt?*' Nowhere. Vanished. Not a black face in sight."

"Bloody *munts*," the boy murmured indignantly.

"I was stuck. What to do? I had to see that movie. I'd never pumped a tire in my life. Stuck. Sure, the cinema was only five blocks away, but what Rhodesian ever walks? Have you?"

"Never."

"I was in a rage. I kicked my bike. I swore. Then I just fell down on the gravel and had a screaming fit."

"You didn't!" He blushed. "I do that."

"Suddenly I snapped out of it. Saw myself, a fat boy screeching in the dirt. G.C.M. — is this me? Such a tantrum, over a flat tire? I got a real scare. I was helpless. I couldn't do a damn thing for myself. I was a real Rhodesian boy."

"Like me." There was harsh honesty in those fine eyes.

"My eyes opened. I began to think, to ask myself, what's happening to me? I began to look around, for the very first time."

"Oh, boy." Lovey stared at me. "What did you do?"

"I started to learn to look after myself. Learnt to pump my bike, to polish my own shoes, get my own breakfast."

"What did the family say?" the boy asked shrewdly.

"They were amazed. 'Paul makes his own bed!' 'Paul folds his own clothes!' 'Paul pumps his own bike!' It was a family joke."

"I'll bet."

"I began to see the world. My world. I saw that Tickey was in rags while my cupboard was jammed with clothes. I gave the kid some pants. 'Who gave the *munt* those new shorts?' my Dad asked. 'The *kaffir* can't afford new khakis on two shillings a month!' When they found out, there was a big row. I was forbidden to be careless. Mom was outraged. 'You think I've got golden nuggets dangling from my nipples?' She always had a salty tongue, your Granny. Net result: Tickey was sacked."

"No!"

"Yeah. I had my first lesson in practical politics: liberalism is self-indulgence."

"I know." He nodded sagely. "My history master told us."

"Did he, indeed?"

Lovey lumbered to his feet. "Got to do my homework, now." He scowled. "Here come the Monsters!"

The "Monsters" were the twins, Lawlene and Eric, now cycling up the driveway. They faithfully repeated the routine of bellowing for Tenja and abandoning the bikes.

Two very hot and sweaty ten-year-olds hurried towards the pool as Lovey scurried off, muttering.

"Hi, Uncle Paul!"

"Hi, Niece Lawlene. Hi, Nephew Eric."

The twins collapsed with glee at this ritual joke. They fell about on the grass, giggling. Eric's stubby fingers were, as usual, plucking at his crotch.

Lawlene's sharp eye scrutinized me. "You're getting black as a *munt*, Uncle. If you aren't careful, they soon won't let you in the European bog."

"Don't worry, I'll flash my lily-white bum."

"You say such funny things." She shouted suddenly: "Grace! Cool drink!"

Grace appeared promptly with two iced Fantas.

Eric looked round as he sucked his orange drink. "Where's the fairy?" This was a reference to Lovey's guilty passion for dressing up in his mother's drag.

"That's not a topic for public discussion," Lawlene snapped. "Mom'd kill you."

"Fairy! Fairy!" Eric crowed. The birds in the tree replied: *go-away, go-away.*

My father's ancient Toyota turned into the driveway. I ran to help my mother from the car. Her face opened in a brilliant smile as she saw me. "Paul. So black?"

I was shocked all over again by the wastage of Parkinsonism on that frail frame. When I was a child she'd been so plump. Now she was a wobbly doll. Her skull trembled, her hands shook, her speech was a croak, but her brown eyes were still sharp. "My boy. You look tense."

"I'm fine, Mom. Truly. And you?"

"Fine."

"She always says that," Dad complained, irritable with concern.

"Don't fuss, Joe."

My father's eyes were weepy. He wore his Matabeleland tennis blazer with the crossed silver racquets on the pocket. His grey flannels were crisp as always. His wavy silver thatch was neat.

He and I helped my mother to a chair beside the pool. She was so tiny it was like guiding a feather.

Grace came out and curtsied. "Tea, missus?"

"Tea," Mom nodded. She added eagerly: "Pineapple cheesecake?"

"The doctor said —"Dad began.

"Pineapple cheesecake!" the old woman cried urgently.

"Too rich for my tummy,"Dad moaned. But he tucked in all the same, when Grace brought the trolley.

My mother buried her face in the cake. In a trice the large slice vanished. There was cream on her lips as she grimaced. "I feel nauseous," she said. *"Naw-zhus —"*

"She's not well, not well at all," Dad complained.

Tenja appeared with a long net. He was skinny as a snake in his denim overalls as he scooped dead beetles from the surface of the pool, and shook out drowned insects on the tiles.

"You really going to stay?"Dad asked me suddenly.

"Sure he is," Mom snapped.

"Yes, Dad."

He stared at me. There was panic in his hooded eyes. He clutched his tummy apprehensively.

"My only son," Mom said. Her gaze was soft and sexy. "My boy."

"Is there work for you?" Dad persisted.

"I was offered a job today. Advising Shaun Connaughton on a new township project."

"Shaun's a brilliant man," Dad said. "Brilliant."

"So is Paul. More brilliant."

"Brilliant man," Dad repeated. All his antennae were frantic with alarm. He knew it wasn't right for me to be at home. He squinted at me in misery. "You were always such an idealist!" he accused.

"Joe, I want to make a wee," Mom said. "Call Grace."

Grace and I helped the old woman to her feet. I felt the thinness of her bones, the agitation of her trembling muscles. My heart sank as she was led away like a mouse.

What a fighter she was. The eldest of thirteen kids from the slums of Bloemfontein, abandoned by their father, she had ruled her family with a rod of iron. Her own mother had been crippled with rheumatoid arthritis. Rachel Silverman was made of steel. But now all her fierce control was slipping away. She was frantic. She was angry. The fury made her fight.

"She's not well, not well at all," Dad moaned. "You don't know what it's been like these past ten years. So much suffering. I can't stand it. My poor tummy —" He cuddled his middle.

I touched his silver waves. "I'm very fond of you, old boy."

He jerked his head as if stung. "Of course!" he exclaimed. He added, with immense relief, "Here comes your sister!"

Leonie bounced across the lawn. "Big brother!" she cried, grabbing me in a close hug.

Her copious breasts, swelling the floral tent that draped her big body, squashed against my naked chest. "Big black brother," she howled, laughing in my ear. She shoved me away brusquely. "You're getting black as a *munt*."

"Hi, sis."

Leonie looked round sharply. "The crocodiles not here today?"

"Don't call your Aunties that," Dad pleaded.

"Green Crocodile Maidens," Leonie giggled. "G.C.M.s." She slumped down on a chair, fanning her face. "Grace! Fresh tea!"

"Grace is helping Mom in the loo," I said.

Leonie's face sharpened. "How is Mom today?"

"She's not well, not well at all," Dad said.

"So what else is new? Paul, what did you do today? I had a terrible day at the pharmacy. Every *munt* for miles around seems to have the fever. And every one wants penicillin, would you believe it? They swallow antibiotics as if they were sweeties. It's the new witchcraft."

"*Tagati,*" Dad said sagely. "Black magic."

Grace led my mother back to the table. As she approached, Leonie reached out and squeezed my hand. My mother noticed this as she was being seated. She scowled.

"Ah, jealous?" Leonie taunted her. "I know you love him best."

"Rubbish," Mom snorted.

"He's your prodigal son."

"Rubbish."

"Who's got the wavy hair, then? Who's got the brains? Who is sensitive and subtle? Paul!"

My mother nodded jerkily. "Paul."

"Who is slim?" Leonie barrelled on, two hundred pounds of floral female in full charge. "Who has fine hands and narrow ankles? Who is fastidious and frugal, and never has to crucify himself with diets? Paul!"

"Paul," Mom agreed, smiling at me.

"Paul," Leonie snapped, and shoved my hand away. "Don't think I'm complaining. Sure, you love him best. Despite the fact he vanished for twenty years. Despite the fact he hardly ever wrote. And when he did deign to communicate, the letters were looked upon as manna from heaven! Me, I'm just Fat Old Lee, the faithful daughter who gives you grandchildren. Fat Old Lee."

Leonie's voice slithered into teariness. Her swollen face, framed by a nest of bouffant, lacquered straw, was brilliant with hurt.

"My tummy, my tummy," Dad moaned, clutching his gut.

"For God's sake, go to the bog Daddy," Leonie snapped, and cut herself a chunk of cheesecake.

*"Baruch atah adenai Elohenu melech ha'olam ... "*

Leonie mumbled her way through the Friday evening prayer for blessing the Sabbath Lights. A serviette was draped over her coiffure. Her hands wavered over the candles. Even through this brief incantation the family fidgeted round the dining table, anxious to feed.

The vestigial prayer ended with an abrupt bellow: "Ray!"

The houseboy ran in at once with the food trolley, as if he had been hovering behind the kitchen door.

"The Monster's got my chair!" Lovey screamed. "Fat Fairy!" "I don't like fish!" Lawlene wailed. "I wanna sit next to Grandpa!" "Where's my cottage cheese, Ray?" Leonie cried. "I feel nauseous," Mom moaned. "Gimme the flank," Dad begged.

"Silence!" David bellowed, from the head of the table. My brother-in-law, David Mandel, was a pudding-faced man with raisin eyes bloated behind thick lenses. "If you brats don't *shtum* I'll belt the living daylights —"

"David, your coronary," Leonie undercut him.

"I can't stand racket at the dinner table."

Leonie shrugged. "Change families."

Ray went round the table, dispensing dishes. Everyone was eating something different. My mother had gefilte fish. My father dumped a great chunk of soupmeat — flank — on his plate and smeared it with horseradish sauce. He tucked in with his fingers, mopping up the gravy with slices of bread and butter.

David carved himself roast beef cooked to the texture and tone of tarmac. Steam from the huge joint clouded his specs.

"David, your cholesterol level," Leonie admonished.

"Aw, it's Friday night, have a heart." He piled up roast potatoes round his beef.

"It's your heart I'm thinking of."

But David tucked in avidly. He had been a German Jewish refugee to Rhodesia in the thirties. He remembered his father, who had died in Dachau, being beaten on the streets of Hamburg. The fright of that memory had given him a hunger he could never seem to appease.

Leonie and Lawlene were munching boiled fish and cottage cheese. They were on diet. "Hate fish," Lawlene mumbled, pulling a face. "You want to be a blob, like me?" her mother asked. Lawlene ate her fish and cheese.

Lovey and Eric tore a chicken apart with their bare hands and fled to the T.V. room with drumsticks.

"Can't we all sit down at the table together, for once?" David said.

"Ach, they're mad about *Teen Scene*," Leonie answered. "Hey, Dad, you're splashing me with gravy!"

My father's cheeks were smeared with grease. "Sorry," he mumbled.

"Paul, you're not eating," Leonie chided. "Trying to show us up?"

"I'm doing very well," I protested.

"Wish I had your willpower," Leonie sighed. "One more thing you have that I lack."

Lovey and Eric dashed in to make another raid on the chicken carcass. "Want another drumstick," Lovey said. "Ray!"

"Go get it yourself, choppychops," Leonie told him. "Ray is busy with dessert."

Ray entered with a second trolley. He scurried about

collecting plates and dishes, replacing them with fresh ones. There was cheesecake, jelly, trifle, fruit and cheese to follow.

The houseboy was a thin man in his mid-twenties. He wore a smart white coat to serve at table. His dark head was narrow and lit up by very white eyes. A boy from the bush, he had been schooled by Baptist missionaries in the virtues of obedience.

While the humans were feasting, Snuggums retrieved lumps of beef, chicken, and fish that dropped on the floor. The rose-figured carpet was her meadow. She grazed voraciously, on a rag bag of all the goodies passing over her head. When the dessert was served, a plate was set for her at the table beside me. The golden retriever lumbered onto the chair and sank her muzzle in a dish of cheesecake. The bitch guzzled, farting with ecstasy.

David pushed his plate away and put his hand to his chest with a look of pain. "My heart."

My mother finished her slice of cheesecake and announced: "I feel *naw-zhus*."

My father hugged his bulging stomach and complained: "My tummy's sore."

"Coffee in the lounge," Leonie said, ending the ritual.

The lounge suite was covered in a tapestry of tea roses. Leonie in her florals made a park of the settee. She wore pink mules with pompoms on her feet.

We drank coffee. My father yawned. David sucked at an empty pipe; the doctor had forbidden him to smoke. Dishes clattered in the kitchen as Ray and Grace washed up.

"Sanctions are killing me," David announced suddenly. His voice still retained a rasp of German. "Business is tight. Can't get new bikes for the shop. Bloody British." He turned on me. "When is the world going to let Rhodesia live? Seven years since independence, and they still hammer us!"

"Our independence is illegal," Leonie reminded him, always quick to contradict.

"I never voted for the Rhodesia Front," Dad said. 'Ian Smith was never my man. Old Sir Godfrey Huggins, Lord Malvern, now there's a true Rhodesian. He'd never have put us in this situation."

"He was deaf," David said. "Without his ear trumpet, he was lost."

"I never voted for the Rhodesia Front," my father insisted.

"Don't say that in front of the *goyim*," Leonie warned.

Dad was shocked. "Of course not!"

David turned his lenses on me again. "When will they let us live?"

"When you have majority rule."

"The war is getting serious," my father worried. "These terrs mean business."

"Bunch of *munts*," David said. "Don't know their arse from their elbow."

"I was chatting to Jock Mallard at the Railway Club. He's in the government. Serious, he says."

"The blacks have never licked us in Africa," David countered. "The countries that went under — Kenya, the Congo, and so on — collapsed because the Europeans lost their nerve. We must have nerve!" He shook his fists angrily. "Look at the Portuguese in Angola and Mozambique. Been fighting for years. Won't give an inch. And look at South Africa. The Afrikaners will never go under. There's a breed for you."

"Nazis," my mother said. "I know. Grew up with them. Beat Jews on the street. Bloemfontein."

"Don't upset yourself, Rachel," Dad warned.

"Nazis," Mom repeated stubbornly. Her head wobbled and sagged. In a trice she was asleep.

"Take her home," Leonie told the old man.

My father and I helped my mother out to the car. She was half asleep. The old Toyota rolled out of the driveway and vanished into the night, through the cloud of flying ants circling the gate lamp.

The air was fresh and cool. Bullfrogs croaked in the dried-out riverbed of the Matsheumhlope several streets distant. A train whistled. A woman laughed somewhere; a deep, female African chuckle, raunchy and mocking.

I stayed out a while, smoking and relishing the soft air. The sky was dense with stars. A chip of bright African moon floated in the darkness to the north.

The raucous voices in the house seemed far away in all

this peace. The stillness was eternal. Killing was unthinkable in this tranquil night. Yet out in the bush, not all that far away, men were hunting one another with all the sly ferocity of jackals.

Car lights glared in the street. A sporty Jaguar XK120 turned into the drive. The open car was white. The driver wore a white safari suit and had a shock of dark ginger hair.

My cousin, Barney Silverman, the chief electronics engineer at the Post Office Telecommunications Centre, swung his leg over the door and hailed me. "Paul! Pissing on the grass, eh?" Barney came up and joshed me with his elbow. His cheerful Silverman face was white as dough. He shoved a package in my hands. "A present, for my hippy cousin!"

"What is it?"

"Open it, man. Made it myself. Just your style."

I pulled the brown wrapping apart. Inside was a shoebox. I opened the lid and saw a jumble of electronic spare parts. Barney, impatient with my slowness, plucked the mess from the box and draped it round my neck. "A necklace, for my hippy cousin!"

I gaped down at my chest and saw a linked chain of bakelite discs on which were set transistors, condensors, and other circuitry. The "necklace" ended in a square breastplate of miniaturized electronic components.

"What on earth —"

"The marvel is, it works," Barney chuckled. He jabbed the centre of the breastplate. African pop music blared forth. "Radio Matopos!"

"A radio?"

"I set it so you can only tune in to the darkies," Barney laughed. "Serve you right. 'And he shall have music wherever he goes,' " he sang out.

"How do I turn it off, for godsakes?"

"Just press this knob, here." He ended the noise. "It's also a transceiver, kind of walkie-talkie, for sending and receiving if you want to communicate with the Martians."

"I don't."

"You don't like it?" His face fell.

"I love it."

"Knew you would — hippy!" Barney cried, and hugged me.

"Barney is a real wit," Leonie said, when the necklace was explained to her. "Is that all you have to do all day in that fancy radio room of yours?"

"Telecom Centre," Barney corrected. He turned to me. "When are you going to come and see my marvellous toys?"

"Soon."

"The Brain of Matabeleland," he said proudly. "Computerized operation. Telephone, teletype, telegraph. Satellite relay. Nerve centre, military and civilian. Marvellous."

"Isn't all that Top Secret?" Leonie questioned.

"Sure. But for my hippy cousin, Category X-1 clearance."

"Soon," I said again.

Grace trundled in a fresh trolley of coffee and cakes. Barney bit into a chunk of pineapple cheesecake. "Delicious, Lee," he enthused. "Your goodies are the best."

Leonie preened at the compliment. "I like to bake."

"I thought Ray made this?" I said.

"He mixes the pastry and the filling, under my orders."

"Ah."

Leonie scowled at me. She turned to Barney. "Seems the war is hotting up, Barn?"

"We lose a damn sight fewer soldiers than the British in Northern Ireland," Barney shrugged. "Or the Israelis."

"This isn't Israel," Leonie retorted. "Do you want your Callum to die for Rhodesia?"

Barney wriggled. "It's given us a good life. We owe the place something."

"Not my son's blood."

"They'd never take Lovey in the army. His balls won't drop."

"Don't be crude."

"Did you take him to that specialist in Jo'burg I told you about?"

Leonie's lip trembled. "He'll mature, in good time."

"Well, I'm not taking the gap," Barney said. "Won't find me on the yellow run. I'm going to see it out."

Grace returned to collect the trolley. Barney was about to go on about his determination to "see it out," but Leonie gestured him to silence. *"Die schwartze,"* she warned, nodding towards Grace.

"Yeah," Barney agreed. He added grimly, "Even stones have ears."

David spoke up, when Grace had gone. "This country saved my life. I'm not leaving."

Barney chuckled. "What he means is, he's a coronary case, a *shmuck* in business, a total *nebbish*. In any other country but Rhodesia he'd be a *munt*."

"Hey," Leonie protested, but grinning.

David bit down on his pipe. "All the same —"

"Look," Barney cut in, " I happen to know, we have some aces up our sleeve, firepowerwise. The Yanks in Vietnam developed some pretty nasty weapon systems. And we have a line into the Pentagon. You think those generals want to see a Marxist state on the Zambesi? Not on your nelly, kid. No goddamn way."

"My boys won't bleed for Ian Smith," Leonie said. "Never!"


"Never!" Leonie cried again, after Barney had left and David had been sent to bed. David's uneasy snoring sounded along the bedroom passageway.

Leonie stood defiant as Boadicea in the middle of her lounge. She had "comfed" — slipped into a baby-blue fluffy gown that clung to her solid ankles.

Her round face was abruptly doubtful. "Where would we go? South Africa? Australia? Israel?" She shuddered. "We can't take money out, anyway."

"I have money," I said. "You're welcome to it."

Leonie blinked. "You mean that?"

"I've made a lot in the last ten years. You're welcome to it."

Leonie's cheeks wobbled with emotion. "That's kind. So kind! But —"

"But, what?"

She gave me a hard look. "What's that scar on your lip?"

I touched the small gouge on my lower lip. "Memento," I shrugged.

"A woman?" she cut in shrewdly.

"A woman."

"Why?" Her tiny eyes were glittering.

"She said she couldn't reach me otherwise. Needed the taste of blood, to see if I was real."

"Oh, you're real all right — but not in the way you think." She grinned. "You really would lend us the cash to get out?"

"I've made my will. Everything goes to you."

"You don't mean it!" She ran to hug me. "Brother, brother," she sobbed, smothering my face.

Fighting for breath, I struggled to my feet. Leonie's eyes were bright with tears, but her tone was sharp.

"Paul what are you up to? What's happening in that clever head of yours? You're such an idealist!" She pushed me back. "In this town I'm still known to all and sundry as Paul Kahn's little sister." Her lip trembled with self-pity. "Just can't shake you off. You're a shadow. A black shadow!"

# 4

## JERUSALEM

I stand in Babi Yar, Russian ravine of a hundred thousand murdered Ukranian Jews. I've come halfway round the world, to collect a lump of bloodied mud from that Nazi-made mass grave of my people.

My father lies there, a corpse melted in the buried mound of rotted flesh. His bones have fused with the communal mud. I've come to breathe life into a chunk of that paternal clay.

In my gullet's stuck the magic Word: *Emet* — *Truth*. If I can spit it out the mud will come alive. My Dad will walk again.

He will succour me. He will validate me. He will love me.

Babi Yar. Grey sky, grey earth. Ghosts, millions of them, dance under my feet. I hear them sighing. I hear them wailing. I hear them hoping.

I scoop up clay with my bare fist. It's cold. Half-frozen. I breathe on it, hard. Steam comes out of my mouth, but no Word. *Emet* is a bone in my throat.

The lump of mud in my palm lets out a shriek — *help!* I suck in sharp air and gasp it out with all my force.

But it's only air. No magic syllable. No miracle.

My cheeks puff hot with shame. Blow! Blow!! Blow!!! Nothing. No power in me. No magic.

The mud stays dead. My father will not live.

My eyes flicked wide in fright. I was choking in my sleep.

But I saw that I was safe in bed in my sister's spare room. I was in Africa.

The night was moonless, but starlight glowed along the blades of the venetian blind. Insects scratched somewhere. In Africa they never seem to sleep. I sat up and lit a cigarette.

Mud.

As a boy I'd made clay cities in the corner of our back yard, behind the chicken run. There were palaces and temples, streets and plazas populated with tiny figures.

Shaun was my assistant. He and I spent many afternoons squatting in the dirt, moulding walls and roofs. In the Great Temple of our city I housed a pair of High Priests — pandinus scorpions. Izzy and Sarah were their names. After I had milked them of their poison, using a big cork as striker, they would doze off in the darkness of their holy house, caressing one another's shiny backs in post-orgasmic tenderness.

The city was called Jerusalem.

The name was unoriginal, but apt. Actually, it was Shaun's notion. He'd always had a very direct mind. That is how we became architects, I suppose, playing in the mud — the mud of Africa.

But the kind of "mud" I was toying with these days was more explosive.

Plastic explosive.

Barney Silverman's hippy necklace lay on my bedside table. I pressed the breastplate knob. The contraption crackled, but there was no music. The station had closed down.

A shadow passed the slatted blind. A cloud? Too swift. The handle of the french window squeaked.

"Who's there?" I croaked, heart hammering.

I slipped out of bed and padded to the window. I listened, ears sharp as nails.

Silence, but for the nocturnal insects scraping away in the grass.

I unlocked the window and slid out round the blind. My only garment was pajama pants. The cool air prickled my spine as I stepped out on the damp lawn.

I crept to the front of the house, keeping in the shadows. All doors were locked, all windows barred: a bungalow under seige. The pool glittered in the starlight. I saw the man.

An African hovered at the edge of the water, as if about to plunge into the pool. There was an ordinariness about his stance, as if the lawn were his. As if the black possessed the place by night, when the whites were dreaming.

The man saw me. He flared white eyes and fled.

I came out of the shadows. The grass was black beneath my naked toes. Light from a sodium street lamp blued the branches of the trees. The sky was punctured with a million sharp stars.

I made a circuit of the house, checking all the doors and windows. It was shut tight as a drum.

In the servants' *kayas* at the rear Ray and Grace lay wrapped in one another's arms on a narrow iron cot. Her face glowed yellow in the dark. Ray's stick insect body was angular even in sleep. The tiny room gave off a warm, dark, sexual smell: that *muntstink* the whites loathe.

Tenja, the garden-boy, was in the adjoining cell, cuddling his pillow. His feet were tangled in a coarse brown blanket. He moaned softly as I looked in.

In the main house the dreaming bodies were embedded in soft sheets. Lovey lay flat on his back, rigid as a tombstone effigy. Next door were Eric and Lawlene. The boy gripped his groin; the girl's expression was severe even in rest. In the master bedroom, Leonie and David filled a kingsize bed. Snuggums linked them, snout nuzzled in Leonie's bosom, rump under David's jaw. All three breathed in rhythm, synchronized in sleep.

In my own bed again, I lit yet another cigarette and sat up in the dark.

I had learned to hate in early adolescence. The fit over the flat bike tire I'd described to Lovey was the flashpoint. It had revealed my rawness.

Hatred was the only defence. My father was the focus. He was weak and I detested him for it. He sensed my revulsion. His spaniel eyes tracked me miserably. He could not grasp why his bright, plump lad had become his accuser.

It had been a splendid time for hatred. The first films of the concentration camps were flashed on the screen of the Palace Bioscope. Between guzzles of ice-cream soda, I'd witnessed Auschwitz.

The images of naked Jewish women flogged on frosty squares on their way to the gas ovens had boiled me with helpless shame and lust. Their pubic tufts had burned into my brain. I'd been sick to the stomach with curdled ice cream and imagery.

My soul was mud. Mud and blood, melted in the mass grave of my people. Mud of my fathers, that I cannot animate, no matter how hard I blow.

I woke late. The family were all out, at Saturday morning synagogue. In the second bathroom, Grace toiled over a tub of washing. Each morning she collected the clothes dropped on the bedroom floors and scrubbed and ironed them immaculately. "Cheaper and better than any laundry," Leonie said.

After showering I made some coffee and took the tray out to the pool. Snuggums padded after me, waggling her stump. She lay beside me on the grass, drooling contentedly in the shade of the tree.

The sprinklers hissed tirelessly. Tenja was netting the pool. Among the pile of corpses he dredged up was the soggy grey lump of a hedgehog.

The front page of the *Chronicle* was dull. No atrocities today. But page two carried the announcement of the promulgation of a new bill by the Minister of Law and Order.

This proposed bill specified a number of new capital offences. The death penalty would be mandatory for harbouring terrorists, for not reporting their presence, for undergoing any sort of subversive training, for recruiting or helping to recruit insurgents, and for encouraging any person or persons to recruit such criminals. The announcement also took the opportunity to remind the public that the State of Emergency Powers Act had been renewed for another year on June 21st 1973.

On page nine, the centre spread, was a large photo of Ian Smith. The Prime Minister was addressing a Rhodesia Front rally at Gatooma, a small town to the north. The Simple Farmer's rubbery, *faux-naif* face was creased with sincerity.

"We are containing the insurgency," he said. "Since we initiated Operation Hurricane, over half the terrs, both

ZANU and ZAPU, have been rounded up or destroyed. I sincerely believe there cannot be more than a handful of infiltrators running about in the bush today. So much for their vaunted *Chimurenga*. Yes, we will subdue all these Kremlin-trained agitators trying to stir up our loyal, happy, peaceful natives. We will make our beautiful Homeland safe again for Rhodesians of all races.''

After Good Old Smithy's speech, the new national anthem had been sung by the crowd. It replaced ''God Save the Queen'' since that royal lady had not responded to Rhodesia's appeals to her heart, over the heads of her socialist government.

The words of the anthem, sung to the tune of Beethoven's ''Ode to Joy,'' were printed in full. They began:

> *Rise, O voices of Rhodesia,*
> *God, may we Thy bounty share,*
> *Give us strength to face all danger and,*
> *    where challenge is, to dare.*

A muffled but derisive snort sounded over my shoulder. I squinted round to see Tenja looking down at the newspaper in my hands. The young man tucked his head in as I looked up at him. His slim body was clothed only in denim overalls. I caught the flicker in his yellow eyes as he backed off.

I held up the photo of Ian Smith. ''Charming, isn't he?'' I said.

A gurgle of laughter bubbled in Tenja's narrow throat. ''*Nyogamhlope,*'' he sniggered. ''White Snake!''

I took a cigarette, and offered him one. The boy glanced round quickly, then accepted the smoke. We lit up.

''How old are you, Tenja?''

''Twenty-two, baas.''

''Don't call me 'baas', okay?''

Tenja scowled at me. He shrugged. ''Okay.''

''Twenty-two, and a garden-boy?'' I wondered.

Tenja drew himself up proudly. ''I have two Advanced Levels. In Mathematics and English. Now I study book-keeping, in night school.''

"Can't you find better work than this?"

"No work. Sanctions. Business is bad. If I go for interview, there are maybe fifty, hundred black people queuing up."

"Economic sanctions have hurt the blacks that badly?"

"Bad. But good. Very good. The Europeans know what other countries think."

"What's it like, working here?"

He shrugged, leaning on the pool pole. "Your sister is okay. Hard, but fair. The man is weak, so he kicks us."

"Can't you leave Rhodesia, to study?"

Tenja gasped at my naivety. "You joke! To start with, my *situpa* is not in order. I haven't got the right piece of paper from the police that states that I exist!"

"But you are Rhodesian?"

"I am a Zimbabwean, sir. I am a socialist."

I peered at him, remembering the cuddled pillow. "A socialist?"

"Yes." He was very firm. "Our *Chimurenga* is not only a national struggle, for freedom from white rule. It is also a class struggle. A struggle to free my people from exploitation of every kind, black and white."

"Is that possible?" I queried mildly.

"Why not? Cabral has done it, in Guinea. Nyerere, in Tanzania. Castro, in Cuba."

"I've worked in Cuba."

Tenja's eyes lit up. "Truly? What's it like there?"

"Interesting."

"I would like to travel." His tone was yearny. "The world has so many things." He frowned at me. "You came back? Why?"

"I'm a Rhodesian."

"No." He shook his head. "I hear you speak, with your family. You are not Rhodesian." He turned and loped off.

The pool was cooling. I came out dripping and stretched out on a towel, face down, to brown my back.

Pools.

The last one I had swum in was in the Hollywood Hills. From that terraced elevation the City of The Angels could be seen, sweltering in its smog.

Molly's pool, setting for a bitten lip:

A hummingbird sips at a honeysuckle as Molly slides out of blue water and sinks her teeth in my mouth. Her incisors puncture my gum through the lip. For one hot instant we're an androgyne — male and female fused.

There's fire in my face. I slam her naked chest. She sprawls on the grass.

"Why?" I blurt, bleeding.

"To reach you. See if you're real, honeylamb."

"I'll need stitches!"

"Tastes bloody. You do bleed, then?"

"Fuck you."

"Anytime. You do it good."

Molly parts her long legs. The vaginal lips open in a vertical smile. Moist pinkness winks through the fair tuft. My cock twitches. Molly chuckles. She shoves me down on the grass. We fuck.

That evening, lying on loungers, drinking screwdrivers, watching the city sky reflected in the pool, I tell her of my recurrent vision of the mud of Babi Yar.

Her pool-blue irises dilate in shock. "So that's what bugs you? I thought it was me!" She shudders. "It explains —" she hesitates, not quite knowing what it explains — "why you're so damn inward." She comes to kiss me, lightly, on my newly-stitched lip. "That's my mark, love. My Magic Word on you, forever. Does it breathe life?" she demands.

"No. It makes scars."

We fall out, soon after. Molly has other marks to make. A month later, I'm on my way home, to my sister's pool.


"God, you're black!"

The voice above me was only vaguely familiar. I rolled round, sat up, saw long legs in flapping green pantaloons. Above these were an emerald tanktop, a pair of bare and freckled bony arms, a cloud of jet hair and a long white face decorated with huge designer shades.

"Mona?"

"That's me." She folded her limbs and sank down on the grass beside me. "Hi, Paul."

Mona Bach was a young widow in her early thirties, a friend of Leonie's. My sister's comment on Mona was succinct: "She likes to think of herself as a rebel, but all she is is a pushover."

"You really are quite black," Mona said again, running her eyes over my half-naked body.

Her stretched purple lips were tense. A narrow nose sprang from black brows, then swooped down to flare out in raw nostrils. She plucked a cigarette from a silver case and stuck it in an ebony holder. Bony fingers with carmined clawtips flicked a gold lighter.

"I suppose your sister's been telling you bitchy things about me," she said, sucking smoke. She flicked her face aside before I could respond and yelled, "Grace! Tea!" She grinned at me. "The shriek of the Great White Madam was heard in the land." She scowled. "Why did you come back here, to this stupid place?"

"I'm a Rhodesian."

Mona removed her sunglasses. Her coal eyes were nakedly myopic. "I know what you're thinking," she muttered. "That I'm a hicktown hoyden who comes on like real cool stuff." Her jaw jutted. "True. That's me, to the life."

"As good a pretension as any," I said.

"You're a card," she blurted. "A real card!" She snaked a finger at my lower lip, not quite flicking the scar. "That wound — a woman?" She nodded instantly. "That figures. Any female who fancied you would have to leave her mark."

"No more marks, please!" I cried out.

Mona laughed. It was a parched, sardonic sound, dry as cracked mud.

# 5

# SERPENTS

The following Monday I started working in Shaun's office. He gave me a drawing board in a cubicle, separated from the main drawing office by a low partition. The days passed. The physical act of putting lines on paper soothed me. The blank sheets on the board were oblongs of white simplicity.

One afternoon Shaun brought in an old cake tin. It had a picture of Queen Victoria on the lid. He dropped it beside my board with a thump.

"Tshabalala mud," he announced, prising off the top of the tin. "I'm sending off a sample for chemical analysis. To test how it reacts with some of the cement mixes we might use for the hut facings."

He took a pinch of clay and rolled it lovingly between his fingertips. "We're playing with mud again, Paul. Just like we used to under the pawpaw trees in your backyard, building the New Jerusalem."

"In Rhodesia?" I teased.

"Where else?" he shot back. "Do you know a fairer place?"

"No."

"Well, then." He leant over my board. I explained my sketches. "Excellent!" he exclaimed. He squinted up at me. "And you're the chap who's given up architecture?"

"It gave me up."

"Architecture's just building, isn't it? Shelter, workspace, playspace. Basic. Everyone everywhere needs architecture."

I stepped back, leaned against the partition, lit a cigarette. "Architecture's not just building. It's a cultural act, a way of seeing yourself, of announcing who and what you are. Your clothes are architecture."

"Huh?"

"Look at you, in your beige safari suit, bare knees, long white socks. What does that outfit say about you? What are you saying about yourself?"

Shaun cracked a grin. "You tell me."

"It says, 'I'm a white man in a hot climate. A colonial, and proud of it.' It says, 'Look at me — I most certainly haven't gone native!' "

"Damn right," Shaun cackled. "Okay, so architecture's a cultural act. Why should that upset you?"

"I no longer know what culture is."

"Culture is — culture!" Shaun protested. "What else?"

"And what is that?"

"Well, I suppose ..." He screwed his face up. "An assumption about the way things ought to be?"

"Right. That's my problem. I haven't a clue about the way things ought to be any more. Haven't had for quite a while. Perhaps I never had, even when we played in the mud in my back yard, building Jerusalem."

It was Shaun's turn to back off a pace. He rubbed his reddish bristle uncertainly. "You doubt that deeply? Why? What was the crunch?"

"My last big job."

"That big project in Caracas? I saw the drawings in *International Planning*. They looked superb." He stretched his spine. "Let's have a tipple, what say? Can't haggle over culture with a dry tongue."

We went through to Shaun's office. He took a bottle of John Jameson from his drawer, and two jiggers. "A drop o' the Irish, son?" he asked jocularly. Shaun was only jokey when he was uneasy. He handed me a small glass. "Smuggled it in, last time I was down South. A mick can't live by beer alone. *Slainte!*" He tossed back his slug and poured another. "So. Tell me." He propped his brown tasselled Oxfords on the corner of the desk and challenged me with his chin. "Caracas."

I sank down slightly in my chair. I had no real pleasure in pursuing this, but he had his teeth into it, I could see.

"I was taken on as consultant by the Venezuelan government."

"Billion dollar housing project, yes, I know. Go on."

"They had these shanty towns — *barriadas* — they wanted replaced with a modern suburb. Half a million people, living in mud-and-paper shacks. Chickens and goats in the alleys."

"Sounds like Mzilikazi," Shaun chuckled.

"The Venezuelans were ashamed of them. Bad for the country's image, when visitors look out of the modern hotels and see such chaos. All the officials were certain the *barriaderos* were just dying to exchange their hovels for bright new highrises. They were not. When the time came to shift them to our spanking new Utopia, they put up barricades. They shot at us."

"No!"

"Yeah. Two cops were killed, ten wounded. God knows how many *barriaderos* died."

"But that's insane!" Shaun's face was flushed with indignation and distress. "Why? Why were those people so adamant?"

"The *barriada* was their home. Their own creation. They didn't want our culture forced upon them. They refused to buy our notion of how things ought to be. And they were right."

"But you were offering decent accommodation, at low rent?"

"Even in that our notions were flawed. In their shanties the people paid no rent. They were squatters. And every hovel was a poor man's home. He'd built it, with his family and friends, in his own style. We were telling him our style was superior."

"Wasn't it?"

"No. How could we ever think so? Except that it's our basic 'white' assumption that, even in our hollowness, we know what 'culture' is."

Shaun waved this aside. He refilled our glasses.

"So, what happened? After the cops were shot?"

"I was shaken. I advised a radical rethink. The government disagreed. They were incensed. They sent in troops and tanks, followed by bulldozers. In a fortnight, the *barriada* was a ruin. The jungles were jammed with homeless refugees."

"Holy Mother! You must've been shattered."

"Yeah. I was."

"What did you do?"

"Resigned from the consultancy, for a start. Returned the balance of my whacking great fee. Took a good look round. I compared our spanking new suburb with the memory of the *barriada*. Even as a ruin it was more apt — visually, humanly."

"But damnitall, it was a slum!"

"What is a slum?"

"A dirty, foul and evil place," Shaun said simply. "Packed with dirty, foul and evil people."

"Very graphic," I smiled. "Sounds like Bulawayo."

"Oh come on," he retorted irritably. "You're such a damn idealist!"

"What the hell is that?" I shot back, also irritated now.

"Someone whose idea of things is more compelling than the things themselves," he countered strongly. "Someone who's obsessed with a yearning for simplicity in all the ripe human confusion. Someone — religious!"

"Sounds like you."

Shaun chuckled. "We're a right pair, eh? Still deciding the nature of existence in short pants."

"Still."

He dropped his Oxfords to the floor and put his bare elbows on the desk. "Do you still have your London office?"

"No. I told you. I turned it over to my partners. They're doing splendidly."

"I'm sorry."

"For what?"

"For the failure of your soul to rise above disillusion." He smiled, mocking his own solemnity. "But then, I'm limited. Some things are clearly beyond me. But at least I'm not burdened with your brand of spiritual pride." He shoved his chin at me. "Anyway, if you feel as you do about architecture, why are you working here, on our New Jerusalem?"

"Old habit."

But Shaun was not that easily answered. "You once fled Africa's simplicities. Now you've returned to them, it seems. Why?"

"A dog must return to its vomit. It's a stink that haunts him."

"Very witty," Shaun said. But his eyes were clouded.

Shaun drove me home, to Leonie's house, after work. I asked him in for a drink.

Leonie, David and my father were in the T.V. room watching the box. My father rose and shook Shaun's hand warmly. "Shaun, how nice to see you. Are you having any trouble with my prodigal son?"

"Your son's a truly gifted man, sir," Shaun said simply. "I'm ashamed of my limitations in his shadow."

"So am I," Dad said, mock-grim. "So am I." He smiled, proud and uncomfortable together. "There's this T.V. report on the fighting up north we're going to watch. Will you join us?"

"For a moment. My wife's expecting me for dinner." But Shaun sat down and received the whisky David brought him.

The television flickered. A narrator's crisp voice crackled from the speaker.

"Our Rhodesian Broadcasting Corporation reporter Doug Fourie accompanies a stick of airborne Fire Force commandos into action in the Zambesi Valley ... "

The reporter's face appeared on the screen, against the background of a dusty airstrip in the bush on which an ancient Dakota was parked, engines spluttering.

"The boys are hunting a bunch of terrs holed up in a rocky hillside forty miles east of here." The camera zoomed in on the plane. "These thirty-year-old Dakotas, backbone of the Rhodesian Light Infantry counter-insurgency wing, are veterans of General Orde Wingate's Burma Campaign. They are well-tried warhorses. The Dak can fly in at five hundred feet and drop a stick of commandos right on top of the infiltrators before the terrorists know what's hit 'em."

The commando stick — twenty armed young men in T-shirts, khaki shorts and tennis shoes — climbed into the plane. Parachutes were strapped to their backs. Their automatic weapons and ammunition pouches were slung with a casual bravado. Their sergeant could not have been more than twenty-two. His head was shaved. He sported a jaunty skull-and-crossbones medallion pinned to his breast.

"Sergeant Maclennan is a veteran of seventeen contacts. Only last month he broke his leg in a drop and had to fight off a squad of terrs with his pistol. He wiped three, and got a bullet in his shoulder. He crawled back to base through the bush."

The sergeant's face came into close-up, grinning. "This outfit is called 'The White Mambas'. The mamba, as you know, is a very deadly serpent."

The Dakota rattled down the runway in a cloud of dust. In the belly of the plane the paratroopers checked their weapons. An eighteen-year-old had wrapped the butt of his FN automatic rifle in leopard skin. He wore a choker of African beadwork. His eyes were grim.

The bush ran out below. From this height the camera picked out kudu loping through the long grass, bright scuts scattering in panic. The deer vanished behind a rocky *kopje* in a puff of dust.

"Contact!"

The pilot's voice leapt metallically from the intercom. The sergeant jabbed his finger at the open door. The paratroopers lined up. The Dakota dipped and the ground came up fast.

"Away!"

The young bodies hurled themselves out of the plane. The camera ran behind them to the gaping doorway. Parachutes popped. In a few seconds the first commandos hit the deck. They shed their 'chutes and scattered into the bush.

The plane swerved, tilting the camera angle. The lens caught a Rhodesian soldier in the act of being cut down by two guerrillas who jumped up out of the long grass a yard or two before him and fired their Kalashnikovs directly into his face.

"Sweet Jesus!" the reporter gasped.

On the ground, where the scene shifted, the bush was loud with gunfire. Everyone seemed to be shooting at once. Two young "White Mambas" ran before the camera, firing from the hip as they wove and ducked. The ground exploded in front of them. The troopers flung themselves sideways into the grass.

"The bush is so thick here," the reporter's voice said breathlessly, "your enemy can be skulking in the grass no more than a yard away. It's face-to-face contact. Fire first, ask second. A real test of nerve, that our boys always win."

The volume of fire put down in the first few minutes was so ferocious the bush was chopped to fragments. Grenades, hand bombs, bullets whizzed and thumped, splintering tree trunks. The ricochets of the lighter Soviet-made ammunition of the guerrillas pinged and zipped. The heavier Rhodesian rounds sliced through everything.

The firepower was ferocious. In a few minutes the contact was concluded.

"Terrs always shoot high in thick bush," the sergeant told the camera, as the "kill" was counted. "They go for the face." Six bloodied bodies were laid out in the dust; five black, one white. "Our usual kill ratio is twenty-to-one," the sergeant shrugged. "Poor old Hennie ran out of moz today. His number came up, that's all." He prodded a dead guerrilla with the toe of his tennis shoe. "Shot in the back, see? The buggers are always chopped running away."

The sergeant picked up a small red book dropped in the dirt. "Mao Tse-tung," he scowled. "'Surround the cities from the countryside,' the old Chink commie says. Well, these *munts* are still a long, long way from Salisbury, man."

In contrast with the casual dress of the Rhodesians, the dead guerrillas were kitted out like regular troops in full camouflage battledress and service boots. One boy had a bullet through his eye. It was a clean hole, a neat scoop in the black face, as if a sculptor had not yet finished off his bronze. Round his lean neck was a battered tin crucifix and a Tom Thumb tobacco bag filled with *muti* — magical charms for protection against the Evil Eye.

A white trooper tore these talismans from the corpse's neck and pocketed them as battle trophies.

The reporter's face repossessed the screen. "A typical contact with Fire Force Nine, 'The White Mambas,' in the Zambesi Escarpment. First the bullets, then the beer —"

An open truck barrelled through the grass towards the unit. The men climbed on, licking dry lips, after tossing in the corpses.

"— with a little blood on the way," the reporter said. The truck vanished into the bush. The reporter's face reappeared. "Operation Hurricane is doing its job protecting our northern bush from red terrorist infiltration. Doing its share to hold the boundary of democracy in Southern Africa, that runs from the Indian Ocean to the Atlantic, along the line of the Zambesi. This is Doug Fourie, with Fire Force Nine, in the northern bush."

The reporter's face faded out. The screen flickered as the heroic strains of the Beethoven chorale welled up.

There was a harsh silence in the room. Lovey entered, sucking a lollipop. He intuited the tension instantly, and parked himself in a corner of the settee without a word.

"Typical?" I queried, finally.

"Yes and no," Shaun said gruffly. "To start with, no black Rhodesian troopers were shown, and our forces are now about eighty per cent African. But this was a special unit, I suppose."

"You mean, it's kind of civil war?" Leonie asked. "Black against black?"

"In a way," Shaun nodded. "In a way. Though army policy is to use Ndebele troops in Shona areas, and vice-versa. The tribes are old enemies." He rose. "I must go."

Leonie shuddered. "I don't want to ever see my sons 'run out of moz'!"

"How old are your boys?"

"Thirteen and ten."

"Oh my dear, this small unpleasantness will be done before your lads are service age. If it isn't over long before then, we've had it anyway."

I saw Shaun to his Citroen. "Nice family," he said, and drove off.

"Nice man," Dad said, when I returned.

Leonie's thoughts were still running on the track of her main concern. "The White Man's Burden," she muttered, gazing at her son with stark eyes. "Are Jews really white?"

"Of course we are!" Dad exclaimed.

Leonie turned to him. "Was Grandpa Kahn 'white' in Russia? Was David 'white' in Nazi Germany?"

"Sure I was," David spluttered, angry and disconcerted.

"We know you were in the Hitler Youth," his wife retorted. "Until they found out you were a yid." She grinned at me. "He still has his Nazi uniform tucked away somewhere. When they were kids, he and his brother Egon used to put on their black duds and parade up and down in the bedroom of their house down on Abercorn Street giving Hitler salutes."

"Rubbish!" David was purple. "Slander!"

"Heil Hitler! Heil Hitler!" Leonie taunted, jutting out her arm.

"Children, my tummy," Dad moaned.

"White?" Leonie murmured, grim again. "In the old days we never questioned such things. Jews were just happy to find a place where they'd let us live. The *goyim* were too busy hating the *schwartzes* to have time to bother us. What do you think, Paul?"

I shrugged. "It's a question of survival, I suppose."

"How do you mean, survival?"

"Jews have survived two thousand years of hostility by being very sharp indeed about their own motives, and that of their masters. It's a kind of clarity that's been forced upon us. We can't afford to be as fuzzy-minded as the English, say. The White Man's Burden can't be ours."

"What are you saying?" Leonie frowned.

Lovey spoke out suddenly. "I understand."

All faces jerked in his direction. He fidgeted uneasily, a scruffy fat boy under challenge. I could have hugged him.

"You?" his father spluttered. "You don't know your arse from your—"

"What do you understand, Choppychops?" Leonie asked tenderly.

Lovey's face reddened. "I want to learn to make my own bed, Ma," he blurted.

There was a communal gasp. Lawlene and Eric, who had just come in, flung themselves on the carpet and howled with laughter.

Lovey jumped up and fled. His cry came to us across the living room. "Make my own bed!"

"I'm so worried about that boy — so worried!" Leonie moaned.

She and I were alone in the lounge later that night. Everyone else was in bed. Down the passage David's snores punched holes in the night's silence.

Leonie stopped pacing. Her eyes were red with tears. "You know, he dresses up? In my clothes? Down to bra and panties?"

"So what?" I said. "Some boys do, at his age. I used to love to clatter about in Mom's old shoes. And see, I'm normal!"

"He's so sensitive," Leonie said, twisting a hankie in her hands. "So sensitive. How can he live? He has no friends. The kids call him a fairy."

"Kids are stupid. And conformist. They always pick on the special ones."

Leonie's cheeks wobbled with joy. "He is special, isn't he?" She smiled shyly. "Just like his Uncle Paul?"

"Exactly."

Leonie came to hug me. Her tears dampened my cheek. "You're a nice man, brother, under all that crabbiness. Yes!" She stepped back and cupped my chin in her hand. "A really nice man," she crooned, flicking my nose with her fingertip as we both laughed.

Next morning, Grace brought me a plain unstamped manila envelope as I was sipping coffee by the pool before going to work. "Paul Kahn, Esquire" was typed on the label.

"Who brought this, Grace?"

"A black boy, baas."

I opened the envelope. Inside was a sheet of cheap ruled notepaper. Its message read: "Great Zimbabwe Cafe, corner Grey Street and Ninth Avenue. Tomorrow, 11 A.M. Please destroy."

Nkabi!
Trembling, I burned the sheet in the ashtray.

The Great Zimbabwe Cafe was owned by a Portuguese family, refugees from the war in Mozambique, but its clientele was wholly African.

The place was jammed with young blacks drinking Pepsis and Fantas. The shouts and laughter I had heard as I pushed the door open ceased the instant my white cheeks appeared. Faced with a pit of silence, I froze in the doorway. Behind me was the bright street, before me a dark hole. I wavered on this boundary, searching the gloom for Nkabi's face.

His deep voice released me. "Enter!"

I jerked forward a step, tugged towards the blunt command. Nkabi's face came into focus as my eyes adjusted to the gloom. "Nkabi —" I mumbled as a plastic chair struck my knee.

"No names," he said curtly. "Sit down."

I sat. Nkabi was at a table on his own tucked away in a corner. He wore black, as usual. His clerical collar cut his big face from his body. Jesus glittered on his lapel. On the chipped blue enamel tabletop before him was a can of Fanta orange.

The other people in the cafe, mostly jobless young Africans, began to talk again when they saw I was with someone they respected. But their banter was subdued by my white face. The cafe's walls were dark green, the floor was blood-red cement. A long glass counter filled with soft drink cans floated dull silver in the gloom.

Nkabi stared at me warily. "What's that?" he grimaced, pointing at my chest.

I was sporting Cousin Barney's hippy necklace for this meeting. The conceit amused me.

"Music." I jabbed the breastplate knob, releasing a blare of *kwela*. Heads turned, and I shut the radio off.

Nkabi glared at me. I saw black flecks of shaving rash on his swollen jowls. I saw his collar was yellowed with sweat. I saw the uncertainty in his jet eyes. And I perceived myself, cool and white, tanned and easy in my open tennis shirt and pale beige denim slacks.

"How is the Great Man?" I asked.

Nkabi leant towards me, shoving the soft drink can aside as if it were a bug. "Is it the truth you have access to the Post Office Telecom Centre?"

"I told you, my cousin is in charge there."

"He will let you in?"

"He's begging to show me round."

"Good." He nodded. "You will do that."

"I will?"

"I have said. He has said it. We must discuss a plan."

I stared at him. So it was on. Just like that!

"A plan," he repeated impatiently. "Ideas?"

Actually, I had not come unprepared. I pulled an envelope from my back pocket, unfolded a small sketch, and laid it flat on the table before him.

"This is my idea," I began, beckoning him closer. Our heads were just a foot or so apart as we huddled over the paper.

He frowned. "What is it? Some garment, it appears?"

"It's a waistcoat. A kind of vest, with inside pockets. Made of quilted rayon. The kind of thing bullion smugglers use."

Nkabi knitted his brows. "Bullion?"

"A sort of lifesaver jacket, if you like. Body-hugging, with shoulder straps, tucked under the arms, so. The straps have poppers, so the vest can be swiftly shed. I can wear it under a loose safari suit. In one second or two, when no one's looking, I can drop it in a corner."

I realized I had explained everything in a jumble. Nkabi's face was a perplexity. "What for?" he asked.

"To carry plastic explosive into the Telecom Centre. Under a jacket."

"Ah." His eyes lit up. "Explosive."

"Yes. I estimate you could store up to six kilos of plastic in the pockets of such a garment without seeming too fat. Bullion smugglers often carry more bulk."

"Explosive," he repeated, as if it were a magic word.

"Yes." I was calmer now. "So far as I can make out, the core of the communications centre is a control and computer room about twenty feet square, packed with delicate gear. Five or six kilos of high-impact explosive in such a tight space should make quite a mess, especially if some incendiary material were added to the blast. Millions of dollars of virtually irreplaceable sanctions-busting equipment would be mangled."

Nkabi stared at me. Respect flickered in his eyes. "You really think it would work?"

"Why not? What are the problems? Let's look at them. One: entry. I could be body-searched. It may well be perfunctory, since I am the chief's cousin. Have to take a chance on that. Two: detonation. How do we set off the blast?"

"Ah," he nodded. "Tricky, that."

"What are the options? One: a time fuse. But that is inexact. We can't leave the thing lying around too long. It might be found. And time fuses tend to be bulky, with clocks and all. Two: delayed-action chemical pressure fuse. Acid in a phial, eating away a copper wire. Too sensitive. I'll be wearing the damn thing and could set it off by accidentally bumping into something. And it's also inexact."

"Difficult," Nkabi frowned. "What other?"

"Suicide or radio," I said crisply.

"What?"

"It's either a kind of kamikaze number, with me as pilot detonating the blast while I'm in there—"

"No!" His cry was emphatic. "We want no martyrs."

"Especially not white ones, eh?" I smiled. "I didn't mean that seriously — the kamikaze bit."

"Bad joke," he grunted. "Stupid."

"Also, I don't want to harm anyone, if I can help it."

Nkabi gave me a look. An incongruous grin parted his prim lips. "You have scruples, sir?"

"Yes. Actually, it's very doubtful if we can be certain to have the place quite cleared. We must detonate as soon as possible after the bomb's in place."

"So what's the answer? Radio?"

"Radio. Remote control." An idea struck me. "We could use this!"

He was startled. "Your silly neck thing?" He jabbed a finger at my breastplate.

"Why not? My cousin made it. He'd be flattered to see me wear it on the day."

"Does it only receive?" he wondered doubtfully.

"Apparently not. It's also a transceiver, I believe. Could be fixed to send a short-range signal to a receiver sewn into the vest. That signal will prime the fuse. All I'd need to do then, from a few hundred yards distance, is press this knob, and —"

"Give it to me," he interrupted. "Our radio expert will fix it."

"You have one? A really good one?"

"First-rate chap," Nkabi said proudly. "Trained abroad."

"Of course he'll have to consider the problem of static from all the electronic gear in the Centre. The counter to that, I'd say, is to build in a wavelength key."

"Pardon?"

"Lock the receiver in the vest to one very precise ultra-high-frequency signal. An absolutely exact key, to unlock the fuse."

"Is there such a mechanism?" he wondered.

"The fuse could be of the tungsten filament type, powered by shockproof batteries. He could also fit a vacuum relay valve, to delay reception of the signal. That would mean the knob here, on my chest, would have to be pressed for fifteen consecutive seconds to turn the key. Just to make sure it's not set off accidentally."

"Sounds very bulky."

"Not at all. A good radio man could miniaturize all that so it's no bigger than a pack of cigarettes. We need it to be effective up to two or three hundred yards, I'd say. A good few loops of copper wire aerial wound round in the vest should do it."

"How do you know all this?" he asked, abruptly suspicious.

"The Bulawayo Public Library has an excellent reference section. This is a mining country, remember. Detonators and explosives are a speciality."

"You did that much research? Since yesterday?"

"I'm used to research. It's part of my profession. It only takes a few hours, if you know where to look. And how to look."

"You are —" He paused, not quite knowing how to express what I was. His eyes clouded. "They will know it is you."

"I doubt it. The blast should destroy most of the bomb itself. I doubt they have such skilled forensic scientists round here, to make an exact analysis of such a sophisticated device from a few scraps. They'll probably think it was a high-tension blowout, or some such."

Nkabi gave me a hard look. "Do you know of the interrogation methods of the Specials? Have you heard of 'The Brickie'?"

"No."

"They make a suspect balance on a pile of loose bricks. He holds three more over his head, up high. They leave you standing there for twenty, thirty hours. If you sag they kick you in the private parts. It breaks many brave men."

"My God!" I blanched.

"Second thoughts?"

"How long will it take you to get all this stuff ready?"

"Some weeks. The Leader — *He* would like the action to coincide with the ceremonial opening of Smith's parliament, on Tuesday October Sixteenth."

"Okay. I can arrange that. The rest is up to you." I removed the necklace and laid it on the table. Many eyes were watching us covertly, but Nkabi did not seem to care. He took the electronic chain and tucked it into his pocket. He folded the sketch and slipped it inside his jacket. "Tuesday the Sixteenth, then?" I queried.

"Yes. And we have a code name for this action." His voice was neutral, but I could sense an undertone of mockery.

"What's that?"

"Operation *Nyogamhlope*."

"*White Snake?*"

Nkabi rose. The meeting was over. He straightened his big body and marched towards the door. The young blacks fell silent. Their faces were awed by his massive presence. Nkabi put his hand on the doorknob and jerked it open.

The brightness of the street burst in. Nkabi's shoulders slumped. As he stepped out onto the sidewalk and entered the White Zone, his black authority melted like butter in the sun.

# 6

# KITH AND KIN

A racing bike almost flattened me as I stepped out onto the sidewalk. Ribbons whirled on the wheels. A wild black face under a white cowboy hat screeched at me in Ndebele. The rider's fringed leather jacket, bright with beadwork, banged against my chest as the front wheel scraped my thigh and crashed into the cafe's plate-glass window.

The big pane shuddered, but held. Spokes and limbs tangled on the pavement as bike and rider collapsed. I bent to help the man up. Under the squashed cowboy hat I recognized Tenja. He unknotted his legs from the wheels and grinned at me.

"You twit!" I shouted, shaken by delayed shock. "You could've hurt me — and yourself! What the hell do you mean by racing your bike on the pavement?"

Tenja's face shut down. His wry grin of apology and chagrin vanished behind a blank mask of deference. "Sorry, baas."

I shook him. "Never mind the 'sorry baas' shit. You're a bloody idiot!" And I burst out laughing.

His mask cracked. "Sorry, Paul," he said softly.

"That's some jacket," I said, admiring the fringes. "Where'd you get it?"

"It's my brother's. He was in Jo'burg, working in the mines. He lets me wear it sometimes, on my day off." He brushed the jacket down lovingly.

"Where do you spend your spare time?"

"In there." He jerked a thumb at the cafe. I offered him a smoke. We lit up. "My friends and me, we meet for a Fanta and a talk. Yes, we talk," he added significantly. He frowned. "You been in the Zimbab?"

I smiled. "I have friends, too."

Tenja scowled at me, disturbed by the thought that I had invaded his haunt. I tapped his shoulder and walked off.

The Main Post Office was a few blocks up, on Main Street. The entrance to the Telecom Centre was round the side, on Eighth Avenue. It was guarded by an African constable in gleaming leather leggings and a khaki pillbox hat. The narrow red sandstone doorway was topped by a bright coat-of-arms.

The constable snapped into an elaborate salute as I walked by. He clicked his boot heels sharply and flicked his stiff right arm to his hat. His eyes looked right through me with a military ferocity. I replied with a casual wave and strolled on.

On the next corner up was the public library where I'd spent the previous afternoon, researching explosives in the Mining Section. It was one of those grey granite buildings a British colonial administration provides to remind the locals of the weight of Westminster.

BULAWAYO PUBLIC LIBRARY was incised in gilded Roman letters over the corner entrance. It was here, as a fat boy of fourteen, that I had one day abruptly discovered books:

This day, a hand seems to grab me by the collar as I'm cycling along Fort Street. It yanks me from my bike, shoves me up the library steps. On the pavement my wheels are left spinning.

It's black inside, after the dazzle of the street. There's a weird smell, of books — hundreds of them, thousands; a guilty, almost sexual stink of knowledge. In my bulging khaki shorts, askew school tie, soiled hat and sagging socks, I'm a plump pubescent Adam in the Paradise of Sin.

I know it's dirty. I sense this revelation will shatter the daze of my soccer-and-bioscope, milkshake-and-masturbation daydream in this Rip-van-Winkleland Rhodesia. But I have to know what must be known. It's my fate.

The librarian is a scrawny snake. Her ice-chip eyes prick

me as I stumble towards the racks. Blindly, I reach out. A book opens in my grubby paw. I drown:

The River Neva gives out a stench as it thaws in the spring of old St. Petersburg. The dark alleys rot where Raskolnikov writhes on his bed of rags, remorseful over his murder of the old hag of a moneylender.

Dostoevsky. *Crime and Punishment.* Russia:

A frozen land, erotic with suffering, randy with despair. The Russia that's the root of my Grandpa's bungled flight half a century before. Russia ... lost true homeland of my young colonial Jewish soul. *Russia!* My chest swells. Joy and terror are bursting in my heart. *Home!*

Hours later, at closing time, I am ejected. The sun blinds me. I don't recognize the street. Africa seems as hostile as the moon.

Every day, after school, I return. I run through all the Russians, too nervous to sit. I fidget, scratch my crotch, pick my nose in ecstatic fright. I cannot borrow these books, cannot take such subversion home. I'm even terrified the Russian reek might stick to me, betray me at the dinner table. I know it would upset my folks.

There is another Russian smell that I know — the odour of my Grandpa's house. But that is clammy: the stink of sour fish and foreignness. When the old man embraces me I'm glad I am Rhodesian. I'm happy to smell of sunlight, steak and soccer. I'm very pleased I'm white.

Grandpa is a European, but in a very alien sense. European is a term used constantly in southern Africa. "Europeans Only," the park benches declare, along with the public toilets. I'm a European, but I sure as hell don't smell like Grandpa!

The most sickening thing about my Grandpa's house is not the odour but the *mikveh* — the ritual bath the old ones use to cleanse their shrivelled bodies each Friday before the first Sabbath star appears in the sky. This silvery slit in the basement of the Main Street bungalow, this glimmering wet hole, sucks me into the darkness I fear haunts all sunlight.

Russia is black. Rhodesia is white.

Russia is dark. Rhodesia is light.

Russia is thick. Rhodesia is thin.

This split hardens in my soft young mind. It cuts me in two, but I read on, even as each book separates soul from body, heart from mind, there from here. I read on, ravenous for *knowledge*.

"Hey! Paul! Dreaming?"

The female derision froze me in mid-reverie. Mona's face was at the window of a lime-green Datsun parked at the curb. Her sunspecs were like the eyebulbs of a giant praying mantis.

"Where were you?" she demanded. "So far away?" Her voice wavered abruptly. "Buy me a drink?"

We drove to the Selborne Hotel. The lounge was cool and dark. A waiter in a white coat and tasselled fez took our order. He delivered the drinks on a tin tray, but with a flourish. For a moment the shabby old hotel had style.

"The chap has class," I remarked.

"So have you," she said. "But you're ashamed of it."

"You think?"

"I know. Cheers." She gave me a sardonic salute and sipped her yellow Advokaat.

"How can you drink that revolting stuff, and at lunchtime?"

"I like it."

"Eggnog and brandy?"

"I like it."

I leant back and lit a cigarette. "What's up?"

Mona's head jerked on the swan neck. "Bad night. Bad dreams."

"Tell me. I'm a connoisseur of bad dreams."

"You wouldn't like mine."

"Like that, mm?"

Mona fumbled in her bright green beadbag for her long cigarette holder, and jammed in a Gold Leaf. I gave her a light.

"My life's a bloody mess," she said.

I kept silent. Mona sucked thirstily at her ebony mouthpiece. The smoke spurted between her teeth like dragon's breath.

She said abruptly: "Help me."

"Me? I can't even help myself!"

She stared at me. Her eyes were very black. "Don't I

interest you, at all?'' She added quickly, ''Well, not surprising. I'm just a hicktown hoyden.''

''Look, love,'' I muttered, ''you don't need me in your life. I'm no woman's meat, these days.''

''You say such funny things!''

''I mean it. Listen to me.''

''I'm listening.''

''You're a sexy woman. Very. Never mind the 'hicktown hoyden' crap. But you don't need me. I'm no one's salvation, least of all my own.''

Her purpled lips twitched round the ebony. ''But you've got to have a woman. I mean, you're the kind of man who really needs sex.''

''Yeah. True. I wouldn't say no to a lighthearted little encounter. But I'm not very light of heart just now. Neither are you.''

''Let's just do it, anyway.''

''Mona! You're not hearing me.''

She touched my lower lip. ''Do women always take a bite out of you?''

''How did you know it was a bite?''

''What else?'' She smiled brilliantly. ''Paul, let's just cut the cackle and do it, okay? No claims, no regrets?''

''I've got regrets already.''

Mona grinned. ''Fact is, I'm randy as hell.''

''So am I.''

''Well, then?''

''I'll think about it.''

''So will I!'' she laughed. ''So will I!''

Mona offered me a lift to my parents' house in North End when I said I was going to visit my mother. ''I won't come in.'' She added quickly, ''Don't worry! Your mom doesn't like me. Neither does your sister. I hope you do, though.''

We drove out along Main Street. As we passed Second Avenue, Mona saw my eyes jerk sideways.

''That's the house where you grew up, isn't it, down there?''

''How did you know?'' I asked, startled by her quickness.

''I know a lot about you,'' she smiled. ''Want to drive by?

But I warn you, it's owned by Hindus now. This whole part of town is Little Asia."

We circled round the block and parked opposite 28 Second Avenue.

It was a modest colonial home. A pair of dusty date palms framed a narrow gravel walk that led up to a columned veranda under a red tin roof. Lizards swarmed in the arid rockery that passed for a garden. To one side were the garage and the *picanin kayas*, as the servants' cells were called. Two Africans were squatting there, beside the porch where I used to sleep, boiling up a blackened pot of maize-meal *sadza* paste over an open fire.

"Not very grand, is it?" Mona smiled.

"Not very," I agreed.

"Ah well, we all have to start somewhere."

A plump Hindu housewife came out to hang a wet pink saree on the washline. Two small brown children rushed giggling out of the sleeping porch and chased one another round the pawpaw trees that led to the back yard.

"Never mind," Mona laughed. "Moses was born in the bullrushes!"

We said goodbye on the corner before my parents' new house, the one they had moved to after I had left home.

"Call me," she said tensely, and spurted away in her Datsun.

My mother's housegirl, Susan, lolled giggling under a jacarandah tree with a dapper swain. She curtsied to me as I went by, as all good mission-trained girls were taught to do. Her suitor, a proud young man in spotless white cricket flannels, looked away as if he had not seen me, to avoid having to call me "baas".

My mother sat in an armchair in the glass-walled lounge, dozing with her feet up. Her head lolled loose on her bosom, trembling a little even in sleep. On the side table was a pile of her staple romantic novels, a glass of water and the bottle of L-dopa, the latest and most potent anti-Parkinsonism drug.

Her eyes flicked open. She was always instantly aware of my presence. "Paul? My boy," she murmured, reaching out for me.

"Hi, Mom." I brushed her dry cheek. "Having a snooze?"

"Just a little nap," she apologized.

I sat beside her. "How are you today?"

"Fine."

"She always says that," I mimicked Dad.

"Don't mock." She squeezed my hand. She peered at me, as if trying to focus down a long tunnel. "You're more Silverman than Kahn, you know? My family—"

"Does it matter?" I queried, but gently.

Her reply was firm. "It matters." Her eyes finally found my range. They zeroed in on mine. "What *are* you doing here?"

I shrugged. "Killing time."

"Can it be? Killed?"

"Sure. If you use the right weapons."

She stared at me. "You always were . . . hard. On yourself, mostly."

"And on you. And Dad. And the rest."

"No more?"

"No more. I've forgiven you for being my parents." I smiled.

She clutched my hand. Her palm was surprisingly strong; the small, adroit dressmaker's fingers were still capable of a hard grip. "You will survive," she said. "You will."

"You, too, Ma. You, too."

"No," she said. "I've had it."

There was not a shred of self-pity in her tone. It was flatly factual.

"We come from a race of survivors," I tried to jolly. "'Survival is the ultimate virtue.'"

Her eyes would not let mine go. "Get my bag," she said, finally, releasing me.

I passed her the big brown bag. She reached in and produced a sheaf of papers. "Remember these?" she asked slyly. "Your dirty stories?"

"My what?"

I took the papers. Schoolboy script covered the ruled sheets, now yellowing. I read a sentence and blushed hot.

"Dirty stories!" Mom chuckled. "Yours! Very sexy."

"You kept this schoolboy trash, for twenty-five years?"

"Very sexy." She shut her eyes and frowned with recollection. " 'Bill put his hard knee between Clara's sweaty thighs ...' Sexy!"

"Mom!"

" 'Clara groaned in trembling passion ... Her ecstasy was close!' " Her eyes flicked open. "You should've been a writer. More your own man."

"You make me blush, old girl."

"My stories. Give them here." She tucked the precious papers back into her bag. "I read them all the time. They comfort me. I have a clever son."

"Mom. Dear." My eyes were prickling. "I'm not so clever, you know."

"You are," she insisted, stubborn as ever. "A Silverman, not a Kahn. Clever." She focused on me shrewdly. "It's the Silverman blood causes you trouble. Kahns haven't the imagination ... to be scared."

"I don't know—"

She cut me short with a gesture. "This house is yours. Your share. Inheritance."

"Pardon?"

"Leonie's had her lot. We bought her her house. This one is yours."

"But Mom, I don't need it!"

"Not the point. Yours. Your share. Inheritance."

I was dumb with amazement. I looked around, at my "inheritance" with a blurred eye.

The mantleshelf over the unused brick hearth was a shrine to my cleverness. Propped there was a leather-bound book in which were pasted all my school reports, from kindergarten on: "Paul is a bright, responsive boy. It is a pleasure to teach him."; "Paul should do brilliantly in his Cambridge School Certificate graduation. The School expects great honour from his future career."; Paul is a natural leader. He commands respect from his peers at all times."

Beside this tome was the silver kiddush cup I'd won for being the outstanding Barmitzvah Boy of Bulawayo in 1948. Ranged alongside were my sporting trophies: Team

Tennis Captain, Milton Senior School; Team Soccer Captain, Milton Junior School; Junior Champion, Parkview Tennis Club, 1950. And then there was the framed award of my Beit Scholarship, that had paid my way to architectural school in London. And finally, framed in silver, set in the place of honour, my graduation diploma from the Architectural Association.

There were framed photographs, too: Of me in my pram, guarded by my black nanny; Of me in short pants, wearing a tie, seated at the wheel of our old Vauxhall; Of me in tennis whites, racquet in hand, the championship cup between my bare tanned knees; Of me holding my Cambridge School Certificate — distinctions in eight subjects — in blue school blazer with blue-and-white piping and silver badge.

"Inheritance?" I mumbled, turning my eyes back to my mother's smiling face.

"Inheritance," she said firmly, dismissing the topic. "Read to me."


" 'Melissa imagined the Count's arrival. Her heart thumped atrociously in her slender breast at the thought of his ravishing dark eyes!' " *The Treasures of Her Heart* was a lengthy epic. We were on page 557 when my father came home from work.

My mother had fallen asleep, lulled by my "rich voice," as she called it. Dad gazed at her with weepy eyes as he loosened his tie and slipped out of his beige cotton jacket.

"She's not well, not well at all," he whispered.

Mom's eyes flicked open instantly. "I'm fine, Joe. Fine."

Dad sank into the settee. He sipped the lemonade Susan brought him, proffering the chilled glass with a shy curtsied bob of the head.

"How's the factory?" I asked.

He scowled. "Trouble, today. Agitators. Had to call the police."

"Agitators?"

"ZAPU boys, stirring up the staff. Threatening them with *tagati* if they don't go on strike. Black magic — the blacks are so superstitious." He gave a very Jewish shrug. "Tragedy is, there's massive unemployment. Every time we put a sign out on the factory gate, there's a queue round the block. And yet these agitators want the boys to strike? *Meshugeh!*" He threw up his hands. "Sanctions! When will the world just let us be? Recognize our independence? This could be one of the richest countries in Africa. We have so many natural resources: chrome, asbestos, coal, gold, tobacco, maize, fruit. Yet blacks are starving on the Tribal Trust Lands. The townships are choked with jobless Africans. *Meshugeh.* A crazy world, my boy."

"A crazy world, Dad," I agreed.

He glanced at me sharply, to see if I was mocking. "They have their ZAPUs and their ZANUs, their ZANLAs and their ZIPAs, their FROLIZIs. What good does it do them, the blacks, all that — that salad of initials? Zimbabwe African People's Union; Zimbabwe African National Union; Zimbabwe African National Liberation Army; Front for the Liberation of Zimbabwe. *Meshugeh.*"

"Crazy."

"Joe, your tummy," Mom warned.

But Dad was in full flood. "When they're finished with us, the tribes will slaughter one another! Ndebele will kill Shona. Karanga will massacre Manyika. Traditional enemies. They've always hated one another. It was only the coming of the European that brought peace and law and order to Rhodesia. And you want us to step aside?"

"Me?" I said, startled by this sudden attack.

"You!" the old man shouted, red in the face. "You British in Westminster! 'One man one vote,' you demand. 'NIBMAR — No Independence Before Majority African Rule.' You send out your Pearce Commissions. You take the testimony of intimidated blacks and say we aren't yet ready to govern ourselves! You listen to the Bishop Muzorewas and the Josiah Nkunzis — those intimidators and terrorists — and tell us the Africans won't accept our constitution!"

"I haven't said a word—"

"Joe! Your tummy!"

" 'Kith and kin' — that's the cry. You British are our very own kith and kin. Yet you listen to a bunch of *schwartzes!*"

"Joe! *Shtum!*"

Mom's voice was peremptory. Its command rang out. My father sagged down in his seat and rubbed his hot cheeks miserably.

"Kith and kin," he mumbled, peeking at me sorrowfully through his fingers. "Our very own kith and kin."

# 7

# THUGS

My niece shrilled: "So, Uncle Paul, you drink in *munt* cafes!" This was delivered at the highest pitch of her ten-year-old voice, instantly silencing the room.

My Dad ceased moaning about his tummy. My sister cut short her loud complaint about the Africans besieging her pharmacy for antibiotics. Lovey stopped bickering with Eric over the game of draughts they were playing on the lounge's parquet floor. My two aunts, June and Rose — the Green Crocodile Maidens — suspended the clicking of their knitting needles.

All eyes turned to me. Even my mother snapped out of her bored doze to stare at my startled face.

"Drinks in *munt* cafes?" Leonie echoed.

Lawlene stepped forward into the centre of the circle on this cue. Her plump round face was pink with triumph. Her light grey eyes were shining. "I saw Uncle Paul in that *munt* cafe on Grey Street, sitting with an African man. He was drinking Fanta orange," she added, clinching the matter.

"Drinking Fanta orange!" Aunts June and Rose exclaimed together.

From the neck down, my aunts were identical: barrel-corsetted women with puffed-out floral bosoms and knotty calves. Above the neck, they differed. Aunt June was sallow, liverish, and hawk-nosed with a coy bow of carmined lips. Aunt Rose had a tiny head with a cap of permed greying hair and hooded, melting spaniel eyes like my father's.

Leonie's attack shifted. "What were you doing in town on your own, miss?" she demanded of her daughter.

"I went to Patel's to get my mended ballet pumps," Lawlene countered virtuously. "And there was Uncle Paul—"

"The man's a friend of mine," I cut in crisply, attempting to tough it out. "He's a Methodist parson. Where else could I meet an African but in a *munt* cafe? He wouldn't be allowed in Miekles!" My voice came out steady enough, but my shoulder blades were shivering. A small town is a difficult place for secretive conspiracy.

"You have black friends?" Dad exclaimed. His face wobbled with shock.

"Surely. Besides, the chap's involved with this project I'm working on with Shaun, at Tshabalala."

"But if the police see you?" Dad persisted unhappily.

"Is it illegal, then? To talk to a black man?" I smiled unconvincingly. "Is this the third degree, family?"

Leonie shrugged, half-apologetically. "Things are a bit tense. 'Specially since those poor Canadian tourists were shot up by Zambian soldiers at the Victoria Falls."

"I have a name in this town!" my father cried. "*A name*!"

"Kahn! Kahn!" the Aunties chirruped.

"Do you want the *goyim* to think my son is a *munt*-lover?"

"Kahn! Kahn!" the Aunties chorused.

My mother cut the furor with a sharp command. *"Hou jou bek!"* she snapped, in the Afrikaans of her childhood. *"Shtum.* Shut *up!"*

There was a shocked silence. My mother's eyes were blazing.

"If my son wants to talk to an African, that's his business. I won't have a pair of crocodiles snapping at his heels!"

That seemed to end the incident. My aunts nervously clattered their knitting needles, inching out yet another of the interminable Fair Isle cardigans they specialized in. "Their cupboards must be hot with jerseys," Leonie often said.

Leonie rose heavily to her feet. "Come, snookumses," she summoned her children. "Time to go."

But Lawlene was not so readily robbed of her big moment. She stared at me with sharp, suspicious eyes. She knew in her bones I was far from innocent. "Uncle Paul," she crooned silkily, "you'll be sure and buy me that little gold watch you promised for my birthday next month, won't you?"

Leonie gasped. "You little gold-digger! Your Uncle will do no such thing!"

But the stern young madam smiled at me with very bright eyes, until I conceded with a fumbling nod.

"I apologize for my daughter," Leonie murmured, later that evening, when she and I were alone in the lounge. "She's a nosy little biddy," Leonie added fondly. Then her face sharpened. "You most certainly are not to buy her any little gold watch, you hear me?"

"We'll see," I shrugged. "Actually, I was going to, anyway," I lied. "She showed me the jeweller's window when we were in town one afternoon. If it gives her pleasure ..."

"Be foolish, if you like," Leonie said. "I must start organizing her birthday hop. Set up a marquee on the lawn, maybe. Hire a disco." Not looking at me she added: "This used to be a pleasant country, before we discovered politics. Or politics discovered us."

I chuckled awkwardly. "When I first went abroad, travelling in Europe, nobody knew where Rhodesia was! Each time I showed my passport, outside England, I'd get a suspicious look from the hotel clerk. Now the whole world knows of Rhodesia. That's fame for you."

Leonie said nothing. She was watching me covertly, swinging one pompommed mule and plucking at the fluff on her baby blue gown.

I hurried on, to fill the silence. My own voice sounded shrill. "You know how I first heard of Rhodesia's U.D.I.? From a man in a pension in Granada!"

"Where's that?" Leonie asked, without interest.

"In Spain. It has this Moorish palace, this marvellous Alhambra, up on the hill. Well, I was holed up in a small hotel in the Palace grounds one rainy November with a woman—"

"The Lip-Biter?" Leonie interjected, perking up.

"Huh? No, someone else. I mean, this was 1965 — years earlier."

"You've known a lot of ladies, huh?"

"Yeah, I guess so."

"He guesses so!" Leonie expostulated the ceiling. "And now he's sucker for another!"

"Pardon?"

"Mona," she said curtly." That small-town siren has set her cap for you, brother."

"Sis!" I protested. "Can I get on with my little anecdote?"

"Get on, get on," Leonie muttered, subsiding into her seat.

"Where was I? Oh yeah, in this small pension in the Alhambra ... a rainy day in November ... This, er — friend of mine and I, came back that evening, after a stroll round the ramparts. The hotel porter comes running out to greet us. 'Rho-dess-ya!' he's screeching. 'En la televisión!' He was out of his tree with glee. And there it was, on Spanish T.V., the face of Ian Smith, announcing Rhodesia's Unilateral Declaration of Independence. Amusing, eh?"

"She's a *paskutzva*," Leonie said sharply. "Our local Mata Hari."

"*Paskutzva*?" I laughed. "Haven't heard that Russian curse since Granny Kahn died."

"That's our Mona," Leonie snapped. "A whore."

"Oh God, sis —"

"Have it your own way, but don't say I didn't warn you!" Leonie declared, and marched off to bed.

I was in the bathroom brushing my teeth when I heard the commotion in the back yard. There were female shrieks and male shouts, and the sound of a blunt weapon thudding on flesh.

Hurriedly wiping my mouth, I ran out into the yard. The hysterical uproar came from the servants' quarters.

I dashed towards the *kayas*. A dozen or so half-naked black men and women were reeling round in the small cement-floor courtyard. The women were screaming with fright. The men were moaning in drunken fear. The night air reeked of *kaffir* beer.

David was in the midst of this melee. He wore striped pajamas, his feet were bare, his hair was on end, his specs were askew. In his fist was a thick *knobkerrie* — a knobbed club made of thornwood a yard long.

He was slamming the club on naked limbs. The brown bodies were stained with dark blood. There was a splash of red on David's blue-striped pajama pants. His face was demented, black with rage, as he lashed out, clubbing everything that moved. "Fucking *munts!* Drunken bastards! I'll kill you! Murder you! *Shicker* thugs!"

As I ran up I caught a glimpse of Ray and Grace cowering in a corner on their haunches. Ray wore no pants. Grace's breasts were naked, yellow in the moonlight. She was without her Afro wig and her scalp was bare but for tight coils of sandy hair.

David lunged at Grace, lifting the *knobkerrie.* I grabbed his arm. He whirled on me — then froze. "Paul?" he blinked, shaken out of his murderous trance.

I took the club away from him. His body sagged like a burst balloon. Seizing their moment, the Africans bolted past and hared off down the driveway, clutching clothing and bloodied heads.

Leonie was waiting for us in the kitchen, arms folded, face stony. I sat David down on a metal chair and brought him a glass of water.

He was shivering. His toes curled pitifully on the bare tiles. He sipped his water like a dying man. Leonie stood over him like Fate. She did not say a word. Her silence was a stone on David's bowed head. Her eyes were nails in his skull. After a long, harsh moment she turned on her heel and departed.

Only then, did David dare raise his face to me. "She hates me," he said. "They all hate me, the kids too."

"David—"

"The family hates me," he repeated. The look on his face was so matter-of-fact it chilled my blood.


"Thugs," Shaun said grimly. "A gang of bloody thugs!"

He crouched over the wheel of the Citroen as we sped out of town. It was Friday evening; we were going to spend the weekend at this ranch.

Shaun wore his camouflage battledress. He had just returned from another short tour of duty in the northern bush. His automatic rifle was on the car's back seat, handy for action, "just in case we run into trouble."

His mood was black. A close friend of his, a young

lieutenant in his reserve unit, had been badly wounded in a contact. The white officer and his black sergeant had been returning to base from a routine patrol when the young man had almost trodden on the face of a ZANU guerrilla hiding in the long grass. The infiltrator had squeezed out a burst at close range, up from under. A bullet had smashed the lieutenant's pelvis. It was likely he would be paralyzed for life from the waist down.

"Thugs!" Shaun shouted, accelerating the Citroen to eighty miles an hour on the narrow Mafeking Road.

I had never seen him so angry. His usually open face was clenched tight as a fist. His green eyes were almost black with rage. The car tilted on the twisting road, struggling to right itself round every curve on its floating suspension.

"I'm sorry," I said, yet again, uselessly.

"Ah—" Shaun let out his fury in a long gasp. He shook his shoulders roughly, to shrug off his mood. "Me, too." He shot a sharp glance at me. "War is hell, eh? But this isn't even war. It's—" He shrugged again, discouraged.

Shaun eased up on the speed. We ran along in silence for a while. The sky darkened swiftly, racing over the Citroen's pale snout. A sharp sliver of waning moon turned the bush silver.

As we passed the Tshabalala district, Shaun asked: "How are the drawings?"

"Done."

"Great. I've got a gang standing by. We can have the prototype house up by the end of next month. The Minister is very interested. He's given us a grant for the prototype. I told him all about you. He is very impressed."

"Jolly good."

Shaun grinned at me. I saw his white teeth flash in the greenish light from the instrument panel. "Like that, eh?" he teased.

"Like that," I agreed.

"Still doubtful?" he taunted.

"Still."

"Of what, exactly? Tell me again. I'm very dense."

"Shaun—"

"Tell me!"

There was a cut of anger to his tone, slicing from the

sadness he was feeling over his young friend's injury. "Doubt of what?" he attacked. "What?"

I tried to answer gently. "That I know who I am. That I know who others are. That I can tell them, through my work, who they are."

"But architecture is just building, damnit. Why go sour?"

"It's not just me that went sour. It's the thing itself."

"Bullshit."

"Must we discuss this, now?"

He shot me a glance of pure malice. "Yes. Now. I need to know."

"Oh, shit."

Shaun let out a laugh, but it was grim. "You owe me an explanation," he said. "Because I love you."

"Well, if you put it that way ..."

"Yes. I do. Tell me. How has the thing itself soured?"

"Look, when we were students, modern architecture made us a promise. It promised a humane idiom for our time. But it failed. It was a false promise. There is no humane idiom for our time."

"If that's so — and I'm far from sure it is — it's our failure, not architecture's."

"We are our architecture. Our architecture is us. And our modern design is an abortion. It's an oppression. So what does it say about us?"

Shaun squinted at me. "You feel that strongly?"

"Yes. It makes me sad. What makes me sadder still is the part I've played in this oppression. I am very ashamed."

The car swerved to miss a truck packed with African police. The truck's horn blared derisively as we flashed by.

"You're such an idealist," Shaun muttered. "Everything human fails. The failure is our glory."

I laughed. "Oh you Papist!"

"Oh you Jew," he countered, but with a grin. His jaw tightened. "You really think 'there is no humane idiom'?"

"It's obvious. Look at our modern cities. They are not humane creations. We seem to have lost touch with that crucial human root. We're adrift on a tempest of technology. All we have are methods. What we lack is meaning. To paraphrase your own St. Augustine, architecture is an activity which gives the opportunity for the divine model to be revealed by human hands. But we have no model, human or divine. All we have is a supermarket of techniques, a junkyard of methodologies."

" 'For just as mothers are pregnant with their young, so the world is pregnant with things that are to come into being,' " Shaun quoted. "Yes. St. Augustine. God as the Architect of the Universe. But even He has his abortions," he added, flicking his eyes at me. "But, surely, ours is not the first age in which architecture has 'failed to find a humane idiom'?"

"True. But our failure is massive. This is supposed to be an age of Human Rights. The gap between our achievements and our aspirations is an abyss."

"You should know," he said sourly.

"Sure I should," I retorted. "I've worked all over the world, in poor countries and rich ones, with capitalists and with socialists, with democrats and with fascists. In terms of concrete and steel, the differences in feeling are marginal."

"How can that be?" he exclaimed, distressed. "Surely—"

"Is the visual style of New York, say, less oppressive than Moscow's? Does it crush the soul any less? Is Lagos, Nigeria, more humane in its architecture than Johannesburg, South Africa? Ask the people who live there."

"Are you political?" Shaun flashed out with abrupt suspicion.

"I've never been political in any formal sense. But, of course, everything a man does is political; it reflects an assumption, exploits a privilege, or suffers from whatever disadvantage you happen to be under. And being an architect or planner is a highly visible political function, however you perceive it."

"You're right, of course," Shaun said tersely. "But that doesn't mean I have to love you for it!"

I laughed. "You don't have to love me at all, old son. Especially not as some kind of sub-Jesuitical spiritual exercise ..."

"Up yours," Shaun snapped, and hunched over the wheel.

The Citroen speeded up. We hurtled towards Plumtree. Just before we reached the town, the car swerved right, off along a twisting dirt road. The headlights swept over arid bushland. Terrified animal eyes flashed in the swerving beams.

Behind us followed a cloud of dust, tinged red by the car's rear lights. A young springbok was trapped between our headlamps for several miles. The small deer galloped frantically, its scut a white flash before us, too frightened to break from our beams. Then the track turned sharply and the springbok vanished into the darkness.

Shaun's profile was grim. His turned cheek was tight with tension. I lit a cigarette, took a deep breath, and tried to break through his harsh silence.

"Shaun, maybe I should keep my distance?"

Shaun's cheek twitched. "Huh?"

"I seem to be depressing you. Infecting you, with my simplicities."

His reply was blunt. "Yes."

"Should we turn round? Go back to town?"

"No," he said curtly. "That'd be cowardly. For me."

"Let's be cowardly."

"You would say that!" he sneered.

"Cowardice can sometimes be the better part of valour."

"Very witty." He squinted sideways at me. "No. You are here. I love you. I must know you. If that upsets me, too bad."

"And if it upsets you too much?"

"Then I'm not the man I thought I was."

"Few of us are, old son."

"But I am, I hope."

"I hope you are, too!"

Shaun chuckled. "You're a real card, matey. An original. A real one-off. They threw away the mould, after they made you."

"Lord, I hope so."

"Me, too!"

"There's a Buddhist prayer I saw somewhere: 'Lord save me from others' ideas about me. Above all, save me from my own ideas about myself.' "

"Nice. I never knew you were a Buddhist." He grinned

mischievously. Then his face darkened. "Look, I have to do my job, in the army. The people we're fighting are thugs. They hurt their own people more than they bother us. They raid villages, torture and terrify the natives, force them to give them food, to inform. Almost all the victims of the guerrillas are innocent villagers, simple folk without politics of any kind. And I detest thuggism — black or white."

"You'd fight white thugs?"

"Certainly. I'm a man of the middle. Someone has to hold the middle ground, when everyone seems to be polarizing right and left. Our weakness is, it's a difficult territory to define. We middlers have no glib dogmas, no passionate atavisms to inspire us. All we have is a sense of balance. An instinct for what's truly humane."

"A rare instinct, these days."

"Right. It's vague, very ill-defined, but it's there, all the same. Without that instinct the world would have polarized itself to death long ago. It's the glue that holds the human thing together."

"Thin glue, here."

"We have it," he insisted passionately. "Just as the British had it in 1940, when things looked very black. It was the nerve Churchill touched, to such effect. The nerve of obstinate hope."

"Ian Smith is no Churchill!" I laughed. "Though he strives for the style. In the paper this morning I read his latest speech: 'I can honestly say, with total candour and sincerity, that never in my lifetime will uncivilized men rule in our Country.' A mite less oratorical than 'We shall fight on the beaches ... We shall never surrender.' "

"Smith is a — " He let out an expressive raspberry.

"The blacks, too, have their nerve of obstinate hope," I suggested. "Trouble is, their instinct for what's truly humane differs somewhat from the white man's."

"I don't believe that. Not for a moment."

"The military jargon expresses the difference. You have your Operations Hurricane, Thrasher, Tangent and Repulse: The guerrillas have their Operations Chaminuka, Nehanda, Takawira, Musikavanhu. You have your Counter-Insurgency Offensive, they have their *Chimurenga*. And so it goes on."

"Just jargon, as you say."

"More than that. Chaminuka, for instance, was a Shona prophet, a famous rainmaker. He foretold, just before the Ndebele killed him, the coming of 'men-without-knees' — white men, in long trousers. Nehanda was a spirit medium who led the first *Chimurenga* — the 1896 Rebellion. And then there is the Ndebele White Snake legend."

"Christ is the greatest medium of them all," Shaun said, and smiled. "Look — I don't enjoy killing people. 'Not my scene,' as my teenage Debbie would say. I'd far rather house them than shoot them. But there are only a quarter of a million whites and six million blacks in this country. Our job is to hold the line. If I have to kill to hold it, so be it. Here's the ranch."

A rough signpost flashed up in the lights: "To Excelsis Ranch," it read.

"Is that from *Gloria in excelsis Dei*?" I queried.

"Right. 'Glory be to God on high,' " he sang out.

The beams cut a tunnel of light through the flat veld. A few miles on, they brushed the face of a tin-roofed and verandaed shack. The car squealed to a halt at the steps.

"Welcome to Excelsis Ranch," Shaun said, getting out. "Wantenaar!" he bellowed. "Where is that bloody Boer?"

A shadow came out of the dark. A gruff voice replied: "Meneer?"

"Joel!" Shaun exclaimed. "Why are there no lights on, man? Didn't you get my message? I phoned the store."

The two men shifted into the headlamps' glare. All I saw of Shaun's foreman was a leathery face under a wide bush hat, and a matted chest revealed by a dirty white shirt unbuttoned to the belly. Wantenaar peered at his boss resentfully for a space, then turned and shuffled off towards the house.

"We're on the Botswana border, aren't we?" I asked, as we collected our bags. "Shouldn't your ranch have a security fence?"

Shaun hefted his rifle. "No cage for me," he said. "I prefer to take my chances. Come."

The house lights came on, a bluish glare of pressure lamps. The veranda boards creaked under our shoes.

The shack's interior was just one room. The hissing

lamps stood on a rough pine table. Their harsh light illuminated a couple of bunk beds, a few wooden chairs plaited with ox-hide strips, a rudimentary kitchen. Spiders scuttled out of the lamplight, dusty webs trembling.

"Home," Shaun sighed, suddenly content.

"Needs a woman's touch," I commented.

"Never!" Shaun retorted fiercely.

He bustled about the room, taking possession like a hound returned to its kennel after a long absence. Wantenaar stood by the table, stolid as a carving. His cheeks were grizzled, his skin was wrinkled with too much sun. It was hard to guess his age.

All at once I noticed a bulge sliding round his waist under the soiled shirt. I was just about to cry out when a small furry face peeped two huge black eyes into the light.

Wantenaar noticed my alarm. He chuckled like the grating of a rusty hinge. "Meet my Jannie!"

He jerked open his shirt to reveal a tiny nightape clinging to his body hair. The minute, humanoid fists clutched at the Afrikaner's chest. The beast was no bigger than a small rat. Its vast eyes drank me in greedily.

"He hates the light, Jannie does," the foreman crooned, stroking the galago's bushy brown scalp between the owlish ears. "Don't you, hey, *ou klonkie*?" He added, informatively: "Jannieboy hates strangers."

To confirm this, the nightape flashed needle-sharp canines.

"So I see," I said.

"He's a very shy chap, is Jannie," Wantenaar said, as the small primate vanished round the back of his shirt.

"*Voetsek,* now, Joel," Shaun said curtly. "Bugger off. See you at dawn."

The Afrikaner grunted. He shuffled out. His steps creaked on the veranda boards, then vanished into the night.

"A charmer, eh?" Shaun grinned. "One part Boer, one part kudu, one part mamba, three parts sheer bloody spite. The only species that can survive in this end of the bush. Let's feed."

The meal was spartan — bully beef and Irish whisky, weighted by slabs of bread. With each swig and bite,

Shaun's face coarsened. His lean jaw seemed to thicken, his light skin darkened, his emerald eyes grew sullen, losing their clear green glow. Something of the Boer's croak rusted his speech.

I ate and drank in silence, awed by the stillness of the night; a solid block of darkness, big as the continent. Africa. A territory of the heart that white minds must mythologize or be crushed by.

"Shit!" Shaun burst out abruptly. I looked up; his glare was green fire. "You were young!" he shouted. "Can't you forgive yourself? Are you that fucking arrogant?!"

I looked him straight in the eye. "I haven't been young for a very long time. And it's not a matter of self-forgiveness."

"What is it, then?" he yelled. "Tell me!" He slammed the table with his fist and the glasses jumped. "A matter of what?"

"Facing facts."

"Ah —" His face sagged. "Fuck facts."

"Yeah, fuck 'em," I agreed.

He flashed me a lopsided grin and refilled our glasses. "Here's to fact-fucking." He saluted me.

I raised my glass. "Fact-fucking."

Shaun's eyes went dark again, after a swig. "My old Grandad Connaughton was a Pioneer," he muttered. "Came up with the Column in 1891. Helped set up Fort Salisbury. Fought in the Matabele Rebellion in '93. 'Towns are the ruin of this country,' he said. 'Breed a race of wets. Live on the land, my boy. Land.' "

Shaun glared at me. The whisky bottle was half-empty. His face was flushed with boozing.

"Land!" he bellowed. "What it's all about. Earth! Soil! Dirt! That's why my Grandad came up here. Why he and his lot grabbed half the farmland in the country — the best half. The land is pure! I love it! As much as any native. More!"

Shaun snarled at me. "How could you ever understand. You're a Jew."

He rose abruptly and shook a hard fist in my face. *"Yid! Yid! Yid!"*

He lurched sideways, staggered to a bunk, fell upon it and was snoring in an instant.

# 8

# WALKING ON WATER

I am climbing towards the Acropolis. The path is steep and rocky. Behind me is a vast fire in the bush. The night sky is hot with flame. A dragon's breath is on my naked back. The crackle of the burning bush is shot through with bursts of gunfire.

Yet, in all this uproar, cattle are lowing, calling out their soft domestic *moos* in the blazing night.

The base of the Temple is constructed of huge mud blocks fitted together with precision. It is the hilltop Acropolis of the Zimbabwe Ruins, and also Jerusalem.

Theo Theophilus is waiting for me there — my old teacher and first architect-boss. He is at the top of a long flight of mud steps hollowed out by centuries of climbing feet. His squat body — head and torso two boulders balanced — is way above me, beckoning. A fringe of bright white hair dances in the firelight. Out of his round mouth issues a yearning *moo!*

Theo wears a warlock's white robe. Magical golden signs are embroidered there: sun, moon, stars, serpents, swastikas, Stars of David. He beams at me as I ascend, beckoning, lowing, *"Moo! Moo!"* I'm sweating, panting, on the verge of fainting. My skin feels thick as a croc's hide, yet supple as snakeskin. *"Moo! Moo!"*

My Master's bellow is insistent. I make it up the last few steps, on the point of passing out. My eyes rise over the edge of the Temple's floor, at the level of Theo's feet. He is standing on water!

Yes, the old Greek is balanced on a slit of silver wetness. His naked, horny feet have crossed toes. *"Moo,"* he urges, smiling. *"Moo."*

My heart hammers. Walk on water — me? But the old

Hellenic Mage is beckoning, urging. I lift my left foot and step out — and wake up.

Cattle were lowing, in the distance. Their *moos* were bubbles of sound drifting through the shack in the still morning air. I laughed, to shake the foolish images from my head.

The questions lingered. Had I walked upon the water? Had I waltzed over that silver gash, or slipped down into darkness? Dancing or drowning — which?

*"Moo,"* I mimicked, and swung my legs off the bunk.

Shaun's sleeping face was lit by a slice of sunlight through the door. He was on his back, in his battledress, an arm and a leg dropped over the edge of the bunk. His mouth gaped; dried spittle glittered on his bristled chin. He looked innocent as a naughty boy sleeping off a cookie binge.

I splashed my face in the sink and stepped out onto the veranda. The daylight was a blow between the eyes. I went back inside to borrow one of Shaun's khaki army hats and tugged the soft brim low on my brows.

The sky was blinding in its whiteness. Flat bushland stretched away to the horizon, stubbled with blasted thorntrees. Tufts of dried grass clutched at the dust, scattered like bristles on a giant's cheek. There were just two tones to this landscape: harsh white and dried dun.

The soil was like solidified powder under my shoes as I walked. My footprints followed me faintly. Even though it was still early, there was no freshness in the air. Its staleness burned my nostrils.

In this vast emptiness my mind was sucked right out of my skull. Africa put its lips to my mouth and drank me dry.

Africa! How many fantasies the white mind has had of you: "Heart of Darkness"; "Lost Eden"; "King Solomon's Mines"; "Noble Savage"; "Black Venus"; "White African"; "Souls for Salvation"; "White Man's Burden"; "Desert into Garden"; "Zulu-Warrior"; "Stone Age Innocence"; "Paradise of the Beasts".

*Moo!*

My brain was jerked back into focus by this harsh lowing. I saw strange beasts.

They seemed big as elephants, yet they were humped like camels. Their sides were beige slabs high as my head. Their legs were pillars planted in the earth.

*"Moo!"* they bellowed from the depths of their swollen bellies.

I stopped dead. Then it hit me: Brahmins! Yes, these were Shaun's proud Texan bulls, a startling sight in the veld.

An old African herdsman was squatting under a tree, wrapped in a blanket to protect him from the heat. A transistor radio was clapped to one ear; a faint whistle of *kwela* came out of his head.

He rose to greet me, nodding respectfully. *"Sakabona, N'kos."*

*"Sakabona, M'dal.* Fine cattle!"

The herdsman nodded gravely. We both gazed in awe at the Brahmins. They were magnificent. Over six feet tall at the hump, they weighed in at a thousand kilos. Their big, soft brown eyes were wary yet gentle as they looked back at us, jaws masticating tirelessly, undaunted by the harsh sun or the clouds of flies.

A dry croak said behind me: "Beauties, hey?"

Wantenaar was there, hands on hips, jeering at me with delighted malice from under the lid of his soiled bush hat. The hidden nightape made a bulge under his shirt at the neck like a goiter.

"Beauties," I agreed.

"Each bull needs thirty acres grazing," Wantenaar said, suddenly chatty. "That big bastard there is Cecil Rhodes the Second." He grinned derisively. "A champ! Eleven hundred kilos. Seventy thousand dollars American. A bank on the hoof," he chuckled, delighted with his own wit.

"Kaffir!" the foreman bellowed abruptly. The herdsman quivered. "Chase off those fucking flies, you lazy *m'satanyok!*"

The old man jumped as if stung by a cattle prod. He ran up to the bulls and swished his blanket at the flies.

"How's the boss this morning?" the Boer asked. He chuckled rustily. "Poor *ou* comes to this arsehole of a place to get away from wife, kiddies and such. In town he has a nice clean missus, nice clean job, nice clean pals. Here there's just the bulls, the bush, and me." Wantenaar gave a snort of laughter, turned, and strode off.

The dried watercourse was a gouge in the bush. I followed it for a few miles, keeping the sun at my back.

A sickening stench was my first warning of the kraal. Rotting in the sun were a dozen ostrich carcasses, piled like punctured bladders. Over the decay surged a skin of iridescent blue flies. Beside this foulness was the rusting shell of an old Buick crawling with naked kids.

In the village compound of thatched mud huts were a dozen women squatting in the dust pounding corn. The pestle-sticks rose and fell in the gourds to the beat of the chorus from an old English folksong:

> Early one morning,
> Just as the sun was rising,
> I heard a maid sing
>   in the valley below;
> "Oh, don't deceive me,
> Oh, never leave me!
> How could you use a poor maiden so?"

The African voices were startlingly High Anglican, almost Home County. The women's perfect pitch mimicked the missionary's. They were naked to the waist, their bosoms were smudged with dust, but their voices were pure public schoolgirl. The lilting song came after me as I walked away.

Shaun sat at the pine table in the shack drinking coffee. He pushed a tin mug and pot at me as I sat down.

There was a silence. Shaun's face was dazed. His eyes looked lost.

"Sorry," he croaked abruptly. "Very sorry—"

"Forget it," I said gently.

"No," he muttered. "Unforgivable."

"Nothing is unforgivable, old son."

His eyes flickered over my face and slid away. "Back to town. Today," he mumbled.

"Okay."

"Shit," he said softly. "Shit."

The drive back to Bulawayo was silent. Shaun did not utter a word, even when he dropped me at the gate of Leonie's house. I made no attempt to invade his remorse. It seemed wiser that way.

Lawlene was alone when I walked in the front door. She pounced at me. "Uncle Paul! There's a present for you, on your bed! A very heavy present some *munt* brought."

"Present?" I bumbled, disconcerted by the girl's attack. Innuendo was oozing from her eager smile.

"Brought by a *munt*," she emphasized. "The boy wouldn't tell me who sent it. It's a very heavy thing, Uncle Paul." She sidled up to me slyly. "You haven't forgotten my gold watch, hey?"

"Gold watch?"

Lawlene scowled. I wasn't being very bright. "My birthday," she said impatiently. "Remember?"

"Ah. Yes. Sure."

"Good." The girl turned away, leaving me standing.

The present was on my bed. It was a large, flat package wrapped in brown paper. A typewritten label read: Paul Kahn, Esquire.

I froze. The bomb-vest? Only Nkabi addressed me as "Esquire".

I ran to the bedroom door and locked it. I lowered the window blinds and locked the french windows. Then I approached the parcel.

The brown wrapping resisted me. I had to tear at it with my fingernails before it came away. Underneath was the lid of a thick cardboard box. It was sealed with tape, which I plucked off. I lifted the lid with shaking hands.

There it was — the bomb-vest. I stared at it for a long moment before daring to take it out.

It was exactly as I had designed it: a quilted rayon lifejacket with padded shoulder straps in rough webbing. It was heavy, perhaps seven kilos in weight. In my trembling grip it seemed to weigh a ton.

I tried on the garment in front of the wardrobe mirror. The vest was a snug fit. A row of poppers fastened it down the front. The tension could be adjusted by rayon loops in the small of the back.

The padded shoulder straps had triple poppers,

anchored to reinforced canvas gussets. When the studs were unclicked, the vest, undone at the front, dropped heavily down over my hips.

"Well done," I muttered. "Very well done."

The lifejacket was weighty, but the quilting lay flat. I felt the rayon gingerly; it palpated like plasticine. As I grew accustomed to its bulk, it seemed to grow lighter on my body. After a few moments I hardly noticed the extra weight. Yet that bulk would be an advantage when the moment came to drop the vest in the Telecom Centre. It should fall like a stone.

A week or so earlier, I had bought a white safari jacket. It had four large patch pockets and a belt. I had chosen a jacket a size or so too large. "I like a lot of air," I explained to the doubtful salesman.

I put the safari jacket on over the vest. It looked just right. Buttoned down the front, the belt loosely tied, it made me seem a trifle overweight, perhaps, but that was no matter. It could easily pass a casual inspection.

"Well done," I murmured again, admiring my reflection.

When I finally removed the safari jacket and unpopped the vest, I noticed that the tailor had sewn a loop high on the back. There was also a flat magnetic plate. This meant the thing could be hung up or stuck on any surface, if necessary.

At the bottom of the box was the electronic necklace. I examined it closely. It looked exactly as it had — a series of linked bakelite discs decorated with transistors, supporting a breastplate. I put it gingerly aside, careful not to touch the breastplate knob, that could now be a radio-detonator.

There was a typed sheet of instructions. I sat on the bed with the vest on my knees and began to read. "*Nyogamhlope!*" it opened, "Herewith your garment as ordered." I paused, lifted the vest from my lap onto the bed, lit a smoke and lay back against the pillows.

The drawn blinds muted the room's light. The house was silent.

"The garment incorporates 6500 grams of plastic explosive," the note continued, "plus a surcharge of napalm jelly isolated in a shockproof casing in the small of the back. This is the incendiary element."

I reached out and felt for the casing. It made a hardish lump in the bottom of the back of the vest.

"The radio receiver-detonator incorporates a fuse of the tungsten-filament type. The receiver is locked to a precision wavelength. To activate the signal key, press the breastplate knob on the necklace for at least fifteen seconds. To repeat, *fifteen seconds continuous pressure*, minimum. The copper wire aerial loop wound round in the fabric of the vest should ensure reception of the signal up to a maximum range of 250 meters, direct line-of-sight. The impulse will activate the delay-action vacuum-relay tube that primes the tungsten fuse."

I reread this paragraph very carefully, making note of the fifteen seconds, which I counted out with my watch several times.

"Store the garment in a cool dark place. Moderate accidental shock or body warmth will not trigger the device, but it is advisable to take care. That is all. *Hamba gahle, Nyogamhlope.* Take care, White Snake. Long live the *Chimurenga!* Destroy this note."

I burned the note in the ashtray, after reading it over and over. It was signed with the seal of a charging black bull. Nkunzi; the Old Bull himself.

"So this is it," I said out loud, watching the paper burn. Very soon now, on Tuesday October Sixteenth, less than a fortnight away, I would be "walking on the water" of a new life. "Will I sink, or will I swim?" I asked the tiny flames. There was no answer.

The loud knock at my door made me jump. The handle rattled noisily. "Uncle Paul! Let me in! What are you locked up for?"

"Huh?" I leapt from the bed and ran to the door. "What do you want, Lawlene?" I asked, through the wood.

"To talk," the young voice commanded.

"Okay, okay — be out in a tick."

The girl did not answer. Neither did she go away. I could hear her indignant breathing through the shut door.

I packed the vest up hurriedly in its box. Where to hide it? "Store in a cool, dark place" ... On top of the wardrobe? Behind it? Yes. The large piece of furniture rested solidly on a skirting. I edged its back away from the wall and carefully inserted the cardboard box.

It would pass. I arranged a chair so that the wardrobe's displacement would not seem so obvious. Then I bunched up the brown wrapping paper and shoved it temporarily under the bed. I opened the blinds and unlocked the bedroom door.

Lawlene had vanished. The house was absolutely silent. But I could sense my niece's suspicious curiosity hanging in the air like thick scent.

The headline in the morning's *Chronicle* was sensational: "Escaped Madman Murders Three".

I sat on the swing seat on the lawn in the shade of the flamboyant and read the story that followed. It seemed that a white inmate of Ingutsheni, the local lunatic asylum, had slipped under the fence and cut the throats of his wife, her lover and his mother-in-law. The police had found him in the act of eating a chunk of his dead wife's flesh.

Tenja was on his knees on the grass shovelling up dogshit with a pan and brush. Ray was shining the plate-glass window of the lounge. His rubbing cloth squeaked like a rusty pedal. He still had purple bruises on his cheekbones where David had walloped him with the *knobkerrie.*

Ray caught my eye as I looked up. "Isn't it terrible, baas," he called out, gesturing at the newspaper I was holding. "Murder." He shook his small black head mournfully.

"Terrible," I agreed. Out of the corner of my eye I could see Tenja pause in his shit-scouring and cock his head attentively.

Ray put down his rubbing cloth. He came up and stared at the headline. His eyes were deeply shocked. "Why?" he asked me, earnestly. "Why do black men do such bad things?"

I blinked. "But the murderer was white!"

Ray shook his head vehemently. *"Aikona,* baas. No. White man don't do such things."

"But Ray, it says here—"

"No. No. Not so. Black man. *Mnyama."*

Tenja, still on his knees, spoke up. "My boy, you are a

real *munt*." The contempt in his tone was harsh. "A typical brainwashed houseboy. A Christian!"

Ray stiffened. His face shut tight. "I am a good Baptist," he asserted. He tugged at the crucifix round his neck. "Jesus saves—"

Tenja got up off his knees. The two young Africans glared at one another with absolute hostility.

"*Munt!*" Tenja snapped. He turned to me. "Until two years ago this boy still wore his *umtondo* "— Tenja jabbed at Ray's crotch —" in a Tom Thumb tobacco bag! He's a kraal kaffir."

Ray looked very sad all at once. "This is a bad boy, baas," he told me, deeply ashamed.

"Christian!" Tenja repeated, as if that was all that needed saying.

Ray was utterly dejected. The purple bruise on his cheek gave him a lopsidedly disconsolate air. He shuffled away on bare feet, leaving the field to Tenja's derision.

Tenja's young mouth jerked in a ferociously bitter grin. He took his shit-filled pan and brush and vanished round the side of the house.

I skipped through the rest of the *Chronicle*. After the lead story, it was mundane: "ACCOR Banquet: Businessman of the Year"; "Stocktheft: Herdboy Gets Nine Years"; "Faction Fight in Lusaka Nightclub: Five Terrs Die in Shootout between ZAPU and ZANU Factions"; "Rhodesian Soccer 'In a Shambles' Says Matabeleland President"; "FRELIMO Terrorists Claim Portuguese Bomber Knocked Out With Russian SAM-2s"; "Border Patrol Welfare Fund Collects Record Xmas 'Glory Bags' for Troops".

"Paul," Tenja's voice cut in. "Try this."

I looked up. Tenja held out to me a cigarette hand-rolled in a long tube of newspaper. A pungency of raw *dagga* — the wild marijuana of the bush — twitched my nostrils from the burning tube. Tenja's expression as he offered the weed was stiff and wary.

This was a test, I saw. I took the cigarette and inhaled deeply. The rawness wrenched my throat, but I kept the smoke down.

"Wow," I gasped, through a scorched gullet.

Tenja chuckled proudly. "Amanzimtoti *dagga*," he announced. "From my home. First class."

"Terrific," I agreed, taking another toke. My head seemed to grow lighter by the second as the bluish vapour burned my lungs.

Tenja nodded solemnly. He took a matchbox from his overalls' pocket. He slid the cover back an inch to show me it was crammed with dark green leaf. "For you," he said, pushing the matchbox into my free hand.

I passed him the joint. "Thanks, Tenja." Tenja squatted on his haunches before me. We smoked in turns, handing the newspaper cigarette back and forth. I was nervous that my sister might return and catch us in this illegality; or that my sharp-eyed niece might see me being matey with a *munt*, and thus confirm her deep suspicion that I was up to something peculiar.

Tenja sniggered abruptly. The dope was getting to him.

"What's funny?" I demanded. I, too, felt very light-headed.

"My Grandpa — he was *isangoma*!"

"Huh?" I blinked. "A witch doctor?"

"Yes! Yes! Witch doctor!" Tenja giggled. "Wore a cap of hyena skin! Wore jackal tails and a *muti* bag!" His slight body shook with laughter. It seemed hilarious, to him, yet there was a thrill of pride in his chuckling.

"My Great Uncle was a rabbi," I countered solemnly. "He wore a *yarmulkeh*, a *tallis*, and *tefillin*."

"Huh?" the young African frowned.

"Skull cap. Prayer shawl. Phylacteries," I explained. "Each day he'd sing the *Shema* — the Hebrew prayer — swaying like a palm in the breeze."

"Ah," Tenja nodded. "My Grandpa sang the *Vumani libokavumi*." He grinned crookedly. "The old fellow stank of goat's blood and chicken shit rubbed on his skin."

"My Great Uncle stank of boiled cabbage and Talmud."

"He needed protection, you see. To smell out *tagati* — evil spells."

"The old rabbi needed prayer to banish *dybukkim*," I countered. "Demons."

Tenja nodded. He stared at me solemnly as he ground out the butt of the joint under his bare heel. "My

Grandpa," he went on sadly, "he was killed by lightning."

"My Great Uncle choked on a carp bone."

Tenja tilted his small face to the sky. *"Nkosi sikelele Afrika!"* he sang out, swaying on his heels. "God save Africa!"

*"Adenai elohenu, Adenai ehod!"* I echoed, rocking in my chair. "The Lord our God, the Lord is One!"

"My father," Tenja said, his voice going harsh, "is a *Mudzimu* Christian Nationalist!" He spat to one side in fierce derision. "He believes in the *amadhlozi* — the ancestral spirits — *and* in Jesus! *And* in Zimbabwe. All this stew in one big pot!"

"Well," I consoled him, "my Dad's a Suburban Zionist Rhodesian. Believes in Tennis, Eretz Yisroel and The White Man's Burden!"

"Fathers," Tenja said sadly.

"Fathers," I agreed.

"My Grandpa said, 'Our land needs the spilled blood of the *Nyogamhlope.* It is thirsty for the life of the White Snake, to wash clean our shame. Only then will our black flowers grow!' " He squinted up at me. "Blood. White blood. To fill that pool."

"What do you think of Josiah Nkunzi?" I asked, to change the tack.

Tenja jerked his narrow shoulders. "A good front, that Old One, for our fight. A mask for the *Chimurenga.* When we have power we will put The Bull to graze. To play with his Mercedes Benz motor car. His Christian toys." He grinned. "But even Christians understand blood. They drink it every Sunday!"

"True!" I laughed.

"That Karl Marx, though ... now there is a White Man."

"Honorary."

"Eh?"

"Karl Marx was Jewish."

"Like you?"

"Like me."

Tenja gazed up at me with new respect. At that moment Snuggums waddled up and rubbed her fur against my leg. I scratched her ear absently; she rewarded me with her customary fart of joy.

"Snuggums — Running Dog of Imperialism," I joked. "Mao Tse-tung would kick your fat bum!"

"I will kill that bitch!" Tenja burst out. His eyes were black with ferocity. "Kill!" He slashed an imaginary knife at Snuggums's throat. "Shits all over the lawn! My lawn!"

"Poor old Snuggums," I soothed. "You hear that? Tenja will slit your gullet, come the Revolution." The bitch waggled her stump ecstatically.

Tenja calmed himself. "Karl Marx," he said tersely. "That is a good man: 'The bourgeoisie forged the weapons that bring death to itself ... Let the ruling classes tremble ... There will be blood.' "

" 'I don't want the blood of the lamb. What I want is the blood of man,' " I quoted.

"Ha. Also Karl Marx?"

"No. A disciple."

" 'What I want is—' ?"

" '— the blood of man.' "

He clapped his hands delightedly. " 'The blood of man'!" He jumped to his feet and did a joyous jig across the lawn, crowing over and over: " 'What I want is the blood of man'!"

9

# HOT PURSUIT

Lovey said: "The Day of Atonement, Uncle Paul. *Yom Kippur.* We don't eat or drink for a whole night and day. Fasting. To ask God to forgive all the sins we've done for the whole year. Uncle?"

All eyes were upon me at the dinner table. All at once I was the focus of concern. Even Snuggums, perched beside me, lifted her face from her dish of tuttifrutti and bared her fangs in an expectant grin.

"Penny for your thoughts," Leonie laughed. She switched tone abruptly. "Wouldn't harm you to atone for once, brother."

"You could wear your new white safari jacket, Uncle," Lawlene said sweetly. "To the synagogue. And you can also wear it to my birthday hop, just after *Yom Kippur.* I want to dance with you."

I blinked at their faces. The *dagga* fumes still fugged my brain. Atonement? Synagogue? Birthday hop? Safari jacket?

"What new safari jacket?" Leonie demanded.

"In his wardrobe," Lawlene reported. "Very smart."

"Are you fasting, Uncle Paul?" Lovey asked.

"Leave the man alone," David ordered. No one heard him. Since the *knobkerrie* incident he had been invisible. He no longer existed.

"The Day of Atonement," Lovey insisted. "Uncle Paul!"

"Fasting?" I mumbled. "At the birthday hop? In my safari jacket? Dance? For my sins?"

The twins gasped, then exploded with glee. Lawlene's cheeks burned with hilarity. "Oh, Uncle!" she howled. "You say such funny things!"

*Erev Yom Kippur,* the feast that precedes the fast of the Day of Atonement, was a meal twice as lavish as any ordinary supper. In anticipation of the coming abstinence, everyone fed frantically, including Snuggums.

After supper the males of the family who were of age — Dad, David and Lovey — went off to synagogue, blue velvet prayer bags in hand. At the very last moment Lovey decided to be awkward. He flung himself on the floor in his new Sabbath suit of sky-blue Dacron and wailed: "*Shul* is so boring!" His father grabbed him by the ear and hauled him to the car, ignoring the boy's agonized squawkings.

The rump settled down in the T.V. room to watch a James Bond movie: *Goldfinger.* The film began with the second reel and ran on for twenty minutes before the screen went dead. When it rolled again, from the credits, this time, it failed after a few moments. "Rubber band's snapped again," Leonie said sourly. "See how sanctions are hurting?"

My mother had fallen asleep as soon as she was seated before the screen. As her head lolled on her bosom she mumbled faintly, "I feel *naw-zhus.*"

As *Goldfinger* finally got under way, Leonie took up her tapestry. She was weaving a seat cover; an English pastoral scene with milkmaids and shepherds. Eric sprawled on the floor tugging at his tiddle. Pussy Galore, James Bond's heroine, sent him into ecstacy.

Lawlene sat at my feet. She propped her back against my knees with serene possessiveness. The girl seemed quite certain now that I was in her power. From time to time she tilted her round face up at me and winked conspiratorially.

The males returned from worship in time for the last reel. They sat down to watch James Bond's triumph over the evil genius Goldfinger. The movie ended late, extended by numerous ads for male deodorants and second-hand cars. The evening's program ended with an epilogue in which a Methodist minister exhorted The Lord to save Rhodesia from the evils of Sex, Drugs, Communism and Sunday Sport.

Stretching and yawning, forsaking their bedtime snack, the family retired for the night.

The next day the sky was dark. The first rains of the new season deluged the town. Great drumcracks of thunder rattled the heavens. Water fell in sheets, wetting the parched earth for the first time in many months. The air was tangy as chilled Moselle.

David and Lovey went off to the synagogue at ten. They rushed back home just before three o'clock, accompanied by my father. All three faces were haggard with fasting, prayer and panic.

"Dad, what's up?" Leonie cried.

"Terrible rumour," the old man croaked. He made for the radio. "Three o'clock news—"

The radio crackled. "News flash! At noon today major hostilities broke out anew in the Middle East—"

"*Oi vey*," David groaned. "Not again?"

"Reports are confused," the female announcer's voice ran on, "but it seems that Egyptian and Syrian armour and air forces attacked Israel today in massive strength. Today is the Jewish Day of Atonement, when many Jews are in the synagogues, praying and fasting — the assault seems to have taken the Israeli High Command completely by surprise. In Jerusalem a shocked and shaken Golda Meir decried the attack as a violation of the sacred festival of *Yom Kippur*."

"*Mizrayim!*" David spat. "Egyptians!"

"In Cairo, Anwar Sadat, the Egyptian President, has issued a communiqué announcing a crossing of the Suez Canal by his forces. He claims his armour has pierced the Bar Lev Line in depth."

"*Oi!*" Dad groaned, cluching his tummy.

"Syrian sources claim the destruction of two hundred Israeli aircraft and an even greater number of tanks. In Washington a spokesman for the State Department called on all parties to the hostilities to negotiate immediately."

"Oil," David snapped. "Oil!"

"In Moscow the Soviet Politburo declared their support for the Arab armies."

David clicked off the radio in disgust. "You see?" he challenged the shocked room, "Everyone hates us."

"*Oi, oi,*" Dad moaned, "what'll happen now, to all of us poor Jews?"

There was a heavy silence in the room. Even the children were oppressed by the shocking news. Images of Arab tanks roaring through the Sinai Desert towards Holy Jerusalem were in everyone's mind.

Lawlene said suddenly: "What about my hop?"

Leonie blinked at her. "Hop?"

"My birthday hop, this week." The girl's eyes were deeply troubled. "My frock is ready. All my friends—"

"Forget it," David snapped.

"But Dad—"

"People are dying. Our people," her father said.

Lawlene turned to Leonie. "Mom?" she appealed piteously.

"Look, I—" Leonie muttered. She took a deep breath. "After all, how will it help Moshe Dayan if a bunch of Bulawayo kids are glum?"

"People are dying!" David cried.

"You hate to see the kids have fun," Leonie shot back. "And her frock is made. And it's so pretty."

"Dying!"

Leonie turned to me. "Paul. What's your opinion?"

"Yes!" Lawlene echoed. "You decide, Uncle Paul."

"Really—" I protested.

"Please, Uncle," Lawlene begged. There was no blackmail in her cry, only pleading.

"Well," I murmured, "people are dying right here, in Rhodesia, all the time."

"You would say that!" Leonie exclaimed.

"But it's true, Mom," Lovey interjected. "Isn't it?"

"He puts in his oar," David said irritably.

Lawlene clutched her mother's bosom. "Uncle Paul is right, Mom. There's a war on here, too. And we were going to have the hop anyway."

"Ah, let the girl have her hop," my father cut in, settling the matter.

"Okay, okay," Leonie conceded. "So long as no one tells Dayan."


"Don't you care about Israel?" Leonie demanded of me, later that evening, when everyone else was in bed. "What sort of Jew are you?"

"A very peculiar one," I replied, trying to deflect her challenge with a smile.

She would not be softened. "I wonder about you, Paul," she said, gazing at me sadly across the lounge. "Are you really one of us?"

"Of course I am. What else?"

"You don't fast on Yom Kippur. You never go to synagogue. You're not that upset about this terrible attack on Israel—"

"I'm not an Israeli, I'm a Jew," I protested. "There is a difference, you know."

"No." She shook her head firmly. "No difference. Israel is our homeland."

"This is my homeland. Rhodesia."

Leonie dismissed this with a gesture of contempt. "What sort of Jew are you?" she asked, again.

"Being a Jew is very important to me," I replied, picking my way gingerly through the minefield of her suspicions. "Jewishness is my only real country. Without it I really would be homeless."

Leonie's eyes raked my face. "You mean that?"

"Absolutely."

"Ah," she murmured, softening a little. "That's a relief."

The Middle Eastern news was grim for the following week. The Israelis were on the run with the Egyptians on their heels in hot pursuit. Newsreel shots of burnt-out tanks with scorched Stars of David on their turrets dominated the television. Arab infantrymen posed cockily on the wreckage of Israeli Phantom jets.

A haggard Golda Meir was interviewed. "This is a sacrilege," she mumbled into the camera. But one of her generals was more savage. "We shall break their bones!" he cried. "The Pharoanic hordes will bleed into the desert sands!"

The Jews of Bulawayo went about with stricken faces under a wash of Gentile sympathy. They had rallies and dances and bazaars to raise money for Israel. The government in Salisbury made a special exception to the strict exchange control regulations to allow these donations to be sent out of Rhodesia.

*"Mamserim!"* my cousin Barney growled. "Bastards! We'll thrash them yet!"

In the midst of all this, I arranged with Barney to visit the Telecom Centre on the Sixteenth, in the morning. In the locked privacy of my room, blinds drawn, I adjusted the fit of the bomb-vest. I practiced unsnapping the poppers and dropping the lifejacket until I was adept. I also trained myself to count out twenty seconds — fifteen, plus five extra — against the watch.

The cardboard box seemed safe behind the wardrobe. There was no sign it had been discovered. Everyone was too distracted with the war news and the preparations for the birthday party.

A large marquee was erected on the lawn, beside the pool. It had a boarded floor to cover the rain-sodden grass. Coloured lights were strung from poles. A portable disco console was set up in one corner, ready for the disc jockey.

Leonie, Grace and Ray were busy in the kitchen. The counters overflowed with freshly baked cakes and pies, and roasts of beef and chicken. Delivery vans brought cases of oranges, bananas, apples and Cape grapes.

Drink was a problem. Sanctions made it difficult to get hard liquor for the adults, but my father used his influence to obtain a dozen bottles of Scotch. "I have a name in this town," he said, proudly, when Leonie called him a "Miracle Man".

Mona phoned one evening. "Am I invited to your niece's hop?" she asked me in a challenging tone.

"Certainly," I said bravely. "You're my guest. But I warn you, I have promised a dance to Lawlene."

"One dance, that's it," Mona laughed. "The rest are mine."

Leonie scowled when I told her I had invited Mona. "It's your funeral," she shrugged, much too preoccupied with the preparations to trouble her mind with her brother's idiocy.

On the morning of the day before the party, I woke to find a brief note pinned to my pillow. "Gold watch, Uncle!" it read, in a stiffly childish hand.

I laughed; that girl had balls. I went to town and bought the tiny fourteen-carat wristwatch Lawlene had pointed out to me weeks before. "My last golden timepiece," Finkelstein the jeweller said sadly. "Sanctions," he added, rolling his bug eyes in despair. He made me pay for all the pain a heartless world had caused him and his business; but it was worth it to see the shock of disconcerted delight on the ten-year-old's face when I slipped the watch to her.

"Oh, Uncle Paul!" Lawlene stammered, blushing beetroot. "Too much!"

"Much too much," Leonie agreed, examining the watch. "Must've cost a bomb!"

"You could say that," I agreed.

Recovering from her amazement with a yelp of joy, Lawlene flung her arms around my neck and hugged me hard. "I love you, Uncle! I love you!"

"Give the gel a gold watch and she's yours," her mother commented drily.

On the evening of the hop the bulletins from the Holy Land were mixed. The Israelis had counter-thrust on the road to Damascus, but the *mizrayim* were still pouring across the Suez Canal, widening the wounds in the Bar Lev Line.

"What's Dayan waiting for?" David demanded. "The Messiah, maybe?"

The flow of food and drink into the marquee was endless. Ray and Tenja had set up trestle tables along one side of the tent. They lugged in crates of Fanta and Pepsi. Leonie and Grace, assisted by Aunts June and Rose, laid out a buffet of beef roasts, tongue rolls, chicken, bowls of fruit salad and tomato, egg-and-onion dips and a bucket of non-alcoholic fruit punch.

The disc jockey tinkered with the sound system. Bursts of Little Donny Osmond rattled the ranks of glasses on the buffet. "Keep the music going," Leonie told him. "We don't want awkward gaps where the kids sit and fiddle, okay?"

"Leave it to me, Mrs. Mandel," the music-master reassured her. "I know how to make a hop swing."

It was a dry night, fortunately. The sky was sharp with rainwashed stars as the first revellers arrived. The children, delivered by fussing parents, tripped in on tiptoe to protect their pumps from the muddy gravel. Lawlene escorted the girls to her room to dump their wraps.

The young ladies emerged with lipsticked rosebuds. They smoothed satin frocks that clung to plump young hips and training bras. Their powdered bare shoulder blades were sleek. Each ten-year-old carried a beaded evening bag and sported a carnation or hibiscus blossom in her gleaming wave-and-set.

The lads were neat in Dacron suits. Brylcreemed crewcuts capped scrubbed cheeks and brows. Their black shoes shone like polished plums.

The boys were more awkward than the girls. They hung about plucking at their flies while the females chattered merrily. Eric was an exception. He marched up to the prettiest chick and dragged her to the dance floor. The couple frugged over the boards to the disco beat, and soon other pairs joined them.

Lawlene claimed me at once. "My dance, Uncle," she said, grasping my hand.

The girl was an accomplished frugger. She wriggled her satined hips smugly, bright round face lifted to me in serious delight. The gold watch flashed on her wrist.

We whirled past my mother, who had insisted not only on attending the hop, but on sitting in a corner of the marquee to watch the "young things". Her old eyes glittered happily as we frugged by.

"Where's Lovey?" I asked Lawlene as the number ended.

The girl scowled. "Sulking. In his room. He hates parties. He hates fun." She squeezed my hand. "Thanks, Uncle. That was super. I want more."

"Later," I begged off, and escaped to join the oldies.

Leonie stood by the buffet, flushed with happiness. "What a great litle dancer that girl is!" she cried. Her body was draped in yards of purple taffeta from throat to hem. Silver toecaps peeped out from under. Her hair was a bright blond bouffant. "Great little dancer!" she exclaimed again.

Mona made her entrance late. She came up to Leonie and me and casually dropped her fox-fur cape. Under it was an off-the-shoulder black-sequinned tube that sheathed her slim figure like snakeskin.

Leonie looked her up and down. "Sensational," she said.

Mona looked Leonie up and down. "Magnificent," she retorted.

My sister turned her back on us. Mona made a face. We wandered to the dance floor. The hop was in full swing. Satin flashed, and young white teeth. Carnations and hibiscus jumped to the thumping disco beat among the bobbing Brylcreems.

Mona came into my grip. She was rigid. Under the tight black sheath, the long muscles in her back were iron. Then she loosened, melting into the rhythm of the dance. Her head lolled, flailing black tresses. The white throat stretched with self-delight.

My mother's eyes were icy as we whirled by. She was jealous. Childishly, I exaggerated my entrancement with the black sequinned snake in my arms.

"Tonight," I hissed in Mona's ear.

She jerked her head back. Her myopic eyes were jet. She nodded curtly, and we danced on.

Later, I danced again with Lawlene. The girl's face was a swoon of happiness. This was her night. She clung to me with a pure eroticism, made innocent by triumphant joy. "Thank you, Paul," she bubbled, hugging me round the waist as the number ended. "Thank you so much!"

Mona needed a drink. So did I. We poured a couple of Scotches and gulped thirstily.

At the edge of the marquee was a row of peeping black faces. I saw Tenja's there. His eyes were greedy. I grabbed a bottle of Scotch and slipped it to him secretively. He took it with a grin and vanished into the darkness.

"You'll spoil them," Mona said severely.

"I hope so," I replied. "Shall we split?"

Mona lived on the other side of Kumalo, in a two-storey square white house built in a pre-war Modern style. "My parents are away down South," she said. "My daughter, too. We have the place to ourselves."

Mona went to powder her nose. I sat on a stool at the corner bar in the lounge and sipped a Scotch. The living room had a gleaming parquet floor and a fawn Bokhara rug. The settees were modern Victorian deep-buttoned burgundy leather. There were two framed Dufy water-colours on the wall that turned out to be originals when I examined them.

"Nice room," I said, when Mona returned.

"Surprised?" she mocked.

Mona had tied her hair back with a velvet ribbon. It hung in a horsetail down her spine. Her eyes were puffy with apprehension.

I held out my hand. She did not take it. Instead, she slid away towards the bar and poured herself a stiff drink.

"Mona," I began.

She whirled on me. "I am what I am, Paul!" she cried out. "I'm me!"

"I know."

"No," she retorted fiercely. "You don't know. You don't want to know."

"Love," I sighed, "I thought this was going to be fun. 'No claims, no regrets,' the lady said."

"I'm sorry. I can't."

"Okay. I'll finish my drink and go."

Mona began to talk. She sat coiled on a bar stool clutching her glass. Her eyes were fixed on it, as if it were a crystal ball. "You have to know — I must tell you — I am frigid. Cold." She emphasized the word harshly. "Been with lots of men; too many. I'm called the 'Bulawayo Bicycle'. Everyone's ridden me. But I've never been touched. Not where it counts. I've never come with any man, ever."

She paused. Her black-sequinned body was stiff. "Not even with Jack, my husband. Even though I loved him. You see, he wasn't real to me. No one's real, not even my kid. No one in the whole world is real to me!"

She lifted her face. Her eyes seemed bruised in the subdued bar lighting. "I live in a kind of bubble. Float along the days inside this balloon. People are there, outside, looking in. I'm looking out. They see me. They see a woman who seems to know exactly who she is. They see what I want them to see. They see what they want to see. They don't see me. Because I'm not here. I'm — "

She threw up a helpless hand. The painted nails flashed black in the light. "God knows where I am!" Her eyes focused on me suddenly. They were very dark. "You know, though. Don't you? What I'm saying? You don't exist either!"

"Oh, I exist all right. But where is quite another matter."

"You're the first man — "

I stood abruptly. "Mona, I am no one's first man," I said. "Last man, maybe. But first, never. Let's get that straight before we fuck."

She blinked. Then a rip of laughter tore through her skinny frame. She got up and reached behind her back. I heard the scratch of a zipper. The black sheath peeled. Flat breasts were revealed, circles sketched on her rib cage. The nipples, purple as bruises, were inverted. They were dark slits in very white skin.

"Okay," she said softly. "Okay, okay." She moved towards me with the sequins peeling from her flesh.

# 10

# HE SHALL HAVE MUSIC

Leonie caught me sneaking into the house next morning. She shot me a look that would have frozen a stone. "Hi, sis!" I said, trying to be breezy. "The hop was a smash, hey?" She turned her back on me and marched off without a word.

For hours I could not shake off a foolish sense of having been a very naughty boy. It was Lawlene who relieved me. I had expected that she, too, would be furious at my early disappearance from her party. But when she woke, late, and stumbled blinking into the lounge in her nightie, she flung her arms round my neck and hugged me passionately. "Oh, Paul!" she cried, "I just love my gold watch! All my girlfriends are so jealous!" Her small, sleep-warm body wriggled against mine in an ecstacy of erotic glee.

Later, I called Mona. She sounded sleepy. "Been in bed all day," she yawned into the phone.

"Lazy slut."

"That's me. Will I see you tomorrow?"

"Depends."

"On what?" Her voice was suddenly anxious.

"I'm visiting Barney Silverman at the Telecommunications Centre in the morning, at twelve."

"So?"

"I'll speak to you in the evening."

"Anything wrong? You sound tense."

"No. Not to fret."

"Where you're concerned, I'm full of fret!" she retorted with a bitter laugh, and rang off.

That evening I kept to my room. I tried to write a letter to my parents. I wanted them to have some explanation of my motives if things were to go wrong next day — Bomb Day.

But it was impossible. There was no way I could jump the gap between their context and my own. If I were arrested, they would suffer horribly. The name of "Kahn" would be mud. It would be the label of a traitor, of a criminal, of a terr.

"One simple, unambiguous act" ... How to explain that?

I smoked a last cigarette in bed before falling asleep and listened to the noises of the house. David was already snoring beyond the wall behind my head. In the distance I could hear the canvas of the garden marquee flapping in the brisk night breeze. Leonie's slippers shuffled past my door.

The phone rang as I was dropping off. Leonie answered. There was a gap of silence. Then her steps approached my door.

Her knock was peremptory. "Paul. Phone. Long distance."

"Phone?" I stammered. "Long distance?"

She walked off without bothering to answer. I pulled on my pants, opened the door and stumbled to the hall phone. "Hello? Who is this?"

The voice that leapt out of the earpiece almost floored me. "Paul? It is you!"

I was too stunned to answer. There was a long gap. In the bakelite the long distance wires crackled with static.

"Paul? Paul?" the voice insisted.

"Theo," I mumbled.

"It is you!" The voice was mocking. "I just knew. So, how is my very best and most famous ex-student-assistant-partner?" He added slyly, "Not happy, eh?"

I sat down heavily on the stool beside the phone. My bare chest was chilled. My guts were water. "Where are you?"

"Johannesburg. I surprise you, no?"

"You surprise me, Theo. As ever." I took a deep breath. "What are you doing in my part of the world?"

"You own it, then?" he shot back, catching the nuance in

my tone. He cackled down the phone. "He owns it — the whole of Southern Africa!" Theo ceased laughing abruptly. "Two things I am doing here. One: I am giving a seminar on urban planning to the South African housing ministry. Two: I am hunting you."

"Hunting me?"

"You, Paul Kahn. You. What is this off-the-wall crap I hear about you chucking it all in?"

I had to laugh. The old Greek's usage of American and English slang was as idiosyncratic as the man himself. He loved to be racy in the language he most adored.

The line hummed with static. Theo's voice was momentarily lost. It gave me pause to get my breath, and to imagine Theophilus at the other end of the line, shaking the receiver crossly. I could see the tiny round ball of a man with his tufts of bright white hair standing up all round the fringes of his scalp. I could see his sharp black eyes that were constantly blinking with an intensity of curiosity about everything.

Theo's timing was diabolical, as ever. He had an instinct for the awkard moment. To have phoned me on this of all evenings ...

"Paul!" His voice jumped at me again. "How are you, really?"

"Fine."

"Bullshit."

"Theo — "

"You have really quit architecture?"

"Yes."

Theo gasped. I could hear this small breath-explosion over five hundred miles of telephone wire. But then, with lightning sleight-of-mind, he leapt over his own shock and raced on to my reasons. "That sad business in Caracas, eh *paidakimou?*"

"That's part of it."

"Sad," he sighed. "But not surprising. Listen to me. Don't let the modern world crack your mind. Remember Nietzsche: 'Without cruelty there is no festival.' "

"Oh, there are festivals, all right," I laughed. "I've got one planned for tomorrow, in fact," I added under my breath.

"Bloody hell," he muttered, not pleased with my tone.

"Hey. You'll burn the operator's ear, Theo. Or shock the BOSS-man who's tapping our phones out of his britches."

"This line is bugged?" Theo exclaimed, abruptly paranoid. "The Bureau of State Security is tapping me?"

"Just joking," I reassured him. I had forgotten for the moment Theo was in exile from his beloved Greece that was suffering under The Colonels' junta.

"*Skatà!*" he cursed. "You can still joke, eh? That, at least, is something. Listen, Paul, Paulakimou ... " his tone slid into the fond diminutive. "I finish here tomorrow. I don't dig this Golden Witwatersrand, this Jo'burg that stinks of money and misery. I come visit with you, yes?"

"*No!*"

The cry sprang spontaneously from my gut. It was out before I could soften it. I tried, but Theo cut me off.

"That bad, eh?" he muttered.

I attempted to laugh it off, but that was foolish. You had to be straight with Theo. He was much too canny to be cozened.

"Theo, I love you, you know that. You are my old mentor. The teacher who taught me what little I know, and what I'm trying hard to forget. I am home, at last. I don't want your sharp eyes here seeing right through my muddled motives, not now. Not here. I simply could not stand your scrutiny. *Katalava?*"

"*Katalava,*" he said, at once. "*Entendido. Compris.* Understood. Oh, Paul, is there nothing — ?"

"Nothing."

"Ah."

A silence. Across the hundreds of miles of line I could almost hear his mind whirring, could almost see him swivel his pinkie in his small left ear, that was eternally itchy, especially when he was troubled. Theo kept the nails on his little fingers long in the old-fashioned Greek manner. The narrow pink elongations were useful for digging out ear wax.

Theo spoke suddenly. "I must tell you. I have recommended you to the South Africans. They need a housing consultant, for their African townships. I tell you, they need you. Oh boy, they are such *malakas*, wankers, you read me? This is an urgent necessity, Paul. These poor blacks live in shit. You cannot refuse. They will contact you."

"Theo!"

"*Yassu, paidakimou. Au revoir.*" He rang off.

"*Yassu,*" I muttered, into the dead phone.

I stood shakily. My chest was freezing but the backs of my knees streamed with sweat. I went back to my room and fell upon the bed.

"Theo," I mumbled into my pillow. " 'Without cruelty there is no festival ... thus the longest and most ancient part of human history teaches.' "

I rolled over with a sigh. *On The Genealogy of Morals* — I had this passage by heart. Theo had bullied me into memorizing it when I was his assistant: "In the days when mankind was not yet ashamed of its cruelty, life on earth was more cheerful than it is now that pessimists exist .... On his way to becoming an 'angel', man has evolved that queasy stomach and coated tongue through which not only the joy and innocence of the animal but life itself has become repugnant to him — so that he holds his nose in his own presence."

"Queasy stomach" — mine was churning. I searched for the matchbox of *dagga* Tenja had given me. I tore off a corner of the *Chronicle* and rolled myself a joint.

The raw weed soothed me. Its smoke was potent. I began to drift off.

Theo appears. He wears his white warlock's toga, his gold embossed magician's robe, as in my weird dream on Shaun's ranch.

"*Ella, paidakimou,*" he beckons, smiling. "Come, my son, walk upon the waters, the silver waters. Breathe life into your mud."

I shake my head sharply. The apparition vanishes —

"Get out of my head, Theo!"

I laughed. Pity I had not told Theo of my Magician-in-Jerusalem dream; he would have been amused. His quick and quirky mind would have leapt upon the corny symbolism and fashioned it into a prophecy. But the last thing I needed was yet another prophecy. My gut was queasy enough.

I rolled another joint. "Bless you, Tenja," I thought as I sucked in smoke. *"Nkosi sikele Afrika."*

Africa and festivals ... Boundaries of cruelty ...

Theo hurries ahead of me. We are climbing the village's steep streets. The cobbles slip under my sandals. Up and up we go, under vines of purple wistaria, up to the ruined castle that crowns the village hill.

"I am born here," Theo pants. "This is the place of my peasant fathers."

It is the Greek Easter. I am twenty-three and working for Theo in his Athens office. We are on Lesbos, Theophilus's home island.

We reach the castle. The view from the crumbling ramparts is splendid.

Below us is Molivos. The village is a pattern of tiled roofs like red dominoes fallen down the slope to the hook of the harbour and the grand curve of Mythimna Bay. Behind us is the continental mass of Turkey. The jagged ranges of Asia Minor overshadow the more subtle island scale.

Theo grips my arm. He swings me round in a full circle. "Here, Europe." He flings out an arm. "There, Asia. Here Christ, there Mohammed. Here Aphrodite, there Astarte." He rivets me with his olive-pit eyes. "A boundary this — between cruelties. Ours. Theirs." He grins. "That is why, so many festivals!"

I smile, too, impressed by his gnomic vehemence.

We descend to the *agora*, the village's tiny square. Theo orders ouzo and *mezè* — appetizers of rubbery octopus and feta cheese.

Theo is in full flood. "Form does *not* follow function," he exclaims, as if I would contradict. "The Moderns are cockeyed! Rather it is, Function Follows Form. *Katalava?*"

"No."

He ignores me. "Forms do not impose their necessities upon us. We impose our necessities upon forms!" He pounds the marble tabletop with his small pink fist. "The forms we need spring from the human heart, the human mind. We impose them on the brute chaos of the world, that we cannot bear to leave unshaped!"

"Delicious feta," I mutter.

"Chaos forces form!" Theo shouts, angered by my

obtuseness. "Chaos *gives* form!" He grips my arm, grinning now. "Sweet paradox, eh?"

"Sweet," I agree, not understanding a damn thing.

"Chaos forces form" ... My lids were leaden.

But then, just as I was sinking into sleep, an abrupt thought jerked me back. How did Theo get my number? *Magic!*

No, no — no such thing. There must be a logical explanation. What Kahns were listed in the Bulawayo phone book? My father, of course. Had Theo called him for my number? At midnight? Poor Dad. He retired early. The shrill ringing in the night must have made his tummy jump, that "queasy stomach ... through which life itself has become repugnant."

Poor Dad.

Tuesday the Sixteenth of October — Bomb Day — began with a dull sky. It had been raining the night before and there was a nip in the morning air.

My appointment with Barney Silverman at the Telecom Centre was for twelve o'clock. I waited till the family had all left the house for work or school before rising. After showering, I put on a pair of freshly pressed white denim slacks to match the safari jacket I would be wearing over the bomb-vest.

I pulled on a skin-tight cotton T-shirt; this would give the minimum of friction to the padded vest. Over coffee in the dining room I practiced once again the counting of the seconds: one-breath-two-breath-three-breath, up to twenty.

Ten o'clock; time to kill. I idled over the *Chronicle*. The Israelis had stopped the Egyptian advance but at a heavy cost. Much of their armour and airforce had been badly damaged. The Americans were engaged in a massive resupply by air.

Locally, the Rhodesian forces had carried out an Israeli-style pre-emptive strike at a guerrilla base in Mozambique. They had attacked the ZANU camp with planes and paratroops. The Rhodesian commander claimed a "kill" of three to four hundred terrorists. "That should cruel the buggers' pitch for a space," he told the *Chronicle* reporter.

Ten twenty-two. The day was warming up. I had hoped it would remain cool as I would be somewhat overdressed.

In my bedroom I put on the bomb-vest. The rayon lifejacket was a snug fit round my chest and under my arms. The webbing shoulder straps popped neatly into place. Their padding was light on my shoulders.

Over this, I slipped the safari jacket, buttoned and belted. I put the electronic necklace on; the breastplate sat comfortably on my solar plexus. To add a touch of colour, and to hide the top of the waistcoat if I chanced to lean forward too much, I tied on a blue and yellow Indian paisely scarf.

In the mirror, the effect was quite Rhodesian — sort of Colonial Hip. Perhaps I looked a trifle musclebound with the vest thickening my chest, but that was in character.

Leonie had left the car for me. A friend of hers had picked her up and taken her to the pharmacy. The keys were on the telephone table, with a curt note: "Be home for supper, please."

It was a quarter to twelve when I parked round the corner from the public library. I smoked a cigarette to collect my thoughts before I entered the post office.

The streets were somnolent. A few cars slid by in the wide avenue. A block away was the statue of Cecil Rhodes. His bronze backside was towards me, set up on the granite pedestal.

"Your hinterland lies there," The Founder's effigy pointed. But my hinterland was at his back. It was a different territory altogether.

What territory was my festival? Good question.

Twelve o'clock! I heard the Town Hall clock begin to strike the midday hour. In my daydreaming I had forgotten the time. I jumped out of the car and hastened towards the post office.

The African constable saluted smartly as I crossed the threshold. In the foyer I was stopped by a white security officer. On his hip was a service revolver in a leather holster.

"I've an appointment with Mr. Silverman," I told him. "My name is Kahn."

The security officer rang through on an internal phone.

He told me Barney would be down in a minute. I waited in the small, cool chamber that was sealed off from the interior of the building by a screen of metal bars. The cold eye of a closed-circuit television camera watched me from a corner of the ceiling.

Barney appeared promptly. Clipped to his lapel was a plastic card with his photo, name and security clearance code. He wore a white safari jacket like mine.

"Hi, cousin!" he cried as the barred gate opened to let him through. "On the dot, eh?" He turned to the guard. "He's with me, George."

"I have to search him," the guard said doggedly.

"Make it short and sweet, man," Barney told him. He shrugged at me. "Security regs."

"Of course."

The guard approached and began to run his hands over my body, from my armpits down.

"Heard the latest news?" Barney chattered. "The Israelis have counter-punched across the Canal! They're racing for Cairo!"

"Marvellous," I murmured. The guard's palms were slipping down my chest, over the padded vest.

"We'll celebrate Hannukah with the Sphinx!" Barney laughed. "Hurry up, George. We haven't got all day."

The guard was patting my thighs. He straightened with a grunt. "Okay," he muttered. Then he frowned. "What about that?"

He was pointing at my necklace.

Barney chuckled proudly. "This is my hippy cousin, you know? They wear beads. The Flower-Power types. Listen!"

Before I could react, Barney jabbed the necklace's breastplate. I almost fainted on the spot. In that instant I realized that I had forgotten to instruct the radio expert to fix the breastplate so it continued to play music. If it didn't, Barney would be suspicious. And if he went on jabbing the knob we would all be vapourized.

The burst of African pop blasted the guard back a pace. He reflexively reached for his pistol. I stood frozen, afraid to move my knees in case they melted.

"He shall have music wherever he goes!" Barney sang out gaily.

The shaken guard clipped a plastic card to my lapel, granting me temporary clearance. I signed the register and we went through the barred gate. As we waited for the lift I gingerly pressed the breastplate knob to cut off the music.

"Gave him a scare, eh?" Barney cackled. "Security is a necessary bind. Anyway, blacks aren't allowed through that gate. Even the cleaners are white. Who's ever heard of a white terr?"

"Yeah," I agreed, beginning to recover from my own fright.

The lift let us out at the top floor. "Brain Level," Barney announced.

We were in a narrow lobby. A sign over a heavy steel door read: Unauthorized Persons Strictly Prohibited Beyond This Point.

Barney spoke into a grilled panel. "Silverman," he said curtly. The door clicked. It swung open, leting us into a second lobby. Another armed security guard sat at a table.

The guard glanced at my clearance card. "Can I have your name, sir."

"Paul Kahn."

"C-A-R-N?"

"K-A-H-N."

My name and time of entry were inscribed in the logbook open on the guard's desk. "Step into the Anti-Static Chamber, please."

"Into the Dust Box, cousin," Barney explained.

He led me to an armourplate glass door whose edges were sealed with a thick rubber lining. The door slid back and we were in a chamber about eight feet in width, height, and length. The walls gave off an eerie blue glow. "Ionized light," Barney said. "Takes out the snap, crackle and pop from your clothes. Won't take a sec."

There was a short, intense hum. The walls pulsed a brilliant blue for a few seconds.

"Okay," Barney said. "Slip these dustcovers over your shoes." As we put on the covers, he added: "The Brain is very sensitive. Very allergic to dust. We have to feed it only the purest air."

A door opened in the wall opposite the armourplate screen. "The Monster!" Barney announced, as we stepped through into the Control Room.

The room was larger than I had imagined. It was about thirty feet square. At first sight it seemed a crammed bazaar of electronic wizardry, jammed with whirling tape spools and flashing computer consoles. A low hum of power made my ears tingle; it sounded like a dragon imprisoned in a cellar.

Barney led me through the electronic maze. He babbled happily about digital landlines, optimum repeaters, satellite linkups, encoding, real-time interaction, analogue circuitry, translents and what-have-you.

Slowly, I began to comprehend the layout.

In the centre of the room was an island of equipment — monitors and control panels. A technician sat before a console of multiple television screens set in a fascia that was dense with illuminated buttons. A narrow aisle separated this island from a phalanx of tall metal cabinets ranged round the walls. The cabinets had tapespool eyes that spun like catherine wheels. Their steel bellies gave out rude grunts.

Along one wall was a large illuminated map of Matabeleland, Rhodesia's southern province. Bulawayo, the capital, was the centre of a network of light-lines that webbed out all over the territory. Beside this map was another of the whole of Southern Africa, from Cape Town in the south, to Lusaka, Zambia, to the north; from Angola, on the Atlantic, to the west, to Mozambique, on the Indian Ocean, in the east. The communication system linked Bulawayo with the entire region.

The lighting in the room was concealed and subdued. The whole scene was bathed in a subaqueous glow, like some cavern of the deep.

"This is the nerve-centre," Barney was saying. "This is Matabeleland's Brain."

"Amazing," I murmured.

"Isn't it just?" Barney exclaimed. He introduced me to the technician: "My cousin, Paul Kahn, a famous architect; John Allardyce, The Brain's Nanny."

We shook hands. Allardyce was in his late twenties. A fresh, suntanned face grinned up at me. Blond, hairy, muscled thighs bulged out from a pair of very short shorts. Wedged in a corner of one of the monitor screens was a colour snap of a young blond woman cuddling a fair-haired baby.

"My Peg," the technician said. "The only human thing in here, apart from me."

"And me," Barney protested.

"He's not human, he's bionic," Allardyce teased. "Cut open his head and all you'll find is circuitry. Mind you, he is a bloody genius. This — " he gestured round the room — "is his baby."

"Well, I helped the Jap experts design it," Barney agreed modestly.

"This stuff is Japanese?" I queried.

"Matsushita Electric," Barney said. "Sanctions Busters Extraordinary. God bless Hirohito!"

"Amen," Allardyce intoned.

"Just the two of you here?" I asked, casually.

"There's a standby night shift," Barney said. "But all it takes it two people! The world's at our fingertips. Want to chat with Washington? Paris? Toyko?" He jabbed a button. A jumble of figures sprang up on a screen. Barney played the piano on the console. "Routine checkout" the screen printed. Under this came the instantaneous response: "Pentagon. Reception Degree One Hundred. X-Bulawayo."

"What on earth does Bulawayo want with the Pentagon?" I exclaimed.

Barney tapped the side of his nose significantly. "Mutual advantage. We also have on stream all the dispositions of military and police units in the region. Watch."

He prodded buttons. A print-out unit began to chatter, *tak-tak-tak*. A long tongue of paper extruded from a slot and folded itself neatly into a tray.

"Can't let you see that," Barney said gruffly. "Classified, you know? Come and admire the rest of our marvels."

He led me round the room again, explaining the workings of The Brain. It was, indeed, like strolling round a monstrous mind. The air was charged with a tension between a kind of superhuman lucidity and sheer nuttiness. Electricity was the animating ghost-in-the-machine. It was at once blind and all-seeing; a humming dumb servant that was also a master.

"There's a sixty-foot radio antenna on the roof just over our heads," Barney chattered. "And a satellite-reception dish. We're linked to the whole world. And if there are men on Mars, we can signal them too!"

"Amazing."

Barney squeezed my waist fondly. "Impressed you, at last, Cousin?" He squeezed me again, frowning. "Say, you're getting chubby, man. Leonie fattening you up for the marriage market?" He winked slyly as I jerked back from his embrace. "She's got some juicy *nafkes* lined up for her clever brother, let me warn you."

Nervously, I took out my cigarettes. Barney shook his head. "No smoking. All this junk is very flammable."

"Are there sprinklers?"

"Sprinklers and heat sensors. Make more of a mess of our equipment than any blaze."

"Must've cost a pretty penny, all this."

"Right. Enough to buy one Cadillac for every *munt* in Matabeleland, just about," Barney agreed.

"And that's a lot of Caddies," Allardyce laughed.

"Look," Barney cut in, brisk all at once, "I've got a bit of paper work to get through before lunch. Why don't you prowl round on your own? But don't smoke, and don't touch anything. It might bite back!"

He went to his desk in a corner. I wandered round the room like a tourist. For a moment I had forgotten why I was here.

The vest! Where to dump it?

There seemed to be no gaps in the cabinets that lined the walls. I had to find a corner out of sight.

I unbelted my safari jacket and undid the front buttons so the garment hung loose. I slipped in a hand to undo the press-studs on the vest. I took my first deep breath in hours.

All at once the lifejacket seemed leaden. The padded webbing shoulder straps cut into my neck.

Where to dump it? It was urgent, now. I had to shed this

extra weight. It was unbearable. My kneecaps jumped with the strain of supporting the six-and-a-half kilos of plastic explosive hanging from my shoulders. My whole body was made of mud.

At last I found a gap. It was barely six inches wide, between two metal cabinets. It was hidden from Barney and Allardyce by a bank of consoles.

I snapped open the shoulder poppers — *click-click, click-click*. They sounded very loud, like gunshots over The Brain's low electronic hum. I caught the vest as it plummetted to my thighs and shoved it into the gap.

*Done!* My body, released from its burden, seemed to float towards the ceiling. My bones were air. I was all silvery light, all pure spirit, floating ...

"Nosh, Cousin?" Barney called out. "I'm starving!"

In a moment we were in front of the lift, having slipped through several doors. "Easier getting out than in," Barney chuckled. In another moment we were in the street, blinking in the sunlight.

*Done!*

I gulped, filling cramped lungs. Behind us, the constable clicked his heels in salute. The post office building was a sandstone cliff I had climbed like a human fly, and then descended safely.

The restaurant Barney was leading me to was across Eighth Avenue. The Beefy Burger, it was called. A smell of grilling meat grabbed my nostrils.

Just as we were about to enter, I paused. I took out my hankie, turned my back on Barney, and began elaborately to blow my nose. "See you inside," I mumbled, waving him on.

Barney nodded and vanished through the restaurant doorway. I turned to face the post office, still blowing my nose. I put my finger on the breastplate knob, pressed hard, and began to count under my breath.

"One-breath-two-breath-three-breath — "

It seemed to take hours. Several passers-by stared at me curiously. Their startled looks made me realize that a *kwela* whistle was blaring from my breastplate. In my concentration upon counting I had not noticed the music.

"—ten-breath-eleven-breath-twelve-breath-thirteen—"

The count seemed to last forever. I exhaled into my hankie to its rhythm and rocked to the trilling whistle of Radio Matopos as if in prayer. My shoes seemed rooted to the pavement.

" — fifteen-breath-sixteen-breath-seventeen-breath-eight — "

It sounded like a loud sneeze somewhere, muffled but distinct. I knew in my bones that The Brain had exploded.

I stopped counting and held my breath. In that instant the street seemed frozen in sharp sunlight. It looked utterly ordinary — the Eighth Avenue I had known all my life — yet at the same time totally strange. It was now the Street of the Bomb.

Yet nothing seemed to change. The constable on guard at the post office entrance still stood rigidly at attention. The cars still rolled by in the road. Cecil Rhodes still pointed north.

Perhaps everything was in a conspiracy to pretend nothing had happened?

It made me angry. I wanted to howl over the whistle from my breastplate radio that *The Brain has exploded!* I wanted it *known* —

Suddenly, things began to happen.

The African constable melted from his stiff duty and began pounding across the avenue towards me. His hobnailed boots clacked on the tarmac. At the same time I heard the clang of an approaching fire engine's bell.

The first unit of the Fire Brigade appeared just as the policeman was dashing by me into the restaurant. The second and third units turned the corner of Main Street just as Barney came out of The Beefy Burger.

He had a napkin tucked into the collar of his jacket. There were flecks of tomato ketchup on his lower lip. His face was grey with shock. *"Blast!"* he gasped at me, and ran off across the avenue with the constable at his heels.

I pressed the knob on my breastplate and stopped the music.

<u>11</u>

# FUNCTION FOLLOWS FORM

The fire engines blocked the avenue. A crowd gathered at once, black and white mingled in buzzing curiosity. African constables held the throng at bay, solemn with their own authority. A tangle of hoses snaked through the post office entrance, pulsing with pump pressure. On the roof of the building the sixty-foot aerial was askew. It leaned out over the parapet at a dangerous angle.

An ambulance arrived. A stretcher team jumped out the back and ran into the building. Beside me was an elderly lady in a straw gardening hat. "Someone's hurt?" she gasped, touching a white-gloved finger to her lips in alarm.

"Hurt!" I echoed. My heart sank.

The old lady tilted her face up to mine. China-blue eyes pierced me. "Bloody terrs," she rasped. "Hang the lot!"

Her innocent English eyes were savage. "If I had my way," she told me, "I'd flay the lot of 'em. Hang, drawn, quartered and castrated — every last one."

I gulped. "But surely — "

"Every last one," she said again, and marched off grasping her straw bonnet.

"Here comes a casualty!" someone shouted in the crowd.

"Oh, shit," I mumbled, and ran across the road to see.

The stretcher men were easing a body down the entrance steps. The casualty bounced on the canvas. His bare legs were black with burns.

It was John Allardyce.

He was unconcious. His fair head rolled on the stretcher

as they eased him into the ambulance. There was blood in his hair.

"Bloody terrs!" a raw voice shouted in the crowd.

There were growls of anger from many white throats. All at once the mob began to separate out into its racial elements. The paler faces hardened with baffled rage. The darker faces melted away under the glare of white loathing. They seemed to vanish into the hot tarmac like a stain.

"Bloody terrs!"

The harsh cry made my blood run cold. I left the scene.

"Twenty baases killed!" the African taxi driver cried out in panic. "Very bad terrs." We drove out towards the suburb of Kumalo. Beyond the taxi's dusty windscreen Bulawayo seemed as sleepy as ever, but inside the car the driver's agitation buzzed.

"Very bad terrs," he moaned again as he dropped me off at Leonie's house. Not even the two-dollar tip made him smile.

None of the family were home. I stripped off my safari jacket and the electronic necklace, drew the blinds, and lay down on the bed with a cigarette.

The image of John Allardyce's blackened bare thighs kept jumping into my head. I could almost smell the sweet stench of roasted human flesh.

*Bloody terrs!*

All the same, Allardyce was a combatant. He had tended The Brain. In his own way he must have had a hand in the deaths of many guerrillas.

But those scorched thighs were very vivid.

I lit another smoke. My heart began to calm down. The pulse in my temple eased up in its throbbing.

It was done. I had blown The Brain. That act was unambiguous. The sense of lightness, of "walking on the water," returned to me. It filled my bones with air. I was floating above the bed.

"Baas?"

Grace's soft voice seeped through the door. I got up and went to see what the servant wanted. Her pale yellow face was a moon in the passageway's darkness. "Telephone for you," she whispered.

"What's up, Grace?" I asked. She looked scared.

She put her fingers to her lips in alarm. "Terrible thing in town, baas," she panted. "Bad black men kill fifty baases with bomb!"

"Fifty?" I smiled. "How do you know? Is it on the news?"

"Moses, Mrs. Levy's boy next door, he tells me. Fifty baases!"

"Not fifty," I said, and squeezed her arm reassuringly on my way to the phone.

"Paul!" My father's voice leapt out of the bakelite. "Terrible — " He choked off, too upset to continue.

"Is it on the news?" I asked.

"News? What news?" He sounded very confused.

"Grace tells me — "

"Mom!" he croaked. "Hospital — "

I froze. "What? She wasn't — ?"

His voice burst forth in a rush. "Came home early from work — found her lying — bathroom floor — broken hip — complications — hospital."

"Dad, Dad — give it to me slowly."

The old man took several breaths. I could hear the gasps in the receiver. "I'm at the hospital, Bulawayo Central. Can you come?"

"Of course. I've got Leonie's car."

Then I remembered. I'd left the car parked outside the library! In my confusion after the explosion, the shock of seeing Allardyce's burned legs, I had forgotten it completely. Would it give me away? My mind buzzed with the consequences of my stupidity as my father rattled on.

"I phoned Leonie at the pharmacy. She wants you to pick her up. Come to the hospital right away. Please, my boy, please?"

"Right away, Dad," I said. "Try and calm down, will you? We'll be there soon."

"Hurry!" he pleaded, and rang off.

I phoned for a taxi immediately. As I waited for it, smoking nervously, I listened to the two o'clock news on the radio.

"A fire occurred at the Telecommunications Centre of the Bulawayo Main Post Office at twelve-fifty this afternoon. The blaze was intense, but the fire services were able to bring it under control swiftly. One technician employed in the Centre, Mr. John Allardyce, Matabeleland rugby wing-half, suffered third-degree burns. He is still unconscious but his condition is reported to be uncritical. A European security guard in a room adjoining the Telecom Centre suffered light bruising from the explosion in the electronic installations set off by the fire. Army and police forensic experts, assisted by Mr. Barney Silverman, Chief of the Centre, are investigating possible causes of the conflagration. Sabotage is not suspected."

"Sabotage is not suspected!" I echoed.

Grace was hovering in the background. "You see," I told her, "Moses was wrong. No baases were killed. There was no bomb."

"No baases killed?" She sounded quite disappointed.

"Not one," I said, as the taxi honked in the driveway.

The taxi driver had his radio on. The news bulletin continued as we drove back into town.

"Due to the fire in the Bulawayo Telecom Centre today, several public services will be temporarily suspended until standby arrangements can be made. These services include telegraph and telex relays, television broadcasts, and long-distance telephone lines. Local telephone services are not affected. On the radio, overseas bulletins will be relayed from Salisbury temporarily. This will involve some delay."

The black driver shook his head sadly. "Very bad business, baas."

"Very bad business," I agreed.

The car was still parked where I had left it. There was not a cop in sight.

I drove down Eighth Avenue past the post office. The crowd had vanished, along with the fire engines and ambulances. The street was quiet. The only signs of the blast and the frenzy that followed were the tilted radio mast and a pool of water spilled from the fire hoses in the gutters.

"Sabotage is not suspected ... "

It hardly seemed possible that the forensic experts could hold that view unless it were a cover-up. Perhaps they wanted to calm the public, avoid a backlash of white fury?

I remembered the china-blue eyes under the straw hat. "Flay the lot of 'em! Hang, drawn, quartered and castrated — every last one!"

One could imagine the hectic phone calls between the local civil and military authorities and the Prime Minister's office in Salisbury: "Martial law, sir?" "Public warnings?" "Massive round-up?" "Crack-down?"

Then I realized — there were no communications!

I had blown them all. I had torn out The Brain's wires, fused its links, shorted all circuits. Its wizardry was now a lump of melted junk.

"Hoo!" I shouted gleefully, giving a long honk of the horn outside Leonie's pharmacy. "Long live the *Chimurenga!*"

Leonie hurried out. Her face was flushed as she rolled onto the seat beside me. "What a business," she panted.

"Yes," I agreed. "Isn't it just?"

"She had to go and do it right now. Right in the middle of our annual stocktaking. She's got to upstage us all — always!"

I sobered abruptly. "She's badly hurt."

"You always take her side," Leonie said angrily as we drove out to the hospital. "You're her blue-eyed boy."

"Hardly blue-eyed."

Leonie pushed her reddened face at me. "Can't you see how she's killing Dad? Can't you see!"

"But she's the one who's suffering."

"Killing Dad," she repeated grimly. "By inches. It's a plot."

"She has advanced Parkinsonism. The trembling makes her wobbly on her pins."

"Parkinsonism is psychosomatic," Leonie cut in, her voice abruptly professional. "It's a stress-related disease. A degeneration of the motor control centres in the brain. 'Control' — that's the operative word. She's always been a controller. It used to be control-by-command. Now it's control-by-crisis."

"That's a cruel thing to say."

Leonie shrugged. "Cruel, but true."

"She's so brave!" my father cried out as soon as we entered the private hospital room. "Not a whimper — "

"Shush, Joe," my mother said crossly. "Don't make so much fuss. You'll upset your tummy."

On cue, my father clutched his middle and groaned. My mother rolled her eyes at me. "You'd think he's the one who fell down the way he's carrying on." Her voice, surprisingly, was stronger and clearer than usual.

The old woman looked minute in the vast hospital bed. The covers were propped off her small body by a metal frame. Her greying brown hair fanned out over the wad of pillows.

"How are you, Mom?" I asked, taking her hand. "How did you fall down?"

"Lost my balance. In the toilet. Pulling up my knickers."

"She went alone!" Dad accused. " She didn't call the girl!"

"Can't call the damn girl every time I need to widdle," Mom said. "Ridiculous."

I squeezed her hand. "Silly old moo," I chided. "Too proud to ask for help in pulling up your knickers!"

"She's so brave!" Dad said again. Leonie put a hand on his shoulder.

The old woman beckoned me to put my ear to her lips. "No freedom any more. He watches me like a hawk. Can't even fart without his cadenza!"

I laughed. "Hey, old thing! Next time fall on your tongue, eh?"

She grinned. Then her eyes sharpened on my face. "What's up?" she asked. "You look strange."

I started. "How 'strange'?"

Her brown gaze was very penetrating. It pierced all my secrets. I had never been able to fool her. She put up a hand and touched my cheek. "Take care, Paul," she murmured. Her lids flickered. She fell asleep.

"How long will she have to stay here?" I asked the sister in the duty room.

"Some weeks," the starched woman replied in a voice as crisp as her uniform. "Her bones are fragile. But she's a brave soldier."

"She's so brave!" Dad exclaimed.

The sister glanced at him shrewdly. She took a bottle of

pills from her drawer. "Take these, Mr. Kahn," she told the old man. "They'll help you relax."

All the way home in the car my father entertained us with complaint. "She's so brave ... It's so hard ... She's not well, not well at all ... "

"Shush, Dad," Leonie cut in irritably, after the fourth or fifth repetition of this litany. "At least you'll have some time to breathe. Will you come and stay with us while Mom's in hospital?"

"Oh no," my father said, shocked. "How could I leave the house? Our house? It'd be disloyal."

Leonie shot me a look. I put my hand on my father's knee. "Would you like me to move in with you, Dad?"

"No! I mean — don't trouble yourself, my boy."

"No trouble."

"That's kind of you. I'll, er ... call you if I need you, okay?"

"Okay."

Tea was served by the pool under the shade of the flame tree. The children came home from school and joined us.

"The terrs blew up the post office!" Lovey panted, racing up red-faced on his bike. "People were killed!" he shouted, dropping his bike on the gravel.

"What post office?" Leonie said sharply.

"Post office?" my father cried.

"There was a fire in the Telecom Centre this morning," I cut in. "It happened just after I visited Barney. One technician was burned. Apparently, he's still unconscious. Sabotage is not suspected, the radio says."

All eyes fixed on me. Lawlene leant on her mother's ample shoulder and stroked her gold watch while smiling at me.

"Bloody terrs," Eric said loudly.

Tenja had come out to pick up Lovey's bike and the spilled school books. He gave me a sly grin.

"Our Head's doing his nut!" Lovey exclaimed. "Called the whole school to Special Assembly. Made a funny speech about 'Holy War' or something."

"G.C.M.," Eric muttered, picking his nose.

"All the time Old Geddie's been saying how the terrs are just a bunch of baboons. Now he wants rifle drill for every class!"

"Talking about Holy War," I said, "what's the news from Israel?"

"The Jews have counter-attacked," Dad replied. "Crossed the Canal into Egypt."

Leonie was frowning and biting her thumb nail. "This is serious," she muttered, "this post office thing." She focused on me. "You were there?"

"Barney and I were just going into The Beefy Burger for lunch when the fire broke out. It was put under control quickly though I believe the damage is considerable."

"You were there?" Dad blurted, just absorbing this fact.

"Barney was showing me round."

He stared at me. "You were there."

"I was in no danger, Dad."

"The technician you say was burned must've been John Allardyce," Leonie said. "He has such a sweet little wife and boy."

"He played rugger for Matabeleland," Lovey informed us. "Wing-half."

"The radio said his condition wasn't critical," I said.

"But he's unconscious?" Leonie asked.

I nodded. There was a silence. The lawn sprinklers hissed.

The thought struck me that Allardyce would know there had been a blast and not a fire, even if the forensic experts didn't discover that. Even if the blaze following the explosion had been, with the help of the napalm incendiary charge, so intense as to have consumed every last trace of the bomb-vest, Allardyce would remember an explosion. Or could that be confused with a short in the high-tension cables, for instance?

"It's a cover-up," my father said suddenly. "It can't be just a fire. They don't want to alarm us. Or give the terrs satisfaction."

"Hard to cover up such a thing in a town like Bulawayo," Leonie objected. "Anyway, Barney will tell us the facts. He's family."

"It's a cover-up," David declared at the dinner table.

"Listen to the expert," Leonie said.

"I know," David insisted. "You think they'd tell us the truth? Fat chance. Everyone'd be stampeding for the next plane out."

"Look, I phoned Linda," Leonie said. "Barney isn't home yet, but he's phoned her. It was just a fire. 'I always warned Barn about all that electricity buzzing round his head,' she said. 'Bound to blaze up some day!' "

"Poor old Barn," David chuckled. "His toys've gone up in smoke." He forked up a chunk of roast beef and chewed on it solemnly. "All the same, I say it's sabotage. The *munts* are beginning to box clever, at last." He swallowed a lump of meat. "Instead of shooting up lonely farmers and chopping up their own people in the Tribal Trust Lands, they're starting to kick us where it hurts."

"In the goolies?" Eric winced, clutching his groin.

"Right," his father nodded. "I tell you, there's a brain behind it. A brain." He tapped his temple shrewdly. *"Eine weisische kop*. A white mind. No darkie would have the *seichel."*

"What are you saying?" my father exclaimed, frozen in the act of gnawing his chunk of soupmeat.

"A white mind," David repeated. His spectacles gleamed. "Just think of the logistics! Getting into the Telecom Centre. Getting out. Making a device — radio-remote-control, I'd guess — sophisticated enough to detonate a bomb once it's been placed. *Seichel."*

"If there was a bomb," Leonie muttered. But she looked disturbed.

"A Rhodesian?" Lovey gasped, chin smeared with chicken grease. "One of us?"

David lolled back in his chair. He pulled out his pipe and sucked on it. For once his family were listening to him. He was visible again.

"Not a Rhodesian. Of course not. But a white man."

"Russians!" Lovey cried. His eyes were wide with fright.

"Yes." David nodded. "Or a Cuban, maybe."

"A Cuban!" Leonie exploded with laughter. "Listen to him!"

David turned to me for support. "Paul, isn't that

possible? The Cubans are all over Africa now, doing the Russians' dirty work."

Once again, all eyes turned to me.

I shrugged. "Could be — if it was a bomb."

"You see?" David was triumphant. "You see!"

The heads sank back into the plates. But Lovey's gaze stayed locked on my face. "Cubans," he mumbled, and shivered.

Ray came in with the dessert trolley. He seemed very subdued. His small face was folded in on itself like a pitted prune.

"What's the matter, Ray?" Leonie asked. "Swallowed your Jesus?"

Ray's face clenched even further. "Very bad business, missus," he muttered, avoiding all our eyes as he began handing out the dishes of ice cream.

"You didn't blow up the post office, did you?" Leonie teased.

Ray's hands jerked with shock. The ice cream he was holding jumped into David's lap.

David leapt to his feet. His trousers were wet with tuttifrutti. "Idiot!" he screamed. *"Shaygetz!* Arsehole! *Pascudnyak! Msatanyok'!"*

Ray cowered in terror. The empty dessert dish in his hands wobbled with fright. He backed off into the kitchen in a crouch.

*"Msatanyok'!"* David bellowed after him. "Motherfucker!"

"Shush," Leonie cut in wearily. "For God's sake go and change your pants."

Barney popped in later, on his way home from the post office. His cheeks were ashen. His usually sleek golden locks stood up in spikes. His white safari suit was smudged with smoke.

He accepted a whisky from David. "Cheers," he muttered, eyes glazed with tiredness.

"So, tell us," David demanded. "What happened?"

Barney shrugged. "An accident, I guess. Perhaps the underfloor power cables shorted ... chafed insulation, maybe ... caused a power surge. Right now your guess is as good as mine — but the forensic boys are working on it."

"David is sure it was a bomb," Leonie said, deadpan.

"Uh-huh," Barney shook his head. "No way. Anyway, it's a total write-off. Millions of dollars of irreplaceable equipment gone up in smoke."

"Irreplaceable?" I queried.

"Sanctions," Barney grunted. "We smuggled that stuff in from Japan, with a hand from the South Africans. A complicated fiddle, with secret bank accounts and false bills of lading, and whatnot." He rubbed his cheeks. "After I've had a bite with Linda and the kids, it's back to the Centre to try and rig up some kind of stand-by system."

Barney smiled weakly at me. "Sorry this had to happen the day you came to visit. By the way, the cops asked about you. Saw your name in the log. I explained you were just my cousin."

"Okay." I smiled back at Barney. "How long will the disruption of services continue?"

"Look, we'll glue up some bypass rigs," he replied, throwing up his hands. "Salisbury can take over Matabeleland. Quite a present for the terrs, eh? This accident is worth more to them than all their incursions put together!"

"Bloody terrs," David muttered, clenching his fists. "If it was an accident?"

"And your assistant?" I asked. "Still out?"

"Still out. He's a mess, but he'll live. Burns and concussion. When he's stronger, they'll have to fly him to Jo'burg for skin grafts. His legs are like charred beef."

"Yeeuch," Leonie grimaced.

"Bloody terrs!" David shouted.

"When he comes to, he'll be able to give you some clues as to how it all started," I suggested.

"Yeah. Maybe." Barney rose. "So what? The Brain's a heap of junk." He walked out.


As I was undressing for bed a shadow passed my window, behind the blinds. There was a scratching at the glass. I pulled the blinds back cautiously.

Tenja was there. He waved a scrap of paper at me. I unlocked the glass door and he thrust the paper at me, grinned wildly, and vanished into the night.

I read the note: "Long live the *Chimurenga!* The warriors dance! *Zhii!*"

"*Zhii,*" I muttered, and went to bed.

# 12

# DANCING WARRIORS

The desert at dusk — a sea of black sand, a sky of red fire. On the line of the horizon a distant warrior dances. One brave soldier does a joyous jig, feet flying inches above the hard line between sand and sky. Pale head tilted, hair a nest of wild snakes — his laughter mocks Heaven.

In the desert no sound but the dancing warrior's joy.

The black sand stirs. Alive, it gathers into limbs, a torso, a head. It's a woman! A huge black Venus rises from eternal sleep.

Black Venus embraces brave dancer. They begin to fuck.

Sunlight striped my chest as I awoke. My skin was hot. Eyes open, I strove to grasp the vision, but the images escaped. Yet a charge of pure joy bounced me from the bed.

On the terrace, drinking coffee, I listened to the radio: "Israeli forces, with tremendous flair and bravery, have punched across the Suez Canal in strength. The Egyptian armies are in confusion. In their panic they are firing on their own troops. Hundreds of Arab tanks are burning in the desert. General Dayan, visiting the battle zone, said: 'This is a dance of death.' President Sadat of Egypt, on the other hand, has dismissed the Israeli counter-punch as 'Nothing but a T.V. show.' Soviet Premier Kosygin is in Cairo for urgent consultations with the Egyptians in seeking a cease-fire resolution in the United Nations Security Council."

There was no further news about the post office fire nor Allardyce's condition. The authorities were clearly trying to play this item down.

After breakfast I phoned the hospital. The sister reported that my mother had had a peaceful night. I phoned my father to tell him this, but he already knew. "She's so brave," he said. I arranged to pick him up at the factory at four and drive him to the hospital.

Mona called. "I'm very sorry to hear about your mother's accident," she said. "How is she?"

"Resting peacefully."

"Meet me for lunch? There's a motel I know about ten miles out of town, on the Salisbury Road."

I laughed. Mona's tone sharpened. "What's so funny?" she demanded. "Why are you so damn happy!"

"Because I love you."

"Don't joke," she snapped. "I'll pick you up at twelve."

The drive out of town was silent. Mona crouched over the wheel of the Datsun as if the little car were a wild beast she had to keep in tight rein. She wore a white satin pants suit that set off her mane of jet black hair. The only colour she allowed was the purple slash of her lips. Wraparound sunglasses swallowed the rest of her face.

The motel was a collection of thatched single bungalows clustered round the restaurant in the bush. A broad neon sign proclaimed it as the Bide-A-Wee Motor Inn.

I waited in the car while Mona went in to register. "Rondavel Seven," she informed me, returning with the key. "I've asked for lunch to be served in the room."

We parked outside Rondavel Seven. The bungalow had its own bathroom. It smelled of disinfectant. The bedspread and the curtains were flowered chintz.

While Mona ordered lunch on the phone, I looked out the window. The bush was bright. The recent rains had added a gloss of green to the scratchy trees. Velvety spring buds softened the thorns. In a wide sky armies of fat clouds did battle.

"Well," Mona demanded as we slid under the covers after lunch. "Why are you so happy?"

"Because I love you."

Her naked body jerked back away from mine. "Don't be nasty," she muttered.

"How do you know I'm happy?"

She gazed at me. "Your face is alight."

"Truly?"

"Yes. But why?"

"Why not?"

I drew back the covers and looked at her long white body. Her nipples were inverted prunes. Her pubic patch was a stark black stripe from crotch to navel. There were freckles on her thighs and arms.

"I'm ugly," she said, shielding her torso with her arms from my lewd eyes.

"Yes. That's why I like you."

She blinked in shock. I pulled her arms away from her body and put my lips to her nipple.

At once she was shivering. Tense spasms shook her from head to toe. Her heels did a dance on the sheet.

I sucked at her nipple, trying to reverse the inversion with my hot mouth. She was shaking so much I feared her thin limbs would snap off, come apart in the bed like a grasshopper dismembered. I could feel her muscles fighting this fragmentation. She was terrified to let go in case she could not put herself together again.

*"Love!"* she shrieked. Her arms and legs flew out like wings as she came.

On the drive back into town Mona's silence was intense. It consumed her. She was eaten up by her own mute terrors.

She broke her silence for the first time as she was letting me off at my father's furniture factory in the light-industrial area.

"Let's go away one weekend," she said abruptly. "I know a quiet hotel near the Zimbabwe Ruins."

"Okay." I got out of the car.

Her shades snapped up at me through the window. "Don't sound so keen!" she mocked.

"But I am keen," I said. "I love fucking you."

"Do you?"

"Yes. Bulawayo has the best Bicycle around."

Her snigger was sharp. She raced the motor and spurted away.

The Bulawayo Beauty Furniture Manufacturing Company Proprietary Limited was a long, low red-brick building with a serrated glass roof. My father's office was beside the entrance lobby.

In the lobby large photographs of the company's prize furniture suites were on display. Each suite had a name. There was the Leonie Suite and the Paul Suite. There was the Rachel suite and the Lawlene Suite. The most opulent of chintz settees and armchairs was titled the Kahn Suite.

My father sat behind a broad mahogany desk that was ancient but spotless. The papers on it were stacked in neat piles. On the wall over his head was a wooden shield with the silver plaque celebrating the old man's victory in the Matabeleland Tennis Singles Championship in 1935, 1936, and 1938.

"My boy," he exclaimed, as soon as I entered. "I'm so worried. So very worried about Mom."

"She'll be all right. She's a toughie."

He plucked nervously at the silver expandable armbands on his shirt sleeves. In the background furniture-making machinery whined. There was a smell of planed wood and glue.

The old man pulled on his blazer and smoothed his silver waves. He made a quick tour of the workshops before we left the factory.

The glass rooflights illuminated a busy scene. Several hundred Africans worked the lathes turning table legs and tended circular saws slicing timber. Others were hammering chintz and moquette over made-up wooden frames. The stench of sawdust and wood glue was overpowering, but it did not subdue the Africans' incessant chatter.

"This is our latest design," my father said proudly. He paused to show me a chesterfield settee being covered in purple velvet with golden braiding. "We've named it 'The Beauty' after Mom."

"It is splendid," I agreed, touched by the feeling in his voice.

"The Beauty," he repeated, eyes damp with tears.

"You're such a lover," I said, and touched his face.

Surprisingly, he did not recoil from my fingers. He allowed me to stroke his old cheek. Several black workers squinted at us slyly, but he seemed oblivious of their mockery.

"The Beauty," he said again, dabbing his eyes with his hankie. He could not seem to tear himself away from the purple settee.

I drove his old Toyota to the hospital. It took him most of the journey across town to recover from his emotion over "The Beauty". He wiped his streaming eyes and blew his nose many times along the way.

He spoke up suddenly as we were turning into the hospital grounds. His voice was all at once very firm. "Yes. I love your mother. She is my life."

"I envy you," I said softly.

He shot me a sharp look, suspecting mockery. Finding none, he gave a crooked smile. "Yes," he agreed, "you ought to. You really ought." He reached out and touched my cheek, returning the tenderness.

My mother was asleep. The sister let us peep into her room. She lay on her back under propped covers. Her eyes were closed, her mouth gaped as she sucked in air. She was snoring gently.

"Brave old thing," the sister murmured, gesturing for us to withdraw.

"Brave soldier," I agreed.


"Oh yes, this came for you," my father said, on the drive back home. He pulled a letter from his inside jacket pocket and handed it to me.

I glanced at the envelope quickly. It had an American airmail stamp. The letter had been readdressed from my London office to my father's house. It was from Molly. I tucked it away at once.

"A lady?" he teased, seeing my cheeks flush.

"No lady," I laughed awkwardly.

"You've had a lot of lady friends in your life, haven't you, my boy?"

"Some." My reply was curt. It embarrassed me to discuss this topic with the old man.

"Too many?" he teased, persisting.

"Too many."

"Why?" The question was asked with absolute simplicity.

"Safety in numbers, I guess. S-I-N," I joked feebly.

"I've only ever had one woman in my life — your

mother. I was a virgin when we met. A thirty-year-old virgin."

"Dad — "

"Not that I didn't have many ladies chasing me," he went on proudly. "I was quite handsome, then — "

"You still are."

"Very athletic. But I knew I had to keep myself for one woman. I just knew it."

"I envy you."

"You ought to," he repeated frankly. "You really ought."


"Dear old Mud Man," Molly's scrawl began, "How goes the nightmare? Breathed any life into your Daddy-*golem* yet? Your tribal incubus? Or is it still huff-and-puff-and-blow-the-house-down?"

I paused and lit a cigarette to calm my nerves. In the distance I could hear the marquee canvas snapping as the workmen pulled down the big tent. Lawlene and Eric were squabbling somewhere, shrill young voices rising.

"You'll be shocked to get these lines from me. Yeah, baby, don't protest. Old ghosts are never welcome, 'specially when they've left their lightning on your lip. Does the scar still throb? Oh, I hope so, I really do!

"But I felt I had to tell you — I'm getting hitched. Spliced. Vowed. *Married*.

"Don't laugh! The guy is beautiful. He's like you, without the mud-dreams. He is clear. He is reachable.

"Yes, I can just reach out and touch solid flesh. He really is there. He exists on this earth. And oh boy, is he sexy!

"Yet you haunt me, Mud Man. You linger in my head, my heart, my cunt. A whiff of your ashes pursues me. I can't get your stink out of my nostrils.

"I hope you've breathed life, for my sake. I'll never be free of you until you do. It'll happen, though. One day I'll wake up next to dear Joel and the mud-and-ashes odour will be gone. Then I'll know. I'll know you're either dead or alive. I mean *alive*. Or dead.

"Be quick about it, for heaven's sake!

"Yours in dust-and-water — Moll."

My first reaction was a hot flash of anger. What need had I to be a "stink-of-ashes" in a Californian's nose? Wasn't it enough for Molly to have left her "lightning on my lip"?

Then I laughed. She needed to get in one last sting before splicing with her solid-fleshed Joel. She'd never forgive me for not having been "real." Dead or alive, I was unforgivable. Even more unforgivable for Molly was her failure to breathe life into my "mud." She'd always fancied she had the magic touch. She was very Californian.

I phoned in an overseas cable to Molly. The telegraph connections had been restored that morning. Barney had been brilliant with his patch-ups.

The message was brief: "Very best wishes marriage. Breathe deep. Am alive. Paul."


"No T.V. tonight," Eric grumbled, after supper. "What a drag."

"Read a book, *bubbele*," Leonie said. "Or is that against your religion?" She ruffled her son's hair. "Look at your Dad. He's reading."

"A dirty mag," Lovey said. "It's banned."

"Shurrup," David mumbled. "Let me get on with my 'Oy' in peace."

Lovey giggled with derision. "It's not 'Oy', it's 'Wee'."

"Don't be a *klutz*. How can O-U-I be pronounced 'Wee'!" David demanded.

"It's French, Dad. We learn it in school."

"Clever Dick," David humphed, and buried his nose back in the tits-'n-ass.

"Let me see, Dad," Eric begged, writhing. "Naked ladies, ooh!"

"Hey, *bubbele*," Leonie warned.

"You can see this cartoon," David offered. "See if you get the joke." David held out the magazine for his son to see. Lovey joined his brother. Lawlene looked haughtily the other way.

Eric started sniggering at once. Lovey frowned. "What's funny?" he asked plaintively.

"Gee, you're a dummy," David grinned. "He doesn't get the joke!" David thrust the magazine at me. "Take a peep, Paul. See if you get it."

I glanced at the cartoon. It showed a pink and naked girl sitting in a meadow of phallic toadstools. "Yeah," I said. "Funny."

"Explain it to me, Uncle Paul," Lovey pleaded.

"Give it here," Leonie demanded. She grabbed the girlie book. "Mm. Juvenile." She frowned at Lovey. "You really don't get it, snookums?"

Lovey blushed scarlet. He shook his head in shame as the others laughed.

Leonie brushed the fair curls back from her eldest's hot brow. "Oh, snooks, what will become of you? You're so innocent!"

"The kid's a dummy," David said. " 'Wee'!"

Lovey slumped. He became a lump of shamed embarrassment. His whole plump body seemed to melt into a pool on the carpet.

"Snooks, snooks," Leonie keened.

"Aren't we going out soon?" David said irritably. "The bio starts at eight."

"In a sec. You don't mind babysitting, Paul?"

"No wild dates tonight?" David joshed, winking.

"No wild dates."

Lovey was still a lump on the carpet. Leonie buried her nose in the boy's exposed nape. "Babysmell," she crooned. "You still smell of baby."

"For Christ's sake let's go!" David shouted, jumping up.

Leonie rose reluctantly. She surveyed her brood. "Well, kids, I leave you in your uncle's tender care."

Leonie gave me a significant look over Lovey's head. I nodded. She went to dress for her evening out.

The children went to bed early, grumbling about the lack of T.V. Ray and Grace cleaned up in the kitchen. After they left I locked the back door, as instructed.

I poured myself a whisky and reread Molly's letter. Her blithe malice depressed me. It gave me an ugly sense of a bad smell lingering from a previous incarnation, a "whiff of ashes". I ended up burning the paper in the ashtray, but the bad smell wasn't entirely banished.

A strange noise disturbed my musings. It sounded like someone pulling out drawers at the back of the house, in the direction of the main bedroom. A prowler? I crept quietly down the passage, not quite sure what I might do if I confronted a black burglar. The light was on under the door. I turned the handle gently.

I saw Lovey.

He was posing before his mother's full-length wardrobe glass. He was naked but for a stuffed bra, Leonie's frilly white cotton panties and a pair of her silver pumps.

I froze.

The look on the boy's face was both prim and entranced. He primped before the mirror, posturing like a starlet, hunching one fat shoulder and wriggling his rear, watching his reflection with self-loving eyes. He slid his palm over his stocking-stuffed bosom and licked his drooling lips.

"Fat Fairy," he crooned at his image. A sneer twisted his rosebud lips, but his grey eyes were bright with love.

I could not move. If he saw me he would collapse with shame. I was transfixed.

He did see me. He caught me in the mirror.

His face crumbled. Lovey's eyes, nose, mouth, chin seemed to smear in a spasm of shock.

I had to act fast. The boy's chagrin was hideous. His face was a frozen scream.

What to do? *What?*

An idea flashed into my head. I lurched forward. Lovey recoiled in terror, as if I were about to attack him. He covered his bosom in very feminine reflex of fright. I flung myself past the child and buried my face in Leonie's wardrobe.

My fist found a frock. I jerked it free of its hanger and tugged it over my head. It was a voluminous floral. I was drowned in yards of cotton print. My body swam in flowers.

I pranced away from the wardrobe and began to dance. I whirled round the room, flaring my skirts. Lovey's mouth gaped. A snort of laughter ripped his flab. His bosoms wobbled with mirth.

"Uncle!" he gasped. "Such funny things!"

As the boy's shame melted into crazy cackles, I danced and danced, floating on air.

# 13

# THE GLORIES OF THE MODERN

For the rest of the week the authorities stuck to their claim that the post office fire was due to a fault in the high-tension power supply to the Telecom Centre. However, the *Chronicle* did report an item in the *Times* of Zambia in which a "senior guerrilla spokesman" claimed that the destruction of the Telecom Centre was "an act of war against the illegal Smith Regime."

*The Financial Times* of London included both versions of the incident, favouring neither. However, an editorial in the same paper remarked that, if the ZANU-ZAPU claim were correct, the fire in the Telecom Centre in Bulawayo "marks a significant and sophisticated escalation of the conflict." *The Financial Times* speculated that this development could lead to "a drastic erosion of the international financial community's confidence in the ability of the Rhodesian Government to guarantee stability and security for potential investors."

Barney had become very close-mouthed about the progress of the forensic analysis of the fire. All he would say was, "The boys are working on it." He did let slip, however, that the South African Army had lent the Rhodesians a blast expert. This specialist in explosives was helping the locals sift the debris.

Most of the public services were soon restored. Television broadcasts resumed, but the transmissions were foggy. A kind of greyish snow seemed to have settled in on the black-and-white screen. The telex and long-distance phones were back. When I congratulated Barney on his skill in patching up these services he pulled a wry face.

"Yeah," he shrugged, "but The Brain will never function again. We've lost all central control. The Pentagon is talking only to Salisbury, now."

There was a photo of John Allardyce's wife Joyce and their baby Darryl in the *Chronicle*. The item under the photo stated that John was "mending well, having recovered consciousness." The hospital intended to fly him to Johannesburg for skin grafts in a week or two. The paper was starting a "John Allardyce Medical Fund" to supplement his government aid. I put two hundred-dollar notes in an envelope and sent it in anonymously.

A letter came for me from the South African housing ministry in Pretoria, from the Deputy Minister. He wrote that Theo Theophilus had recommended me highly as a consultant for the proposed multi-million-rand mass African housing project in the Witwatersrand Region. The Minister offered to pay me a fee and all expenses if I would fly to Pretoria in the near future, at my convenience. I replied with a brief note declining the offer on the grounds of heavy prior commitments.

The next day I received a cable from Theo, from New York. It was brief, just two words: "Remember festivals!"

I remembered.


The Israelis were encircling the Egyptian Third Army in the south of Suez. Their armour overran the western bank of the Canal. An American general was quoted in *Time* magazine: "The Zionists," he stated, "are the best damn tankers in the world."

U.S. Secretary of State Henry Kissinger flew to Moscow to discuss a Middle East cease-fire with Leonid Brezhnev. Meanwhile the Arab oil states were cutting back production to force the West to abandon the Jews. This did not bother the Rhodesians. They had survived sanctions for over seven years. "Let Harold Wilson have a taste of his own *muti*," David gloated. "Watch that Englishman lick black *tochas!*"

In Uganda, President-for-Life Idi Amin announced his conversion to Islam. "The day of the white man is over," he declared. "Long live Black Power!" The *Chronicle* printed a photo of Amin being carried through the streets of

Kampala on the shoulders of four Europeans. "Disgusting," my father said. *"Zhii!"* Tenja crowed, showing me the picture.

"Paul." Shaun's voice was terse on the phone.

"Shaun," I answered warmly. "I've been meaning to pop into the office. How's the prototype house proceeding?"

"That's what I'm calling about. It's well under way. I'm going to Tshabalala this afternoon. A reporter from the *Chronicle* will be there. Would you like to come?"

"Surely."

"Be at the office at two."

"Okay."

"See you."

"Yes."

Shaun's face was stiff when he saw me. I went straight up and hugged him. His body was rigid, at first, then it slowly relaxed. I did not release him till he hugged me back.

"Shit," he said softly, cracking a boyish grin. "Stupid. Punishing you for my own drunken crassness."

"You're a Papist, mate."

"Okay. I deserved that."

"Yes."

"Jew bastard," he laughed. "What do you think of the Warriors of Zion? Aren't they amazing? Turning the war round so dramatically!"

"Amazing."

Shaun glanced at me shrewdly. "You're not a Zionist?"

"No."

"What are you, then?"

"A Rhodesian."

"The hell you are," he said, punching my arm. "Come on, Rhodesian, let's get out to our Modern Mud Hut.

"Listen, I'd like your advice," Shaun said in the car. "I'm thinking of taking on a young African as a trainee draughtsman. What do you think?"

"Excellent idea. But what will your clients say?"

"Sod my clients," he retorted. "They won't have to deal with him, not for some years, at least. I mean, it'd be a pretty humble start, at first. He'd have to learn the ropes. But in a year or two he could study for the Lower Technicians Exam at the Tech."

I had a sudden thought. "I think I might know someone for you. He has two Advanced Levels, in English and Maths. He's very bright."

"Who's that?"

"A young man named Tenja. He works in my sister's garden."

"A garden-boy with two A-levels?" Shaun exclaimed, shocked. "Send the lad to see me."

"I must warn you — Tenja is no Yes-baas, No-baas type. He can be a little awkward. But he's bright, and he's got fire."

"Sounds like my sort of chap," Shaun smiled. "Send him along."

The prototype house consisted of three huts put together, three interlocking circles under one thatch. One circle was the living space, with a small stoop. The second was divided into two bedrooms. The third contained the kitchen and a simple bath and toilet, opening onto a covered yard.

The construction was simple. Rings of stripped acacia staves were planted in a concrete base. Bark laths and dried grass were interwoven through the staves as a key for the mud plastering.

When we arrived at Tshabalala the walls were in the process of being sprayed with the finishing coat of patent cement bonding inside and out. The roof was still an open frame of staves.

David Llewellyn, the Location Superintendent, waved as we drove up. The three of us inspected the work in progress. "We've put the whole house up, base to roof, in twelve days!" Llewellyn enthused. "Tomorrow we begin the thatching."

"What do the locals think of it?" I asked.

"Not much," Llewellyn grinned ruefully. "They call it 'the picanin kraal.' They suspect it's another sly European trick to keep them in their place."

"I'd move in like a shot," Shaun said staunchly. "They can have my suburban bungalow in exchange any day."

"Don't offer," Llewellyn laughed. "Ah, here's our lady from the *Chronicle*."

A plump young woman climbed out of a Renault and came up to us. Untidy blond hair stood up round a pink face that framed a pair of sharp green eyes. "Shaun.

David," she murmured in greeting, but her eyes were on me. "Is this our famous architect?"

Shaun made the introduction. "Paul Kahn. Georgina Halesworth."

The green gaze raked me shrewdly. "Shaun's been singing your praises, Mr. Kahn."

"Ah, but he's a terrible liar," I smiled.

"Shaun is the most truthful man I know," she corrected me. "If he says you're first rate then it must be so."

"Hey, hey," Shaun mumbled, blushing.

"See what I mean?" Georgina laughed. "Can we get out of the sun?"

We went into the half-constructed house. It was cool inside. There was a smell of mud and cement.

"Why does wet cement always stink of sperm?" Georgina asked, wrinkling her snub nose. "Is there any connection?"

Shaun didn't know where to look, but Llewellyn chuckled. We found a few empty fruit crates and sat in a circle while the work went on around us.

Georgina took a notebook out of her capacious leather shoulder bag. "Now, Mr. Kahn, explain all this to me — in words of one syllable, please?"

I explained. " ... and so we end up with a house that takes a quarter of the time to erect, costs a fraction of your conventional unit, and is also more apt. Though the people who live here might not agree on that."

"Not agree?" she queried, pausing in her note-taking.

"It's not a shrunken copy of the white man's house."

"How sad!" the reporter exclaimed. "What have we done to them? I think this house is splendid. Wouldn't mind living in one myself."

"Me, too," Shaun said. He laughed awkwardly. "They want to live like us, and we want to live like them. As you say, sad."

Georgina focused on me again. "Tell me something about yourself, Mr. Kahn. Some personal details." She smiled, to soften the impertinence. "Shaun tells me you've been away from Rhodesia for twenty-two years. Why did you come back?"

"I'm a Rhodesian."

"Oh, I see."

The reporter stared at me. Outside the labourers shouted over the hiss of the cement hoses and the clatter of the compressed air engine.

"Yes," Shaun said suddenly, "Paul is a Rhodesian."

"There you are," I smiled. "The truth."

"Ah." The reporter sucked her pen top. "How do you see the role of the urban planner in a context such as ours?" she asked. "I mean, with thousands of blacks coming in off the Tribal Trust Lands into the towns, with limited resources facing increasing expectations, and with a rapid breakdown of old tribal traditions — what techniques have we to cope?"

"We're not short of techniques," I replied. "Or ideas."

"We're short of something," Georgina insisted.

I shrugged.

Shaun answered for me. "Paul feels our real lack is a humane idiom." His voice was deliberately casual. "He feels modern architecture has failed us."

"But an architect must build, surely?"

"Yes," I said. "I know."

"So what's the answer?" the reporter demanded, pen poised over pad.

"You tell me."

Georgina shut her pad with a snap. She seemed quite cross. "I'd like a few shots," she said crisply. "You three, in front of the house."

We all trooped out of the house to oblige. Georgina clicked rapidly with her camera. "Ta," she said. She fixed her stare on me. "Whatever you say, sir, I am impressed. Very much so."

"I'm glad."

The reporter let out a sharp, short laugh and walked off to her car. Llewellyn watched her go with greedy eyes. "Wouldn't mind tearing off a strip of that some time," he murmured.

"Not a chance," Shaun said shortly. "She's Tom Halesworth's wife."

"The M.P.?" Llewellyn scowled. "That Commie!" He shrugged. "I've set up the Ministers' visit for Friday week, November second. Midday. Housing and Labour will be here. Okay?"

"Sounds fine," Shaun said. "Should be wrapped up by

then. Just the thatching to do, the wiring, the granolithic floor, and digging the septic tanks."

Llewellyn tilted back his broad-brimmed bush hat and scratched his scalp. "Dreadful mess at the post office, eh? You think it was terrs?"

"Impossible," Shaun said at once. "How would they penetrate the security?"

"The buggers are getting to us," the superintendent muttered. "And, speaking of security, keep the timing of the Ministers' visit under your hats. Not a word, to anyone. We don't want any messes here."

Shaun invited me to join him for a drink in his office when we got back to town. "Private roof-wetting," he said.

When we had our whisky, and he was comfortably foot-propped on the edge of the desk, he tossed a magazine at me. "Remember this?" he asked. *The Architectural Review*, October 1963. Read the lead essay titled 'The Glories of the Modern.' It was written by a very bright and keen young architect name of Paul Kahn."

"Oh my gawd," I mumbled, turning to the page.

Shaun tilted his head back and shut his lids in concentration. "How does it open? Let me see; ah, yes: 'Form Follows Function is the slogan of our times. It is Reason's ultimate cry — the belief that every function dictates its innate design. Accident, arbitrary decorativeness, nostalgic excresence of every kind is sliced away as Form is stripped to the bone. Efficiency is Harmony. Truth is Function, Function Truth. "That's all ye know, and all ye need to know," as the poet says.' "

"*Oi vey,*" I groaned, hiding my head in my hands.

But Shaun was merciless. "Paragraph Two of 'The Glories of the Modern': 'In his 1928 essay, "The New Vision," Laszlo Moholy-Nagy wrote: "The basic biological needs are very simple. They may change or be deformed by social and technical processes. Great care must be taken that their real significance is not distorted ..." This "real significance" lies, as always, in the Law of Economy of Means, which is harmony. In design the new Truth is the old one: Function dictates Form. We have a new architecture for the function of our time ...' "

"Have a heart," I pleaded.

Shaun relented at last. His eyes were bright with malicious gaiety. "Brilliant piece of writing," he murmured. "Very uplifting."

I slid the ten-year-old *Architectural Review* back across the desk. "Where did you dig that corpse up?"

"From my private graveyard. Where all the skeletons are buried."

"Burn it," I suggested. "Scourge it with fire."

"Oh no." Shaun took the magazine and tucked it away on a shelf. "I may need it some day. As evidence."

"Of what?"

He shrugged. "Just evidence."

Tenja listened carefully and in silence when I told him of the possibility of training as a draughtsman in Shaun's office. His yellow eyes flared for an instant, and then were hooded.

"What do you think?" I asked. "Will you go and see Shaun Connaughton?"

Tenja shook his head. "No."

"Oh? Why?"

"Charity," the young man snapped.

"Look, Tenja, don't be foolish. Take what you can get, from anyone."

"Does this man serve in the Rhodesian Army?"

"Yes."

"You expect me to work for a murderer?"

"I expect you to grab a chance to stop having to shovel dogshit."

"There are worse things," Tenja retorted.

"Well, yeah, I guess so."

Tenja smiled at me. "You are beginning to think, my baas."

We grinned at one another. I handed him a cigarette and we lit up. Tenja squatted on his haunches beside the pool and I sat on the grass.

"Still, one day, maybe, I will be an architect," Tenja murmured. "One day in Zimbabwe."

"There are worse things," I teased.

He squinted at me. "You are a famous man, in architecture?"

"Famous, no. Successful, maybe."

"Is it very difficult to study?"

"No. Just impossible."

Tenja grunted and rocked on his heels. He held his cigarette by the tip as if it were a *dagga* joint. Smoke curled up through his hand.

"We will need architects in Zimbabwe," he said solemnly.

"Yes. So why not begin now?"

"Work for a murderer?" he repeated, but with less conviction.

"You shan't learn murder from the man, only drawing."

"I don't know," he muttered.

"Think about it."

"Okay. Okay."

A silence. The air was still and hot. Tenja was curled like a question mark on his toes.

"Paul?" he began.

The crunch of heavy tires on the gravel cut him off. We both jerked round. A khaki Landrover rolled up the driveway. On the door was stencilled in black: British South Africa Police.

Tenja leapt to his feet as a white officer got out of the front of the Landrover and two black constables jumped out the back, brandishing truncheons. He backed off a pace or two, swivelling his eyes for an escape route.

I rose as the white officer strode towards me. He halted a yard or two distant and saluted. His flat khaki cap cut his brow in two. The Sam Browne belt made a leather slash across his uniformed chest. Blond hairs sprouted from the vee of his open-necked tunic.

"Are you the master of the house, sir?" he demanded. His voice was harsh with an Afrikaner burr. The African constables edged round behind Tenja, cutting off his flight. I noticed the young man was shivering.

"What can I do for you, constable?" I enquired, as politely as possible.

The policeman plucked a fat black notebook from his top pocket. He consulted it solemnly. "Do you have a native by the name of Tenja Mbala in your employ?"

"Yes, but — "

"I have a warrant here for his arrest under the Law and

Order Maintenance Act of 1960." He handed me the document.

"What's he accused of?" I asked. Behind me Tenja was shaking. The two black cops closed in on him silently. Their polished leather leggings glinted mahogany red in the sun.

"We have reason to believe he is the leader of a Communist cell in Mzilikazi."

"That's ridiculous!"

"We have evidence. One of his conspirators confessed. He was named."

"Confessed under torture?" I sneered.

The officer's face tightened. I was an awkward customer. "Is that the native?" he demanded, jabbing a thumb towards Tenja.

My ready lie was forestalled by Tenja's soft, deep moan. It was like the death-sigh of a calf in an abattoir. He sank to his knees on the grass and buried his face in greenness.

The black constables fell upon him at once. One grabbed Tenja's arms, the other his legs. They hauled him to the Landrover and bounced him onto the truck bed. Flesh and bone thumped on steel. The two cops jumped in after and rested their hobnailed boots on Tenja's back. The young man's bare, horny feet stuck out of the Landrover. They were twitching in terror.

"Don't be so brutal!" I cried.

The white officer shrugged. He swung smartly on his heel and marched back to the vehicle.

"Where are you taking him?" I shouted, running up.

"Central Police Station," the officer replied, slamming the door. Beside him was another African constable, the driver. I stuck my face in the Landrover's window. "What's your name?"

The answer came back sharply. "Fourie, L.S. Number 2491." He turned to the driver. "Move it!" Tenja's jutting toes gave a final jerk as the police Landrover sped away.

Shaun answered the phone himself. He listened in silence as I poured out my outrage. "Can you help?" I asked, finally, ending on a more controlled note. "You know people in this town."

"I'll get back to you at once," Shaun said, and rang off.

I chain-smoked as I waited. The image of Tenja's bare, twitching toes haunted my head. Was he really the leader of a Communist cell? "I am a socialist," he had told me.

The phone rang. I grabbed it. "Yes?"

Mona laughed in my ear. "Never heard you so eager, Paul," she said.

"Ah, how are you?"

"How are you? You haven't phoned me since the motel, yet you said you liked it."

"Look, love, I'm expecting an urgent phone call. Can I get back to you?"

"Do what you like," Mona snapped, and slammed the receiver down.

The phone rang again, almost immediately. "Yes?" I said, more reservedly this time.

It was Shaun. "I've spoken to Jock Wilson, at Central Police. He's the Colonel-in-charge. Tenja Mbala has just been booked there. He's charged with conspiracy to foster subversion under the Emergency Powers Act. Any conviction under that Act carries a mandatory death sentence."

"Oh hell — but he's only a kid!"

"So are boys I meet in the bush up the Sharp End," Shaun said drily. But I could sense his concern. "Look, I went out on a limb. I told Jock Wilson I was about to take on Mbala as a trainee draughtsman. He said he'd see what he could do."

"That's kind of you," I said warmly.

"Thing is, it's a comb-out, you know? A general round-up of agitators and such after the post office fire."

"Oh my God — "

"The Special Branch has orders to detain anyone remotely suspected of subversive activity, political or military."

"But he's just a kid," I said again, uselessly.

"Paul, my friend," Shaun replied gently, "it's a war, you know. Boys fight wars. Look at the faces in the Middle East newsreels. All boys."

"Was Tenja really a Commie?" Lovey asked me that evening. "I mean, really?"

"I don't know," I said. "Anyway, what is a Commie in this situation?"

"A bloody terr," David cut in crisply.

"He could've slit all our throats!" Lawlene wailed in delicious terror.

"Yeah," David agreed. "Especially yours, miss."

"David!" Leonie cried. "Don't be vulgar."

"Rape and murder, that's their style," David persisted.

"What is a Commie?" Lovey frowned. "No one ever explains."

"What's mine is mine, and what's yours is also mine," David rattled off. "That's the Reds for you."

Lovey looked baffled. "Ask your clever uncle," Leonie told him. "He knows everything."

"Uncle Paul?"

"Well, Lou" — the boy blinked with pleasure at the use of his proper name — "Communists believe there should be no such thing as private property. They hold that the state should control a country's resources. That is the theory; in practice things work out rather differently."

"I'll say," David agreed.

Lovey's eyes were fixed upon me. "If we're not Commies, what are we?" he asked.

"In Rhodesia, capitalist."

"Democratic," David corrected.

Lovey frowned with concentration. "Commie and capitalist — are there only two kinds of people in the world?"

"Two basic systems, yes. With shades in between."

"Only two kinds. Like — " The boy searched for a metaphor. "Like fighting dogs?"

"Like fighting dogs," I agreed, smiling.

"Tenja is one kind of dog, and I am another?"

"If you like. But you're both just boys."

Lovey shook his head. "No. He is my enemy-dog. He is, you know."

"Fat Fairy," David hissed, irritated beyond bearing by his son's painful thought processes.

Leonie blinked. She was about to blast David when Lovey cut her off.

"So what?" he challenged his father. "Fairies are also people."

There was absolute silence in the room. The awful secret was out in the open. The only one who did not seem stunned by this was Lovey himself. He winked at me calmly. I winked back.

"Yes," the boy repeated, "Fairies are also people."

No one dared contradict him.

# 14

# DEADLY POISON

My photo gazed back at me from the middle page of the Saturday morning *Chronicle*. I was caught standing alone before the half-constructed Mud House. The article beneath the photo was titled "Back to the Kraal": "Paul Kahn — Bulawayo-born town planner of international repute — has designed the prototype house model for a proposed new African township at Tshabalala," the piece began. "He sees the solution to the urban native housing problem in terms of one basic material — mud!"

The article ran on in the same jovial vein, sharpened by strokes of derisive deference. Georgina Halesworth sent me up tongue-in-cheek as a pompous prig striving to impose "native ways" upon the blacks, who only yearned for "decent European-style housing, not Mr. Kahn's 'picanin kraals.'"

The reporter did go on to mention that the Mud House was cheaper and faster to build than the concrete-block type, but "what use is such a marvel if the Africans detest it? But of course," the final paragraph ran, "Mr. Kahn has a global reputation. Who are we poor hicks — black or white — to say he's babbling through his bonnet? And if it amuses the authorities to spend our tax dollars — in the middle of a war — on such fancies, who's to deny them their bit of fun?"

"Oh, delicious!" I exclaimed to the go-away birds in the flame tree over my head. "Oh sweet bitcheries of life at last you've found me!"

Tucked away in a back page of the newspaper was a short item: "Township-Wide Comb-Out Continues". The one paragraph stated that "Several hundred suspected local agitators have been detained for interrogation by the police."

I went indoors to phone Shaun at his home. "Shocking!" he exclaimed, soon as he recognized my voice. "What a bitch!"

"Ah, that," I laughed. "I was really phoning to ask if you had any news about T — "

"Why was Georgina so awful?" Shaun fretted, cutting across me. "She seemed sympathetic at the time."

"Standard reporter's bitchery," I reassured him. "It makes good copy."

"I'm very sorry, Paul. I didn't know — "

"Not your fault. Any news about Tenja Mbala?"

Shaun's voice was suddenly wary. "I spoke to Colonel Wilson last night. Marxist literature was found at Mbala's house. His father and two brothers have also been detained."

"Oh shit. Where is he? Can I see him?"

"Political detainees are not allowed visitors. Not during the interrogation period, anyway."

An image of "The Brickie" sprang up in my mind. I saw Tenja wobbling on a pile of bricks, hands up in the air, overalls rank with urine.

"How long does that period last?" I asked hoarsely.

"Depends." Shaun's tone was very reserved.

"Is there nothing we can do?"

"Nothing."

At the pool-side I smoked many cigarettes. "The Brickie" vision would not leave my head. Poor Tenja. Just a fragment of the fallout from my "simple unambiguous act."

"More coffee, baas?"

Grace's shy voice slid between the cracks of my black thoughts. I looked up to confront her gentle yellow face framed in the Afro wig and bright blue headscarf. "More coffee, baas?" she repeated.

"What do you think about Tenja's arrest?" I blurted.

Grace shrugged. "Policemens catch him," she said matter-of-factly.

"But he's just a boy!"

"Garden-boy," Grace agreed, confusing my use of the noun. She added conclusively: "Bad boy."

"Why bad?" I demanded.

Grace's reaction was odd. She shrieked, flung out a pointing finger, clapped a hand to her mouth, and fled, clasping her scarf and wig.

I looked towards the gateway, where Grace had pointed. An African woman stood there, hovering beside one of the scrollwork iron posts. She looked as if she had been waiting for some time, not daring to cross the threshold.

She was a slight figure with a small oval high-boned face that was almost hidden by a headscarf. The scarf looked as if it had been through countless rinsings, yet it had the ironed air of Sunday best. The woman's blue floral frock had the same much-rinsed-and-pressed look. Her brown feet were bare. They seemed planted in the gravel with a peasant's timeless patience.

She was plainly a kraal woman. The open gateway — entry to the domestic White Zone — was a barrier she dared not cross without an escort. As soon as she felt my gaze upon her, she slid out of sight behind the gatepost. I could sense her there, hovering. I was about to go and ask her what she wanted when Ray came slouching out from behind the house. He went down the driveway towards the gate, dragging his feet.

At Ray's approach, the kraal woman emerged from her hiding place. Ray wandered up to her and halted. They faced one another in silence.

Ray wore his dazzling white serving jacket. The countrywoman's print seemed to fade even further by contrast with this splendour. She seemed totally overawed by the man. Her slight body bent forward in a semi-bow, acknowledging his mastery. Her eyes rose no higher than his naked toes. Her scarfed head was offered up to his mercy.

Ray rocked on his heels. All at once he let out a lash of clicking Ndebele. The woman trembled, but her submission was unbudgeable. Ray cursed his mouth dry, swung on his heel and marched back up the driveway. The woman hastened behind him, at a distance of several paces, taking small running steps. The couple vanished behind the house.

"Who was that woman?" I asked Grace, when she came to collect my tray.

Grace's face was wooden. She did not want to answer. It was none of my white business. But she was too well-schooled in politeness. "Kraal wife," she growled. She clutched the tray to her bosom like a horizontal shield.

"Ray's?"

"Kraal wife!" she burst out, eyes flashing. "He hate her! She don't even know to eat fork-and-knife! Use her fingers — same like baboon!"

"Grace!"

She struggled to master her rage. "Her father sends her to town. For the *lobola*. If Ray want to throw her away, the father must give back the dollars."

"Ray wants his bride-price back?" I asked, a trifle confused.

"He pay good dollars, baas," Grace explained, patient with my stupidity. "Good dollars for bad woman. *Sifaza impisi*. Hyena girl!"

"Have they any children?"

Grace's face shut down. She distanced herself from my nosiness with a servant's obtuseness. "Some," she muttered.

"Still, it must be a terrible disgrace for a girl to be 'thrown away'?" I murmured.

"*Sifaza impisi!*" Grace snapped, and marched off with the tray.

My mother's hip bone was mending very slowly. The doctors weren't worried, but my father was. "She's not well, not well at all," he said over and over as we drove to the hospital that afternoon.

"Saw your photo in the paper today," my mother said, soon as we entered the hospital room. "You look so handsome!"

"Did you read the article?" I asked. "A regular hatchet-job."

"So handsome," the old woman repeated, gripping my hand. Her eyes melted with proud tears.

"When are you getting back up on your pins, old girl?" I demanded. "We miss you."

"Soon, soon," she muttered. She drew me down for a conspiratorial whisper as Dad and Leonie hovered in the background. "How's the old boy? Are you keeping him busy? Play tennis with him. He's got ants in his pants."

"Tennis? I haven't played in a year. Anyway, he always used to wipe the court with me."

"Play tennis," she hissed. "Ants in his pants!"

"Love-forty!" the old man crowed. "One-five, love-forty. Teach you to play this game one day!"

I limped to the back of the court for the ball. My legs were stiff, my serving arm ached, but my father was unruffled. He stood planted on the far baseline, bandy muscular calves wide apart, belly bulging over the belt of his knee-length white shorts. His silver waves flashed in the sun as I geared up for my last serve.

It was fast and straight. I threw every last ounce of power I had left into the downswing. The ball zipped over the net, hit the clay court with a spurt of dust, and flashed straight to the old man's racquet.

The ball came back slowly. His strings seemed to kill its speed. It slid over the net and corkscrewed sideways. It was out of play before I could even begin to dash forward.

"Game. Set. Match," my father declared. "Six-one. Six-one. Six-one."

I sagged over the netpost panting. In the pavilion several spectators clapped. "Bravo, Joe!" a voice called. "Still the Champ!"

"Game. Set. Match," Dad repeated, jabbing his racquet at my chest.

"Too good for me," I gasped. "Too foxy."

"I was a champion before you were born," he said.

"True," I conceded. "True."

"You'll never match me on court, my boy."

"True."

We walked off the court arm in arm. His strength supported me. I was drenched; he was cool as a cucumber. I sank into a cane chair on the pavilion terrace. My father sat opposite, acknowledging the smiles of the other players in their tennis whites.

The waiter brought us two large tumblers of frosted lemonade. I gulped mine thirstily. My limbs were beginning to lock with fatigue.

"It's a good life, here," my father said. "A very good life." He sipped his lemonade with relish.

On Monday morning, October twenty-second, the United States and the Soviet Union submitted a joint Middle East cease-fire resolution to the United Nations Security Council in New York.

Resolution Number 338 called for an Israeli-Egyptian-Syrian "cessation of hostilities" by 6:52 P.M. Monday evening. All parties to the conflict had agreed to accept it.

"Dayan is stupid," David snorted. "The road to Cairo is open. Why stop now? Unless Nixon has twisted his arm."

Later that morning a messenger brought me an envelope. It was addressed to "Paul Kahn, Esquire." The note inside said simply: "Hurry Up Cafe. Lobengula and Selborne. 12.00 P.M."

It was almost eleven o'clock when I received the summons. I would have to hurry up to get to the rendezvous on time.

Lobengula Street, on the edge of town, was already liberated from whiteness. Few pale faces were to be seen among the crowds outside the record shops that blared *kwela* and Jo'burg rock. Black shouts and laughter dominated the sidewalks. The store windows were jammed with displays of Afro wigs, zooty suits and jars of cheap cosmetics with names like "Zulu Princess," "Black Lily," and "Pink Power."

The Hurry Up Cafe was full of diners. A waft of boiling maizemeal and gravy grabbed my nostrils as I entered. Steam spurted from the iron pots on the open kitchen ranges. The chatter was raucous and thick as the smells.

Elijah Nkabi sat alone at a corner table. He beckoned me with an imperial wave. The Methodist parson was enthroned like an *induna* — a Ndebele regimental commander — at the chipped white plastic square.

"Morning, Elijah," I bowed.

"Sit," he ordered. "You will eat."

It was an order. Dutifully, I scanned the menu chalked on the blood red wall: Beans — 10 cents; Soup — 8 cents; "*Sadza*-and-gravy — 20 cents; *Sadza*-no-gravy — 15 cents.

"*Sadza*-and-gravy," I said.

He scowled at me. "You like *sadza?*" he demanded.

"I used to, as a boy. Haven't had it for twenty-five years, though."

"You ate *sadza* at home?" he asked in disbelief.

"My picanin shared his dinner with me. It was delicious. Much tastier than the singed steak or chicken the cook served our family."

Nkabi shook his head at this example of the white man's endless perversity. He summoned the waiter, who came at once, wiping his soiled palms on an even grubbier apron. "One *sadza*-and-gravy. One chops-and-chips," he ordered.

"*Yebo, 'Nkos,*" the waiter saluted, and scurried off.

There was a silence as we waited for our food. Nkabi was remote, removed from my presence. I lit a cigarette and gazed round the room.

It was dark in the cafe. The sunlight did not penetrate the plate-glass windows grimy with condensation and peeling adverts for Fanta and Pepsi. The people passing by on the sidewalk were vague as ghosts.

"Must you smoke?" Nkabi said suddenly.

"Pardon?"

"Don't you know the body is the temple of the soul? Not to be willfully polluted?"

"I'm sorry." I stubbed out the cigarette. "I'm afraid my 'temple' is beyond cleansing."

"Don't joke."

The arrival of the food saved me from further admonition. It was awful. The maizemeal was stodgy with an aftertaste of chalk. The gravy, boiled up too often from cuts of "boy's meat," tasted of sump oil.

Nkabi saw my grimace and laughed. His big body shook with chuckles. "Not so delicious, eh?" he joshed, released from sternness.

"Why didn't you warn me?" I demanded.

"What for? If you want to be foolish, that is your business. You are a baas."

"Is the coffee here worth polluting my temple for?" I asked crossly.

"No," he replied, and wiped his plate with bread. He pushed his plate away and dabbed his lips with a hankie. "Tasty," he declared. He stared at me. "The Leader is pleased," he murmured. "It went well." He nodded. " '*Nyogamhlope* is a real pro,' " he quoted. " 'The White Snake is well turned ... ' " He leant forward abruptly, shoving his face across the white plastic square. "Any trouble?"

"None."

Nkabi searched my eyes. "You are a man of courage," he said quietly. His voice was neutral, but there was an undertow of puzzlement.

"You still suspect my motives, Elijah?"

"Your motives are not my business."

I drew back from his stiff visage. "Why did you call me here? Just to tell me The Leader is pleased?"

"That is not sufficient reason?" he frowned.

"No. It's dangerous for us to meet. The Special Branch is on the alert — 'Comb-out of local agitators.' My sister's gardener was arrested."

His head jerked back. His eyes swivelled in a spasm of panic. "Arrested?" he gasped.

"He's charged with being the leader of a Communist cell in Mzilikazi. Tenja Mbala. Just a kid. Can you help him?"

Nkabi's eyes flashed with anger. "A Commie? Are you mad?!"

"A boy — "

Nkabi's big fist grasped my hand. He squeezed hard. "Keep out of it. Right out. That is an order!"

"I can't just abandon — "

His grip crushed my knuckle bones. "Listen to me, sir. A home truth. Once an African is in the power of the Specials, he is poison. Deadly poison. Understand? A few days in the hands of the police and a man will say anything to stop the torture. This is not a game." He gave my palm one last bone-crushing squeeze and released it. "Deadly poison," he repeated, leaning back. "Remember that, *Nyogamhlope*."

I blew on my squashed hand. "I'll remember."

"Young hotheads like this Tenja are not what we need in the *Chimurenga*. What we need is cold minds, like yours."

"All right."

"You may smoke."

I accepted the concession gratefully. I badly needed a cigarette. Nkabi waited till I had lit up, then leaned forward again.

"The Leader asks, have you any more ideas?"

I gaped at him. "More ideas?" At that instant inspiration flashed upon me. "Yes!"

"Ah." The grunt was self-satisfied. "Tell me."

I took a deep drag of smoke and blew it out straight up in the air. "You may or may not know that I am involved in the design of an experimental housing project in Tshabalala."

"I read the *Chronicle*," he said curtly. "Yes?"

"In a few weeks, when the prototype house we're building is finished, the Ministers of Housing and Labour will come to inspect it."

"So?"

"You can ambush them."

Nkabi's eyes widened. His teeth flashed with glee. "*Zhii!*" he crowed. "*Ngizakabulala zhii!*" He slammed the table with his fist so hard the plates jumped. "Crush my enemy to dust!"

"*Zhii,*" I echoed, nodding. "To dust."

"Both together, at one stroke. Oh, ho! At the place they think they are safe — surrounded by army and police! We strike the enemy down at the very heart of their arrogance!"

"Indeed."

He sobered abruptly. "Details. Give me details."

"November the second, midday. Tshabalala."

"They will have an armed escort, of course."

"Of course. But the road has a narrow bridge, just outside the township. The convoy must cross it in single file. Mine the bridge, and you can pick off the Ministers' car like a sitting duck."

"Sitting duck," Nkabi echoed. "Splendid. I will inform The Leader." He grinned at me. "Your poison is truly deadly, *Nyogamhlope*."

"No poison like white poison, Elijah."

"Truly spoken," he agreed promptly. "Will we ever learn to have such venom?"

"Oh, I'm sure you will. Africa learns fast."

He scowled at this, but let it pass. "My little brother Jonathan, he was shot by the police in the riots of 1960" — his eyes darkened — "along with eighteen other boys." He shook this sadness from his mind. "That was their *zhii*. Now we have ours." He nodded curtly. "The Leader wants to see you some time. He likes talking with you," he added, a trifle perplexed.

"I'd like to talk to him."

"He is the only one who can unite Zimbabwe. Without him, we should be as a herd without a keeper."

"Would the other factions agree with that?" I wondered. "Sithole, Mugabe, Muzorewa; ZANU, ZANLA, the ANC?"

"Their leaders are in Smith's jails, or in exile. Muzorewa is free because he is a stooge. Josiah Nkunzi is the Father of Zimbabwe."

"How goes the *Chimurenga?*"

"It goes."

"The security forces claim they are 'on top of the situation.' "

"Yes," he said bitterly, "they are on top — in helicopter gunships! That is a terrible weapon of counter-insurgency. We've lost so many men." His face was dark with mourning. "I must tell you, your action was worth many encounters in the bush. And yet it was so simple."

"That's the point."

He shrugged. "So, you are making mud huts at Tshabalala. Why?"

"Because they are cheaper, cooler and African."

"So is the kraal," he said flatly. "But the spiders fall on your neck, the night cold freezes your back, the smoke burns your eyes. Only a white would admire the kraal!"

"Only a white knows the poison of whiteness," I retorted.

Nkabi blinked at me. "True," he said. "Too true. It is deadly."

*Deadly.*

The word rang in my head as I walked up Selborne Avenue away from Lobengula Street. There were no taxis around, so I decided to hike the three miles home to Kumalo.

*Deadly.*

At Grey Street I turned left and then went down Second Avenue to avoid the traffic. The lightness I had felt for almost a week after Bomb Day seemed to have seeped away. My bones were dense. There was mud in my blood.

The thought of the ambush of the Cabinet Ministers I had suggested to Nkabi gave me no lift. It was not nearly so "simple" an act as blowing the Telecom Centre. It was not nearly as personal. My part in it was too abstract. All I had supplied was the idea and a few bare details. It was a sketch for an action. It lacked festiveness. It lacked personal *zhii*.

The Bulawayo Main Jail was at the foot of Second Avenue. In the governor's garden outside the walls two black convicts were spading the flowerbeds. Their red-and-white striped uniforms were stained grey with sweat. An African prison guard leant on his rifle dozing. He seemed to be propped asleep.

I paused a moment to contemplate this oddly domestic little scene from across the road. The guard sensed my presence at once. He cracked a lizard eye, registered me as a harmless white gaper, and returned to his daydreams.

Was Tenja in there somewhere? Was he behind those high white walls topped with broken glass? Was he at that very moment teetering on a pile of bricks, pissing himself? Or had he already been broken?

What did he have to confess? A passion for Karl Marx? "From each according to his ability, to each according to his needs." The *Critique of the Gotha Program* was being wrenched from his flesh with whips.

*Deadly.*

"This one's for you, Tenja," I said out loud. "Two Cabinet Ministers for one homegrown Marxist!"

But that was vulgar. I was posturing. Poison does not buy blood.

I was crossing the bridge over the Matsheumhlope when I saw Mona's car parked down by the trickling river under a willow. It was hers all right. Even at this distance I could read the licence plate: B10957.

Under the willow's drooping tracery the lime-green Datsun was a giant toad. Looking down from the bridge, I could clearly see two heads in the front seat — male and female. They were pressed close as two blots on a folded page.

"Aha," I thought, "the plot sickens." Soon as I said this to myself, the heads parted. The car door opened. A man stepped out.

He was tall and lank. His hair was grey. He wore a dark pinstripe suit that denied the heat of the afternoon.

The man walked away along the riverbank. I lost sight of him under the willows. The Datsun's starter whined. The car climbed up the track to Borrow Street and turned towards the bridge.

I leant my elbows on the parapet and waited. If she saw me she saw me.

She saw me. The Datsun jerked to a stop. Mona pushed her face out the window, leaning over from the wheel. "Paul!"

"Mona."

"Can I give you a ride?"

"Thanks."

I got into the car. She was smiling. Her eyes raked mine, discovering that I had indeed witnessed the riverbank rendezvous. "So," she murmured, idling the motor, "you caught me *in flagrante*."

"*In flagrante* what?" I asked evenly.

"With my lover," she said.

"Ah."

She took out her ebony holder and wedged in a Gold Leaf. She offered me one. We lit up.

"I must tell you," she began, blowing out smoke.

"Not unless you want to."

"I want to." She paused. "We've been lovers for years. That is, he loves me; I respect him. He's married, you see. He is very high up in the government — but behind the scenes. A sort of Grey Eminence."

"Very grey," I agreed.

"Yes. He's much older." She smiled at me. "I've told him about you. Or rather, he was asking. He knew, you see."

"What does he know?"

"That we were dating."

"Ah. Is that what we're doing?"

"You're being snotty."

"I'm sorry. I feel a bit snaky today. What else does your Grey Eminence know about me?"

"Who you are. What you're up to. Everything."

"Oh!"

"He watches over me, you see. So you better be nice."

"Is he nice? In bed?"

Mona took this question seriously. "He is — brutal." She gestured with her holder as if to say, "So what?"

"I've booked for next Friday, the twenty-sixth, at Zimbabwe Ruins. Are you on?"

"I'm on."

"Ha!" Mona put the car in gear. We drove on towards Kumalo in silence for a while.

"Brutal?" I murmured, as we turned into Leonie's street.

Mona stopped the car to let me out.

"Brutal," she confirmed, and drove away.


"There's a very brutal side to the black," Barney said as he dealt the poker hands. "It's in his culture."

It was a four-handed game round Leonie's dining room table: Barney, David, Leonie, and me.

David was the first to bid. "Chip," he said eagerly.

"Double," Leonie raised at once.

"Part of the manhood process," Barney went on, separating his cards with infinite care. "Tribal machismo. Males are schooled out of gentleness by the elders. They delay circumcision till a boy is thirteen."

"Barbaric," David shuddered.

"*Spiel, kinder,*" Leonie said impatiently. "Play cards."

"I pass," I said, chucking in my hand.

"No balls, brother?" Leonie jeered.

"I had nothing."

"My hand is also *dreck*," Barney said. "But I'll stay with you hotshots."

"I'll buy two," David said promptly.

"Two to the lying buyer," Barney teased, dealing David cards.

"How's Allardyce?" I asked.

"He's in Jo'burg, waiting for his op. Do you know his fund has collected over three thousand dollars already? Amazing."

"Three cards for me," Leonie demanded. Barney gave them to her. "I redouble blind," she declared.

"You're speaking out of turn!" David protested.

"Then stop jabbering and play," his wife retorted.

Barney bought four cards. He scowled at his hand. The betting ran round the table. Leonie raised the limit.

Barney threw in his hand, but David said nervously to Leonie. "I'll see the three-card buy."

"It'll cost you ten dollars. Where are your chips?" Leonie asked.

"I'm good for the money," David protested.

*"In drerd,"* Leonie snapped. "No dollars no play. The pot is mine."

"But I've got a flush in hearts!" David wailed, spreading his cards on the table.

"You bought two to a flush?" Leonie exclaimed, shocked.

"And made it!"

"Too bad." She scooped in the pot. "You know the rules. No dollars no play."

David shuffled the deck miserably.

"The black's cultural brutality is transferred to the battlefield," Barney went on. "Mutilation of the fallen enemy is part of the manhood thing. What we call 'atrocities' to them are actions of manliness. It's important to understand that."

"Can we change the subject?" Leonie demanded.

Barney ignored her. The subject was on his mind. "Too easy to label it 'barbarism' — 'cultural cruelty' would be a more accurate description. And then, who is the European to accuse other races of barbarity? Our savagery is all too efficient. We have the subtle techniques. We have an advanced technology of savagery."

"I chip blind," Leonie cut in, before inspecting her hand.

"She always bets blind!" David said.

"And I always win," she retorted. "Your call, brother."

"I pass."

Leonie shot me a look of contempt. Barney made his bet.

"Do you think the Middle East cease-fire will hold?" David asked. "I don't know why Dayan and Golda lay down for it. We had the *mizrayim* by the goolies!"

"The Yanks twisted their arms," Barney shrugged. "Scared of the oil sheiks."

"Wish they'd twist some in this part of the world," David said darkly. "Don't they know Southern Africa's vital to the West? Especially now the Canal's been shut."

"What do you think Ian Smith's been telling Washington for seven years?" Barney asked.

"For heaven's sake, *spiel!*" Leonie shouted. "Play cards!"

"The Commies are all over the place," David went on, dealing out the buys. "Even our bloody garden-boy's been charged with Marxism!"

"Things are bad," Barney said. "The war is hotting up."

"Yeah," David said eagerly. "Look at that bomb in your place."

Barney looked uncomfortable. "If it was a bomb — "

"Ah," David attacked. "So you're not so sure now, eh?"

"Nobody really knows," Barney confessed.

"Time to leave," Leonie said suddenly.

We all turned to her. Her face was grim.

"The blacks hate us. We deserve it," she said tersely. "Let the gentiles waffle about multi-racial societies. White *goyim*. Black *goyim*. What's the difference? We, at least, should know better."

There was a gap of silence. No one present could counter this flat statement of fact.

"If the terrs did blow The Brain," Barney began slowly, "they begin to deserve respect. I mean, I could work with professionals like that."

"What cockeyed reasoning!" Leonie exclaimed.

Barney shook his head stubbornly. "I mean it. Look, we've always had contempt for the *munts*. Maybe it's time to think again?"

"Too late," Leonie said crisply. "They hate us too much."

"I don't know. Nkunzi is an impressive figure."

"Impressive, my arse," David said. "All he ever impresses is a lot of fancy suits."

Leonie ignored this jumbled remark. "Too late," she repeated. "Time to leave, or lose everything."

"Just run?" Barney asked.

"Just run," Leonie confirmed. "As fast as our little yiddish legs will carry us."

"What'll you use for money?" David asked sourly.

"Money's no problem," Leonie said, smiling at me.

Barney lifted his head. "What's that racket?" he asked.

We all listened, chilled by his tone. From the back of the house there came an outburst of delirious screaming.

"The *shegotzim*," David exclaimed, rising from his seat in instant anger. "Bloody *munts!*"

"David," Leonie cautioned. "Ray's kraal wife showed up the other day. Grace is chokker."

David dashed into the kitchen for his *knobkerrie*. He swung the club over his head. "I'll fix 'em," he promised. He ran out of the back door.

"Go with him," Leonie urged us. "He's a madman!"

Barney and I followed David. Snuggums padded at our heels, startled from her after-dinner doze by the sudden excitement. The screaming peaked as we approached the servants' quarters.

There was a strange tableau in the small cement courtyard. Ray, Grace, and Ray's wife were frozen in terror against the far white wall. David was opposite them, *knobkerrie* jutting from his fist. The blue bulkhead light glinted on his glasses.

On the red courtyard cement was a long grey snake.

Barney and I stopped dead in the gateway. There was a moment of absolute silence. Even the bitch froze at our heels.

The serpent lifted its flat skull. Its bright yellow eyes flashed in the lamplight. The dull scales gave a subtle shiver that ran the length of the reptile's spine.

Ray broke the silence. *"Tagati!"* he gasped. "Tenja!"

"Tenja?" David croaked.

Ray flared white eyes at us. "Bad boy — Terr — Send bad *muti* — "

Barney burst out laughing. "The bugger thinks its witchcraft! Hey, you fool, it's just a common old snake."

"No, baas." Ray was adamant. *"Tagati.* Tenja. Bad boy. Bad *muti.*"

Barney stepped forward. He jerked the club from David's fist. "I'll show you *tagati*," he jeered. "Watch!"

"Hey!" David screeched. "Could be deadly, man!"

"It's only a grass snake," Barney laughed. "Harmless. Poisonous serpents hardly ever come into the town. Too nervous."

He made a jab at the reptile's head. The snake jerked back, hissing. The Africans screeched in fright. David gave a deep moan of fear.

Barney reversed the club. He held the sharp end and lifted the knob over his head, aiming for a downward strike. But before he could swing, Snuggums moved. She shot through my legs and buried her fangs in the serpent's neck right at the base of the skull. The snake lashed its tail, but it was helpless. The bitch bit its vertebrae clean through with one snap of the jaws.

"Good old Snuggums!" Barney cried. "She's some fat bitch!"

Snuggums looked up, growling proudly, as the Africans did a little jig and David clapped for joy. The snake was still writhing in her mouth, but she ambled over to me and dropped the trophy at my feet. She gazed up at me with adoring eyes, yearning for a pat.

"She loves you," David exclaimed. "Snuggums adores her Uncle Paul!"

"Yeah," Barney chuckled. "The bitch loves you, Uncle. Give her a kiss, man. She is deadly!"

## 15

## *ZHII!*

As we drove north on the Salisbury Road, on our way to the Zimbabwe Ruins that Friday, Mona quoted: " 'Miles and miles of bugger all.' Isn't that how old Edward, Prince of Wales, once described Matabeleland?"

In the dusk the bush was desolate. The sun had just set and the sky was lit from below with slashes of red fire. Bare-branched trees forked up from black grassland. Starlings stained the heavens with a spatter of inkblots.

The light died suddenly. The sky went dark. The starlings vanished, replaced by brittle stars.

The Datsun's lamps were torches running ahead of us in the night. Mona whistled tunelessly, clicking her lacquered nails on the wheel. The green glow from the speedometer lit her long face from below.

" 'Miles and miles of bugger all,' " she chanted again.

"Don't be so damn cheerful about it," I harrumphed.

Mona chuckled. Her good humour was invincible. We sped on. She drove with tranquil ease and control, at one with the wheel.

At Gwelo we turned east, towards Fort Victoria. There was about a hundred miles to go to the Ruins. The car was a small glass and metal capsule in the African darkness, racing from nowhere to nowhere.

"We don't sleep together now," Mona said suddenly.

"Don't we?" I puzzled, startled from blankness.

"Him," she corrected patiently. "And me."

"Ah. Him." I lit a cigarette. "Why not?"

"He's become impotent."

"Brutal but impotent?" I queried.

"I don't mind if you're jealous," Mona said serenely. "I like it."

"And if I'm not jealous?"

"He wanted to marry me, but divorce would've ruined his career," she said, ignoring my silliness.

"What is his career?"

"I told you, he's a — "

"Grey Eminence."

"Yes. He pulls the strings and Ian Smith dances."

"The Simple Farmer's choreography's far from brilliant," I said drily.

"You think you know everything," she rasped, irritated by my levity. "What you don't know is that there's a Plan. Behind the scenes things are being worked out, at a very high level."

"Oh? Tell me?"

"I wouldn't tell you. You're a terrorist."

"Pardon?"

"An emotional terr," she said crisply, and shut her face right down.

A bright beam came towards us out of the night, a cyclopean eye without a body. There was a high-pitched whistle. Then a train flashed by, shaking the car with its wind. Lighted windows zipped past like a string of luminous beads, leaving a rich aftersmell of coal smoke.

"Help!" Mona screamed.

Her yell synchronized with a sickening thump that jolted the Datsun's body. I felt it in every bone. The car wobbled and screeched as the brakes jammed.

We came to a stop off the road up against a thorn bush. Out of the dust lit by our lamps an animal lurched. It was a half-grown kudu, about the size of a calf. The deer staggered upright, shook its striped brown body, jerked its curling horns, and limped off into the bush. The last I saw of it was the flash of its white scut.

Mona was quaking. Her own lean body shuddered with the beast's shock. Her teeth were chattering with its echo. "Bad luck," she gasped. "Such bad luck!"

I squeezed her hand. Her knuckle bones were sharp in my palm. "It's okay," I soothed. "The kudu wasn't hurt."

"Bad sign," she moaned, inconsolable. "Bad, bad sign."

"Come, love," I chided, "not everything's an omen, you know."

I got out and walked round to the front of the car. The chromium grille was in tatters. Loose metal shards splayed out like strips of flayed hide. The left wheel cover was punched in as if by a giant fist. One headlamp was gouged to the eyeball.

The motor was still purring serenely. I tested the front tires. They were sound. The front axle was not bent.

"Some damage," I told Mona. "We can still run, though."

"She peered up at me through the open window. Her face was white as flour. "Let's go back," she blurted.

"Nonsense," I retorted. "Move over. I'll drive."

She shifted obediently. I slid into the driver's seat, put the car in gear and eased it back onto the narrow tarmac. The Datsun ran smoothly, though there was a rattle from the loosened grille. Mona let out a spurt of abrupt laughter. "I thought it was terrs — a rocket shell!"

"The only terrorists around here are in this car," I reminded her.

We both laughed.

The King Solomon's Mines Lodge was set in the bush a few miles from the Ruins. The main building housing the public rooms was a tin-roofed bungalow bounded by long verandas. The bedrooms were separate rondavels; thatched whitewashed huts scattered round a garden of proteas and flowering cacti.

A black porter in a white jacket carried our bags to Number Thirteen. "More omens," I teased, taking Mona's arm. I tipped the porter and shut the pine door. "Have a shower, love, to calm your nerves," I suggested. "Then we'll go and have a drink on the veranda."

Mona obeyed meekly. I lay on the bed and smoked as she showered. The night was very still. The cabin was an island of light in the darkness.

Mona emerged from the bathroom in a robe of white towelling. Her rinsed raven locks hung loose down her back. "More omens!" she announced gaily. "I've just started my period!"

"Come here," I said.

She recoiled. "You must be mad! Men hate women's blood."

"It turns me on."

Her face was stiff with revulsion. "Pervert."

"Look Mona, is this a dirty weekend, or isn't it?"

She burst out laughing. "Yes!" she exclaimed. "Dirty!" She threw herself upon me.

We had a late supper in the timbered dining hall. The menu was all game. Ferociously horned mounted buck heads glared down upon us as we chewed on their kinfolk.

"I wonder if it's still alive?" Mona murmured. "That poor kudu."

"If he's managed to join the herd. If the jackals and hyenas haven't got him."

"Oh no!" She pushed her plate of venison away. "I'm not hungry."

"I'm starving. Fucking is the best aperitif there is."

"Don't be crude." She drew her crocheted black woollen shawl about her shoulders. "I'm cold."

I finished my meal with relish. Smoking, I looked round the empty dining hall. "Do you think the Queen of Sheba shacked up here with old King Sol?" I wondered.

"That's just a story. Zimbabwe wasn't built by King Solomon."

"Funny. Rider Haggard was certain of it."

"The Ruins were built by the Shona, a few hundred years ago," she said didactically. "The Europeans don't like to believe that, but it's so."

"I prefer the cheap romance."

We ordered coffee and brandy. The white-coated waiter withdrew to the sideboard and settled into a stance of infinite patience.

Mona sipped her South African cognac. Her black eyes skittered over my face, not quite sure where to settle. "You're up to something," she muttered. "What?"

"Oh, I'm always up to something."

"I'm puzzled about you, Paul," she said frankly. "So's my friend."

"What puzzles His Eminence?" I asked.

"He wonders why a man like you is here."

"This is my home, damnit. I'm a Rhodesian!"

"Paul." Her mouth jerked. "I'm hooked on you — you know that. But it's a dead end. With you there's nowhere to go."

"Yes there is," I yawned. "Bed."

"Oh, sure. That's terrific. You're the best lover I've ever had."

"Why do women always feel they have to say that?" I asked testily.

"Because it's true, with you. You know your way round a woman's body. You really like female flesh."

I raised my brandy snifter. "I'll drink to that."

"But, still, there's nowhere to go."

I jerked a thumb at the antelope head trophy suspended over our table. "You're embarrassing our horned friend here. Antelope are very prim, you know. They have that Victorian Aunt expression."

"What are you up to?"

I looked at Mona hard. Her wide mouth was wobbling with an earnest unhappiness. Her vulnerability was raw. My hand shook with an abrupt spasm of lust. My lips throbbed with it. But her head was churned with the enigma of being human, the anguish of loving.

"Mona," I said harshly, "don't moan."

Her left eye twitched. The slash of black eyebrow jumped like a cricket. She hurled the brandy in my face.

We left the hotel before breakfast next morning. Mona insisted that we go as soon as it was light. In bed she had been rigid as a stick all night. I had not dared touch her. The comedy was over.

We limped away in the Datsun. The motor had developed a painful whine. Every so often the car jerked as if the road had hit a sore spot, but it ran on willingly enough.

A few miles from the Lodge we passed the Ruins. I had a glimpse of the stone Zimbabwe "Acropolis" perched on its bouldered hill. The road curved round the great elipse of the "Temple" with its chevron-patterned dry masonry walls and conical tower beside a giant baobab tree.

"Houses of Stone," I murmured. "Great Zimbabwe."

Mona's jaw tightened. She accelerated, putting the Ruins behind her as swiftly as possible.

The bush flashed by. We went through Fort Victoria fast. In an hour and a bit we were in Gwelo. The car turned south down the road home.

"Miles and miles of bugger all" — Matabeleland. My home.

The outskirts of Bulawayo popped out of the bush. To the right, in the distance, was the flat blue hill of Tabas Induna, "The Table of the Chiefs."

Bulawayo, "The Place of Slaughter," my home.

We rolled into the suburban streets of Kumalo. Many of the trees were in flower; their blossoms were squashed on the tarmac. The lawns were dark green, the pools bright blue. The bungalows were low and white.

Mona dropped me at Leonie's house. I took my bag from the back seat. She drove away without a word.

Leonie rushed out of the house to meet me as I ambled up the drive. Her big face was wild with panic. "Mom!" she gasped, flinging her full weight into my arms.

I staggered, but managed to hold us both upright. I pushed the sobbing woman back a pace. "What's up?" I demanded, but my heart sank.

Leonie's cheeks were wet with tears. "Had a stroke — " she sobbed. "Last night — Intensive care — "

"Oh, shit."

Leonie smudged her eyeshadow on her short floral sleeve. "We've been up all night. Poor Dad."

"Poor Mom. What do the doctors say?"

"She's not well, not well at all." Leonie took a couple of short breaths, to calm herself. "Everyone's amazed at her will to survive."

"She's a fighter."

"She's so brave," Leonie agreed.

My father was in the hospital waiting room. His face was crumpled with anguish. The hooded eyes seemed fused to the high hooked nose. "My boy!" he cried, and fell into my arms. His whole body was shuddering with sobs. "She's so brave," he whimpered. "So brave, so brave."

He shoved me away suddenly. "Where have you been? We tried to phone you!"

"The King Solomon's Lodge."

"We tried to phone you!" he accused again.

The specialist entered. He wore a carnation in his buttonhole.

"The chances of surviving?" he murmured, in answer to my question. "Who knows? The stroke has paralyzed her throat. She has to be fed through a tube. Her limbs have locked. Parkinsonism's final stage." He gave a weary shrug. "Survival, in this case, is rather an irrelevance. It is marginal. Survival for what? To be a helpless paralytic? I'm sorry, but that's how it is. Your mother is a brave woman, Mr. Kahn. Perhaps she's suffered enough?"

"Yes," I said.

"No!" my father croaked.

"May I see her?" I asked the doctor.

"She won't know you," he replied, and left us.

My father plucked at my sleeve. "Don't go in there, my boy. It's too sad."

"It's my mother," I retorted. "Look after the old boy," I told Leonie. "I shan't be long."

She lay in a coma in a darkened room. Tubes ran from suspended plasma bottles into her arms. There were more tubes up her nose. Electrode wires ran from her chest and temples to monitoring screens on which faint pulses throbbed.

The old woman's face was shrivelled and toothless. The grey hair crawling on the pillow was dry as straw to the touch. Her sunken mouth gave off nauseous fumes.

"Mom," I murmured, stroking her cold cheek.

"She's comatose," the sister whispered at my back.

"Mom — "

Her eyelids fluttered. For one instant the lids unstitched. She took me in. I bent to kiss her brow. Her skin was chill and sallow. She smelled sour. Under the cover her body was a small bag of bones.

The sister gestured me out. I hung on a moment, gazing down at her. Perhaps this was my last look at her alive? Maybe her brief glimpse of me was the last?

She'd been ill when I was born. She was in bed for almost a year with phlebitis, an inflammation of the leg veins. Giving birth to me had almost killed her.

What had been her first sight of me — her "handsome son"?

Some thirty-eight years separated those two instants. It was the blink of an eye.

We put my father to rest in my bed at Leonie's house. She forced him to swallow a massive sleeping draught. The old man began to snore as we tucked him in.

We ate lunch dumbly. Even the kids were silent. Ray crept in and out with the trolleys on barefoot tiptoe.

Lawlene spoke to me when we were having coffee in the lounge. "Paul, someone phoned for you this morning. Someone black."

"Black?" Leonie frowned.

"Was there a message?" I asked.

"Just one word. I wrote it down." The girl fished a scrap of ruled school paper from her pocket. "A funny word. He spelled it for me." She scowled at the paper. "Zee?"

I took the scrap. On it was pencilled, in a schoolgirl script, the word *zhii*.

"What does it mean?" Lawlene asked. "Is it kaffir?"

"Your uncle's messages are none of your business, Nosy," Leonie cut in sharply. She cocked an ear. "The old boy's snoring well."

"Should we keep him here?" I wondered. "Or should I move in with him?"

"That'd be kind," Leonie said, relieved. "If you could bear it? He'll get so morbid on his own."

"I can bear it."

That night I moved in with my father. He insisted I sleep in the same room with him, in a narrow bed under the window. "I need you close," he said. Each evening at eight, after we had returned from the hospital and had a light supper, he changed into his striped cotton pajamas and went to bed. A couple of Mogadons helped him sleep.

I tucked him in and smoothed his silver waves. "She's so brave," he murmured, as his lids fluttered. He slid into an uneasy doze that lasted till five the next morning. He left for the factory at six.

The evenings were long. The old man insisted I stay in. "I need you close." I sat in the living room listening out for his snores.

The house was locked up tight as a drum. He was terrified of intruders. *"Tsotsis,"* he said. "Bad boys. Cut your throat as you sleep." Every window had iron burglar bars.

Some evenings Leonie or Barney came in for an hour or so. My aunts June and Rose came over one night with their knitting and trays of gingerbread biscuits. "Joe loves gingerbread," they declared, though he did not touch one. But the servants enjoyed them.

Leonie was very subdued. Her natural ebullience had deserted her. She looked almost guilty as she entered "Mom's house." Guilty?" she exclaimed, when I teased her about this. "Why should I be guilty!" But she was. It showed in her face at the hospital. She could not bear to look at the tiny, comatose figure in the intensive care room. "It's too sad," she mumbled in excuse. "Too bloody sad."

The old woman remained in a coma all week. By Thursday evening, though, there were some small signs of recovery. Her eyes would open for a few minutes at a time. She seemed to begin to be able to recognise us when we visited. "I think she's going to pull round," the specialist said cautiously. "But most of the paralysis is irreversible, I'm afraid."

Shaun phoned that evening, after my father was in bed. "Shall I pick you up tomorrow?" he asked.

"Tomorrow?"

"The Ministers," he murmured apologetically. "Or can't you face it under the circumstances?"

"I can face it."

"The mayor'll be there, too; our old school chum Ralph Biggs. I'll fetch you at eleven."

"Ah, wait." I thought fast. "I'll get there under my own steam. Borrow my Dad's car. His plant manager picks him up these days. He's too upset to drive."

"Okay. I can cadge a lift in the official car. Have a chance to chat up the bigwigs on the way."

"No!" I blurted, abruptly panicked. "I'll pick you up."

"Better if I ride with them."

"Please. I need to talk."

"Okay." Shaun's tone was gentle. "Georgina Halesworth has asked to be present. Do you mind? I think she's caught contrition, after that bitchery."

"Let's hope it's fatal," I laughed. "Pick you up at eleven."

"You said you needed to talk," Shaun prompted as we drove out to the township next morning.

"Ah. Yes. But I can't," I muttered lamely.

He squeezed my shoulder. "It is sad, a parent's death."

"She's not dead yet!"

Shaun blushed beetroot. "So sorry — "

"So am I," I said. "So am I."

Shaun, David Llewellyn, Georgina Halesworth and I waited on the stoop of the prototype house for the Ministers and the mayor to arrive. The area was cordoned off with metal barriers. Beyond these was a throng of blacks. They chattered and laughed, accepting the bullying of the township police with good humour. Only white faces were allowed within the guarded ring.

"They're late," Shaun said, looking at his watch yet again.

"Ministerial privilege," Llewellyn grunted.

I looked out over the heads of the African crowd towards the road leading from the city. The narrow bridge over the dried-out watercourse was a few hundred yards distant.

Had it been mined, as I had suggested? If so, would the guerrillas blow it as the Ministers' car arrived, or as it left?

It irritated me that I did not know the details of the ambush. Apart from the telephone message — *zhii* — Nkabi had told me nothing. In a sense, this was not really my "action." My part in it was ambiguous; it wasn't "simple."

"Forgiven?" a voice said beside me.

It was Georgina. She had avoided me up till now.

I jerked my attention away from the bridge. The reporter's swelling bosoms were trapped in a tight white T-shirt sporting a cute big-eared elephant and the slogan, "Rhodesia is Super!"

I nodded. "Witty bitchery is always forgivable."

Georgina flushed. Her green eyes were milky with chagrin. "You got under my skin," she muttered. "Something about you — "

"Yeah," I agreed readily. "I know."

"Here they come!" Shaun shouted.

The Ministers' motorcade approached the bridge in a cloud of dust. The convoy was led by an armoured scout car with a heavy-calibre machine gun mounted on its turret. Behind this was the ministerial black Mercedes 450SE. Eight police outriders on powerful Yamahas flanked the limousine.

Even at this distance I could see that the escort police were all white. No black constabulary could be trusted with the Ministers' security.

The scout car rolled onto the bridge. The clatter of its thick tires on the concrete planking of the span made my nape hairs prickle. "Now?" I thought.

The bridge was about twenty yards long and barely seven feet above the dry riverbed. It was no more than eight feet wide and had no parapet. The scout car was almost across when the Mercedes' front wheels touched the concrete surface.

*Now?*

The motorcycle outriders fell back in double file behind the limousine. The bikes' motors coughed as they throttled down to less than twenty miles per hour.

The big black car was now in the middle of the span. It rolled forward serenely. I could see the uniformed chauffeur in the front seat, flat cap tilted rakishly. In the back were three plump white faces.

*Now?!*

No. The Mercedes passed over the bridge in safety. My nape hairs began to settle.

The scout car entered our cordoned zone. It pulled to one side and stopped. Its fat-barrelled gun sniffed the air suspiciously.

The Mercedes drew up before us. The outriders came in behind and parked their machines. The police fanned out round the perimeter of the cordon with their backs to us and faced the black throng with automatic weapons at the ready.

The Ministers and the mayor emerged, beaming. Introductions were made. They were affable chaps, affecting the "Simple Farmer" style of the Prime Minister. "We are ordinary fellows," their modest smiles said, "shoved into power by duty and demand." Their hand-shakes were manly.

"Well," I wondered, as we chattered on the stoop, "you've come through safely. But will you get out?"

"Let us inspect this marvel," the mayor said. He and I had had a brief but chummy reunion as Shaun was introducing the township superintendent. Georgina they all knew. She was the wife of a prominent Member of Parliament and a character in her own right.

We went inside. Shaun did all the talking, with the easy grace of a professional used to bulling the brass. We inspected the house and then the visitors examined the sketches I had made for a model township, that Shaun had pinned up on the living-room walls.

"Impressive," the Minister of Housing declared at once. "Most interesting."

"Very sound scheme," the Minister of Labour agreed. "A most sensitive response to the practicalities."

"Cheap, too," the mayor said tersely.

"I only hope our natives will appreciate it," the Housing Minister went on. "There's no pleasing some people." He grasped my hand in both of his. "A very great pleasure, Mr. Kahn. I hope you've enjoyed your visit to Rhodesia. Perhaps you can tell your people back home that we're not as black as we're painted."

"I'm a Rhodesian, sir."

The Minister blinked at me, quite put out. "You didn't tell me Mr. Kahn was one of us, Shaun," he accused.

"Paul is a Rhodesian," Shaun confirmed, with a wink at me. "A true Bulawayo boy."

"Mm..." The Minister scrutinized my face. "Kahn — I know that name."

"Joe Kahn, my Dad, was Matabeleland Singles Champion in the thirties."

"Of course! 'Tricky Joe'! He could make a ball dance!"

"Still can."

" 'Tricky Joe' — and you really are his son?"

" 'Son of Tricky Joe,' to the life."

"First-rate sportsman, your father. A true Rhodesian."

We left the house. On the stoop, we posed for photographs. Georgina's camera whirred and clicked. As he was getting into the Mercedes, the Housing Minister pumped my hand again.

"I'll fill the P.M. in on your excellent scheme. We'll wangle funds for a pilot project. Count on me. Regards to 'Tricky Joe'!"

"May I cadge a ride with you gentlemen?" Shaun asked, already opening the front door opposite the chauffeur.

"Shaun!" I blurted, before anyone could answer.

His head jerked round. "Huh?"

"Deserting me?" I croaked. It was all I could think to say.

Shaun conceded reluctantly, touched by something in my tone. I noticed Georgina's curious eye upon me. However, as Shaun stepped back from the limousine, she slipped round him and took the seat beside the chauffeur.

The escort formed up, scout car leading, outriders flanking. The motorbike engines roared, and the convoy nosed forward through a gap opened in the African mob. There were a few ironic black cheers as the motorcade retreated.

Beside me, Shaun was grinning. "Went off smashingly, eh? We'll get our money. The clincher was that bit about 'Tricky Joe'." He slapped my shoulder. "You may be a Rhodesian, yet, old chap!"

Once again, the convoy approached the bridge. Again, my nape hairs prickled. Now? Surely?

The scout car crossed first. The Mercedes entered the bridge. The outriders fell back in double file.

*Now?!*

The big car was in the middle of the bridge span when it exploded. There was a dull *thump!* The Mercedes jumped up into the air as if it had been stung. It fell over the edge of the parapetless bridge and crashed into the dusty river-bed.

Flames shot out as the gas tank exploded. A black spume of oil and sand billowed into the air.

The Ministers' limousine was a ball of fire.

"G.C.M.!" Shaun gasped beside me.

In the background I heard an African voice shout, *"Zhii!"*

# 16

## SON OF TRICKY JOE

**S**haun and I ran towards the flaming gush of oily mud. The roar of the fire was in my ears. Smoke stung my eyes. A spray of pungent dust spattered my clothes and clogged my nose. The African crowd scattered before us, fleeing aimlessly as ants in a violated nest. They waved their arms like stunned antennae and ululated in fright.

The blazing car was a hot breath in our faces as we reached the edge of the riverbed. The cloud of smoke darkened the sun before our eyes. Shaun was cursing. His face was black with grime. His fair hair was spotted with oily specks.

"Napalm," he gasped. "Smell it?"

A sweet chemical stench wrenched our nostrils, like the stink of a burning rubber factory, or the smell of ash from a crematorium. The bridge had been blown clean in two. There was a ten-foot gap in the span. Chunks of the concrete planking were scattered over the riverbed like big broken teeth.

"G.C.M.," Shaun muttered. He focused on me with stunned eyes. "You saved my life?" he said, with an oddly questioning lilt.

"Yeah," I mumbled, and shuddered.

The scout car was invisible through the smoke on the far side of the riverbed. Behind us the motorbikes of the escort had been flung about by the blast. One machine was on fire on the bridge, its motor still coughing. The police outriders who had survived were only now picking themselves up painfully out of the dust.

"Alive!" Shaun screamed.

His finger was pointing at the wreck of the Mercedes. A blackened figure was stuck halfway out the front window. An arm writhed like a dying snake.

It was Georgina.

I rushed down the slope towards the car. Shaun stumbled along behind me. The flames were fading but the heat scorched our faces.

Georgina's head and torso were hanging out over the jammed door. She lay on her back, breasts heaving. The elephant on her T-shirt had lost its trunk. There was a hole burnt through to her chest, but the "Rhodesia is Super!" slogan was still intact.

I slid my hands under her armpits and lifted her body off the hot steel of the door. Shaun slipped his arms under her back and we eased her trunk and legs out through the window.

Georgina's eyes flicked open. She saw me. "Help," she mumbled. Her green eyes were stark with shock in the blackened face. Patches of her blond hair had been singed to the scalp. On her cheek and chin were blots of blistered car paint.

Shaun had the wounded woman in his arms. He staggered up the bank with her weight. On the edge of the riverbed was a rim of black faces staring down at us. As Shaun rose up towards them they fell back wailing in horror.

A constable — one of the outriders recovered from his shock — was beside me. "Survivors?" he panted, peering through the smoke into the limousine's interior.

I squatted down and tried to see in through the cracked windscreen. In the front seat of the Mercedes the chauffeur seemed to be peacefully asleep over the wheel, his black cap at a jaunty angle. In the back were three torched corpses. The charge must have exploded just under their seat; their severed and roasted legs were resting on their bloodied heads.

The policeman turned away and retched into the dust. I pulled him away from the burnt-out shell. I felt like puking, too, but the vomit stuck in my gullet. It tasted like sour pickle.

On the bank Shaun, Llewellyn and several more constables were gathered round Georgina whose body lay on the ground. Llewellyn's Welsh face was smudged like a coalminer's. "Jesus, sweet Jesus," he mumbled, over and over, with an odd jerk of the hand, as if brushing away flies. "Jesus, sweet Jesus — "

"Amen," Shaun muttered, crossing himself.

The sergeant of the motorcycle police spoke up hoarsely. "Any more survivors, sir?" he asked me.

I shook my head. "Any of your radios working? Have you called for help?"

The sergeant was about to answer when a clatter of heavy calibre machine-gun fire cut him off. The scout car reappeared on the far side of the riverbed, its gun spurting flame in our direction.

The burst of bullets zipped over our heads. The throng of blacks, which had begun to close in on us, scattered and fled, howling.

"Fucking idiots!" Shaun bawled, shaking his fists at the scout car. The gunner must have seen him, for he ceased firing at once.

Shaun turned on the sergeant. "You," he snapped, "get a first-aid kit. You must have one in your saddlebag, I hope."

"Yes, sir," the sergeant said. He ran off.

We all gazed down at Georgina. She lay quite still in the dust. Her breath was very weak. It hardly lifted the burnt T-shirt.

One of the constables suddenly became chatty. He looked very young, barely twenty. One of his leather leggings hung loose on a singed calf. "I was in the last rank. Felt this kind of fist in my face. Bashed me clean off my bike. Ended up on my back in the dust." He flung his arms wide. "But look — not a scratch!"

We all looked at the happy boy. He was beaming. The relief of survival gave him a grin from ear to ear.

At our feet, Georgina groaned. She was trying to say something. I knelt down and put my ear close to her lips. They were swollen, as if she had been punched in the mouth. There was blood on her gums. "Yes?" I prompted.

"Camera," she gasped. "Cam-raaa — "

"Sorry, love. In the car. Burnt."

The reporter fluttered her lashes at me almost coquettishly. "Get, camera, please?"

"Sorry," I murmured. "Sorry."

"Olympus SLR — " she babbled. "Computerized shutter — Synchronized — Auto-winder."

"Don't fret," I soothed. "I'll buy you another."

She shook her head. "Can't. Sanctions."

"I'll order it from abroad."

Her lids flickered. "Ta," she sighed, and sank back into coma.

I rose. Over Shaun's head I saw flames licking up from the thatch roofing the prototype house. Sparks from the blast must have set it alight. "House!" I blurted.

Shaun and Llewellyn jerked round together. "Shit," the superintendent cursed. He ran off towards the house. In a moment he had a hose going and was spraying water on the thatch.

The whine of a distant siren penetrated our daze.

"Thank God," Shaun said, and crossed himself again.

A wide pillar of dust came spinning towards us along the road from the town. Out of it emerged a convoy of military vehicles led by an armoured halftrack. The convoy fanned out along the far side of the riverbed. Out of the camouflaged trucks jumped scores of armed troops. Led by a major, the infantry swarmed across the riverbed and surrounded us. Their automatic weapons made an iron ring round our small group.

"Freeze!" the major bellowed.

"Don't be an ass," Shaun said curtly. "Order up an ambulance for this casualty here."

"Ah. Major Connaughton," the officer muttered. "Sorry." He turned on one of his men. "Get the stretchermen," he ordered. "Pronto!"

The trooper ran off. The major tilted his bush hat back with his pistol point. "What happened?" he asked. "Looks like a bloody mess."

"Two Cabinet Ministers, the mayor and a chauffeur were killed in a terr ambush," Shaun summarized crisply. "This lady — a reporter on the *Chronicle* — is the only survivor."

"G.C.M.," the officer gulped. "How?"

"They mined the bridge. Must have been detonated in the vicinity. The lead scout car crossed safely. The ambushers must still be around. I suggest you round up every black in sight."

"Sir!" The major saluted and ordered his men to follow. The troops ran towards the township, arms at the ready.

The stretchermen arrived. They lifted Georgina gently onto the canvas.

"Be very careful with her," Shaun warned them. "Her husband is a V.I.P."

After Georgina had been taken off, my knees felt all at once very weak. "Can we sit down?" I gasped. The sting of unvomited puke was sour in my throat. Shaun took my arm. He led me towards the house. We went into the living room and sat on a couple of the cane chairs that had been provided for the Ministers. The air smelled of singed thatch.

I lit a cigarette with a shaking hand. Around us were my sketches for the model township. "Metropolis of Mud," I muttered absently.

Shaun was scrubbing the grime from his cheeks with a spit-dampened hankie. He laughed sharply. "You saved my life!" His cry was an accusation.

Two police officers entered. One had three pips on his shoulder. The other was in plain clothes. "Captain Williamson, Special Branch," the uniformed officer introduced himself. "You gentlemen are ... "

"Architects," Shaun replied. "This is Mr. Paul Kahn. I am Shaun Connaughton."

"Of course," the captain said, relaxing a little in his recognition. "We've played a foursome once, sir. Hillside Golf Club?"

"Ah, yes. Bill Williamson. I remember," Shaun murmured. "You beat us three and two."

"We were lucky," the captain said modestly. He sat down in a cane chair. His assistant remained standing and took out a notebook. "Could you give us any details of this shocking affair?"

"The Ministers? The mayor?"

"Dead."

The word fell like a stone. There was a thud of silence.

The Special Branch captain cleared his throat. "You begin to see what we're up against? First the post office business, now this. They're beginning to hit us where it hurts."

Shaun frowned. "The post office? Was that — ?"

"Definitely. True, we have no hard and fast forensic evidence to that effect, but the injured technician is quite certain there was a definite blast. 'The cabinets suddenly jumped at me off the walls,' he says. There was also a stink that could only be napalm."

"G.C.M.," Shaun grunted. His head jerked back. "I smelled napalm here, too. It was like a — " he searched for a simile — "burning kraal, after a contact. Sweet and sick."

"I've noticed that," the captain nodded. "These chaps are beginning to fight dirty." His Adam's apple jerked like a thorn in his throat.

"No dirtier than we are," Shaun countered, with a spasm of his reflexive honesty.

The captain waved this awkward truth aside. "What exactly did you gentlemen see and hear?"

"Not much. We were here, just outside. There was a thump, then the car went off the bridge and caught fire."

"What did you do then?" the officer asked, as his assistant scribbled in his black notebook.

"We — Mr. Kahn and I — ran towards the fire. He led." Shaun flicked me an acknowledgement of my speed of reaction. "The Mercedes was already almost burnt out. We saw a survivor — the lady from the *Chronicle*. We went down into the riverbed and pulled her free. How is she?"

"Amazingly unharmed, it seems. Minor burns on the face and chest, a few scratches on her limbs. She'll be up and about in a day or two."

"Unharmed?" I mumbled.

The captain turned to me. "The blast went off under the back seat. Perfect timing. The Ministers and the mayor were killed instantly. Mutilated. The chauffeur was unfortunate. A chunk of metal from the car floor sliced through the back of his seat and severed his spine clean through."

"God."

"Bad luck, eh? Well, Mr. Kahn, what did you see?"

"Much the same."

"What came first, the fire or the blast?"

"I don't really know."

"I'm interested to know if the napalm was detonated before or after the charge. It could reveal the ambushers M.O. — Method of Operation, that is."

"Have you investigated the bridge?" Shaun asked. "Found anything?"

"I only had a chance for a quick look. It seems the explosive was packed in a couple of acetylene cylinders of the commercial type. About a hundred pounds of the stuff, at a guess. The cylinder casing became shrapnel in the blast, but most of this was deflected downwards by the concrete planking. The thing was detonated from a hide about a hundred yards on the far side of the span. We've found the leads and the detonators abandoned by the terrorists. The ambushers must still be in the vicinity. Melted into the crowd, most like. We've cordoned off the whole township. A house-to-house, person-to-person search is in progress. But," the captain paused and scratched his cheek, "this was a most skillful operation. It's likely the types involved prepared a clever out."

"They're getting cleverer and cleverer," Shaun muttered.

"Too clever by half," the policeman agreed. "Who all knew of the Ministers' visit? Timing and details."

"Myself," Shaun said. "Mr. Kahn. David Llewellyn, the Township Superintendent. Georgina Halesworth. That's it, so far as I know."

"Let me ask you an embarrassing question: Did you mention this visit to anyone in your family? Or your office staff?"

"What?" Shaun frowned.

"What I'm getting at is, could any African servant or office boy have overhead you talking?"

Shaun's eyes flashed anger. "I don't chatter," he said curtly.

The captain was unruffled. He turned to me. "And you, sir?"

"Me neither."

"Ah, well. The leak could have come from the other end. One of the Ministers or the mayor, or any of their staff might have chattered." He smiled at Shaun, apologizing.

"Even at that high level, people haven't yet fully grasped the need for absolute caution. They can't get it into their heads that we are at war, that careless talk costs lives. Maybe, after this, they will."

"You have a point," Shaun conceded. "So you think it was a leak?"

"What else?"

Shaun shrugged. "Don't know."

"It is either an unwitting leak, or a traitorous act," the captain said succinctly. "Take your pick." He rose. "Thank you, gentlemen. I may need to get back to you. Would you give my colleague your addresses and phone numbers."

We did so. Shaun walked the Special Branch officer to the door. "Do you think your investigation will get anywhere?" he asked anxiously.

The captain shrugged. "Who knows? We can trace those cylinders back to the point of origin. Stolen, probably. The detonators are standard mine equipment, also probably nicked. Apart from those scraps, we have nothing. But we'll push hard. We'll make someone talk, I promise you. This sort of caper has got to be crushed. If we have to break a few bones in the process, so be it." He saluted laconically, and left.

"Charming fellow," I said.

"Just doing his job," Shaun retorted. He looked round the room and his eyes came to rest on my sketches. "As we've tried to do ours." He turned to me. "So, what now, 'Son of Tricky Joe'?"

"You tell me."

The green eyes tightened. "No," he said, very distinctly, "*you* tell *me*."

When we were at school together — I remembered as we drove back to town in my father's old Toyota — Shaun had penned a piece for *The Miltonian*. It had been titled: "The Question of Grace in Striving to Win at Games".

Shaun was a brilliant sportsman. He'd had caps for rugger, cricket and track. He might well have been Rhodes Scholar material, but for his rather plodding exam performance. Possibly, too, doubts had been raised in the Head's mind by an essay that promulgated the heretical notion that it might not be entirely "graceful" to win too well too often.

"One can be a trifle *too* scrupulous, Connaughton," Old Bones had scowled, shooting up his question-mark Scots eyebrows. "For God's sake, man, try and be a bit less Papist!"

The school's motto, after all, was: *"Dulce et decorum est pro patria mori."* — " 'Tis a sweet and graceful thing to die for one's country."

"Shaun, you know something?" I said, as I was dropping him off at his office. I smiled at his frown. "You're such a *goy*."

"What's that mean?"

"It means you should wash your dirty face."

"You, too," he retorted, and slammed the car door.

In the rearview mirror I saw him staring after me as I pulled away. The sunshine struck ginger from his hair.

An ambulance was parked in the driveway of my father's house. I ran inside. In the hall my father and Leonie were talking to an African woman in a white nurse's uniform.

"What's happening?" I cried.

"We brought Mom home," Leonie said. "The specialist said we might as well. There's nothing more the hospital can do for her." Leonie's lips quivered. " 'Let her die at home,' the doctor said."

" 'Survival is irrelevant', eh?" I mocked bitterly.

"She's so brave," Dad moaned.

"I tried to get you at Shaun's office, but you weren't there. What happened to your face?"

"Is she in the bedroom?" I asked." Can I see her?"

"She's sleeping," Leonie said. She gestured at the African nurse. "This is Josephine. She's going to look after Mom."

"Hello, Josephine."

"Good afternoon, baas."

"Don't call me baas," I said irritably. "My name is Paul."

The nurse blinked. Then she gave a shy smile. "Yes, sir," she said gravely. She had high, almost Slavic cheekbones in a heart-shaped face.

"They've suspended all medication," Leonie said. "L-dopa, anti-congestants, vaso-dilators, tranquilizers — the lot. 'No point in bothering her now,' the specialist said." A tear ran down Leonie's cheek. "She looks so tiny. A little mouse."

"With the heart of a lion," I countered grimly. "Let me see her."

The shrivelled old woman was asleep in the wide matrimonial bed in the darkened room. The close air smelled sweet and sick.

"Mom," I murmured. "Mom."

I gripped her hand. Her eyes flicked open. Her fingers squeezed back strongly.

"My boy ... "

It was a long sigh.

"Welcome home, old thing."

Her gaze focused on my face. "Dirty," she whispered.

"Dirty," I agreed.

She shut her eyes and slept again. The breath rattled in her paralyzed throat. I eased my hand free of hers and tiptoed out.

I saw Leonie out to her car. "Look after the old boy," she said. "He needs your strength now." She flashed me a crooked grin. "Here's your chance to be a good son."

"To 'Tricky Joe'?" I smiled back.

"The kids miss you, Uncle Paul. Lovey, especially."

"Louie, you mean."

She nodded. "Louie. Yes. You're right. We must stop using that baby name. He's almost a man, now."

I held the car door open. "Your son is very much his own man, my dear. Let him be who he is."

"He respects you, Paul. He trusts you. He doesn't trust easily."

"I'll come and see him, soon."

Leonie gazed into my eyes. Her own were stark. "You could save my son's life," she said, with great care.

"My dear, I don't know if I can save my own life, let alone anyone else's!"

"I'd kill for that boy," Leonie said simply, and slammed the car door.

My father required three Mogadons and a Besserol to get to sleep after supper that evening. I put him to bed at seven and tucked the covers in round his shoulders. In a moment he was snoring peacefully.

I looked in on my mother. She, too, was asleep. The nurse sat on a chair beside the bed holding the old woman's hand. Her high-boned black face was set in a mask of profound patience.

There were two items of interest on the television news. One had to do with the doubling of the world oil price by the Organization of Petroleum Exporting Countries in the wake of the Yom Kippur War. "The Arabs are holding the world to ransom," the newsreader said grimly. "This action will make things even more difficult for Rhodesia."

The second news item he read concerned "a fatal car accident in Bulawayo's Tshabalala African Township in which the mayor of the city and two Cabinet Ministers were mortally injured." The accident was ascribed to "a defect in the steering mechanism of the Ministers' Mercedes that caused it to swerve off a low bridge and explode." There were no shots of the scene, only stills of the Ministers and the mayor.

The reader went on to say that "The Prime Minister has expressed his deep regrets at the tragedy, and the loss of two valuable colleagues 'at a time when the Country is most in need of their services.' The Ministers' chauffeur and two members of the police motorcycle escort were also killed in the accident," the reader added, "but a reporter on the Bulawayo *Chronicle*, who was accompanying the Ministers, escaped with light burns and superficial injuries. She is in Bulawayo Central being treated for shock, but will be released in a few days."

The Ministers were to be buried in Salisbury on the following Monday with full military honours.

So, it was to be an accident, officially.

The authorities were clearly concerned not to rock the raft on which the white community floated. Yet rumour was bound to ripple the Rhodesian pools. Too many people had witnessed the event. True, most of them were black and therefore irrelevant, but the shockwave of their gossip could not be dammed by official lying. Servants chatter. The pools would be choppy for a while.

But the Rhodesian gift for dreaming was inspired. Rip-van-Winkleland would not be woken from its long, deep doze by a few blasts.

My father was snoring as I slid under the sheet of my narrow cot by the window. The small flame of his nightlight made delicate shadows on his sagging cheek. In between each rasp there was a grumbled whimper, like an old dog having bad dreams.

My eyelids fluttered. Sleep was a stone dragging me down. I synchronized my breathing with the old man's rasp-and-whimper.

"Son of Tricky Joe," I sighed, sinking.

<u>17</u>

# SURVIVAL IS IRRELEVANT

In the next few days the house settled into a routine of waiting for death. Josephine was with my mother twenty-four hours a day. She slept on the carpet at the foot of the matrimonial bed, under a single blanket. At least twice a night she got up to change the old woman's sweat-and-urine-soaked sheets, and clothe her in a fresh nightie. My mother wore a large diaper, but even this thick cottonwool padding could not contain the fluids draining from her body.

She was melting away by the hour, tissue turning to water, bones softening to butter. Her skin hung loose and folded, a bag made for a bigger being. She was fed pap spoon by painful spoon, dribbling like a baby.

My father could not sleep without heavy medication. He lay in the bed near me, snorting in uneasy rest, kicking off his bedclothes. I had to get up and recover him several times a night. He still had the old habit of sleeping only in his pajama top. His bum was bared to the night air; his curled-in cock shrivelled in its nest of grey hairs. Like Noah's son Ham, I looked upon my father's nakedness and did not turn my face backwards.

The old man woke promptly at five, at first light, with a sigh of relief at having seen out one more night. His very first act, even before he put on his pants, was to shuffle through to the sickroom. He peeped in there, putting only his nose and eyes round the door, out of modesty and apprehension. "Did she sleep?" he whispered to Josephine, who had already shifted to her daytime chair at the bedside. "Granny had a good night," the nurse replied, already aware of the family reflex of soothing Grandpa.

"She's so brave!"

The factory manager picked my father up at six. Without his work, the old man would have gone mad. The problems of furniture production, the upsets of agitators, the delays in getting imported cloth caused by sanctions, drained off his nervous tension. As it was, he phoned the house a dozen times a day to ask how Mom was doing.

"She's so brave!" He always rang off with that cry.

After he had left for the factory, there was a quiet hour. I had my coffee and toast in the kitchen. It was the crispest moment of the day, a breathing space before the sun baked the sky blue. I smoked a tranquil cigarette and read the *Chronicle*.

On Monday the Ministers were buried in Salisbury, the mayor in Bulawayo, along with the chauffeur and the two escort policemen who had died.

Ian Smith presided at his colleagues' funeral. He made an impassioned speech: "The world does not grasp the nature of our struggle to preserve civilized standards in Southern Africa. Even our powerful ally to the south, the Republic of South Africa, begins to compromise its support. The Nationalist government in Pretoria is cosying up to our black neighbours to the north, in the foolish hope of softening those folks' hatred for everything white and decent. America is turned in on its own navel. Britain is floundering under Socialism, whether Pink or Blue in complexion. Only Portugal — that brave little land — fights alongside us to the east and west, to sustain the beacon of Christian civilization in the advancing Marxist night."

The Premier's rubbery features were stiff with bitterness in the photo accompanying this graveside oration.

"The world is hostile. It is corrupt. We must learn a hard lesson from the tragic deaths we've come here today to mourn: we have only ourselves to honour! And what we must honour is the last candle of true Britishness left on a darkening global stage. To quote the poet: 'There is some corner of a foreign field that is forever England.' Rhodesia is that 'corner'. It is the last flame of true Englishness. To those many foes who hope we will flicker out with a whimper, to those few friends who fear our failing, to the concerned and the indifferent, I say we will not be snuffed out. No — never in my lifetime!"

The Monday paper also reported that Georgina Halesworth had been discharged from Bulawayo Central. It seemed she had made a rapid recovery from her burns. She was convalescing at her Hillside home in the care of her husband, "the prominent local Member of Parliament, Tom Halesworth."

I looked up Georgina's address in the phone book and ordered her a large bouquet of flame lilies from a flower shop. The accompanying note read: "To one of 'the last candles of true Britishness' from one who babbles through his bonnet."

The flower shop must have been very prompt in its delivery, for Georgina phoned me just after lunch. "Thanks for the flowers," she said. "And thanks for saving my life." Her voice was still a bit thickened with the after-effects of shock.

"My pleasure, Mrs. Halesworth."

"But you still owe me a camera."

"True."

"A promise is a promise."

"True."

"I need to talk to you, Mr. Kahn."

"What about?"

"The candle of true Britishness, and other matters."

"I see."

"Do you? I wonder." Her voice was clear and sharp all at once. "Could you meet me tomorrow, Tuesday, at three, at the Mug and Jug on Abercorn Street."

It sounded more a command than a request. "Are you strong enough?" I asked.

"Oh, I'm very strong," she retorted, with a grim chuckle. "Tomorrow, three o'clock, at — "

" — the Mug and Jug. Agreed."

I had no time to ponder this exchange, for Aunts June and Rose arrived just then to take up their daily vigil at my mother's bedside. "She's so frail," they exclaimed ritually. "She's so brave!" They sniffled and dabbed damp eyes before settling down at the foot of the invalid's bed to an afternoon of morbid muttering and needle-clicking.

Leonie popped in on her way home from work. A

reflexive scowl disfigured her face at sight of the planted Aunties. "Ghouls," she hissed to me, certain they would overhear. "Green Crocodile Maidens!"

"Is that the real meaning of G.C.M.?" I asked, to deflect her boundlessly fresh venom.

"Huh?" She frowned at me, irritated by my lack of loyalty-in-hatred. She shrugged. "Who knows?"

"I always thought it meant, 'Great Christian Madness.' "

"I'm going home," she said, and departed, leaving the field to the triumphant "ghouls".

My father returned from the factory at five. He went straight to the sickroom, stuck in his nose, asked Josephine: "Did she sleep?"

"Granny had a good day."

"She's so brave!"

After this, he took his evening shower. Then he relaxed with me on the terrace in an outfit familiar from my childhood: a net tennis cap, soiled with the sweat of many sets, to keep his hair neat; a striped and collarless shirt inherited from Grandpa Kahn; a short maroon cotton gown, much mended by countless housegirls, that bared his sportman's calves.

We had drinks — whisky for me, lemonade for him — and watched the sun set behind the pawpaw trees. In one large drooping leaf two weaver birds were starting a nest. The male tied neat knots of straw with his beak while the female flitted across the garden ferrying scraps of dried grass.

The old man's face was grim. He cried out abruptly: "If I'd known then what I know now!" His eyes were harsh with baffled rage. "God is a fool," he said. "A bloody fool."

"Mom, you mean?" I ventured.

"Mom. And other things. You know." He stared at me. "You know."

I nodded. There was a silence. The air was so still I could almost feel his breath in my own chest.

"You know," he said again, and began to weep.

After my father went to bed, I persuaded Josephine to watch television with me for an hour, as a break from her duties. The nurse was reluctant to leave "Granny" even for so short a time, but the old woman was sleeping peacefully, and Josephine really needed the relief.

She was awkward at first, sitting alone with me in the living room, but slowly she relaxed with a cup of coffee and a cigarette. The bones in her face were strong. They pushed the skin out and up under the black almond eyes. Even at ease she was all there, ready to answer any call.

Josephine began to talk as an old American soap opera gave out its canned laughter on the telly. She told me she was a Zambian, a "foreign native". Her husband had been killed in a road accident, leaving her with two young sons. There was no work in Lusaka, so she had come south.

She had no family in Rhodesia, and the local blacks were hostile to a foreigner. "They are lazy," she said simply. "They don't like that I work hard." She took off her nurse's cap and parted her straight jet hair to show me an ugly scar on her scalp. "The other nurses hit me with sticks," she explained. "I cannot work in a hospital any more, only private. I have no man to protect me here. I am alone." She smiled, averting sympathy. "It is the way things are, sir."

"Paul."

"Paul." She glanced at me, then looked away. "You have scars, too," she murmured shyly, touching her lower lip.

"Also a jealous woman," I laughed.

Her eyes were grave upon my face. "Bad girls, too many," she said.

"Bad girls, too many," I agreed.

Josephine started up. "Granny!" she cried, and ran out of the room.

I ran down the passage after her. The old woman was gagging. Spume and phlegm clogged her stricken throat. Her lips frothed with it, her face was blue. The breath rattled in her chest as her wasted body jerked in terror of death.

"Forward!" Josephine said, pulling at my mother's arms. "Hold her forward. Clear the throat."

I jumped on the bed and lifted the choking old woman from the pillows. I got behind and propped her body upright with my chest. Josephine pushed a wooden spatula down her throat to scoop out the muck. It seemed endless, the junk that came out of that small gullet. The phlegm was bright yellow and stank of rot.

In my arms, the old woman fought to survive. Her stringy muscles shuddered with that last-ditch battle against nothingness. Her body jittered and jolted, wrenching at the air locked out of her lungs. It took all my strength to hold her.

Even as I held her, I was torn with conflict. On the one hand, all my energy and will throbbed out to aid her fight for life. On the other hand, her stubborn grip on survival for its own sake enraged me. "Hold on," I grunted. Then, "Let go!" I wanted both at once — survival and release. It was tearing.

She survived.

A gap was opened in her throat by Josephine's swabbing. The breath began to break through. Her face faded from blue to white. In a while she was resting easy.

Josephine sank down on the chair in deep exhaustion. I lay on the bed beside the now-peaceful old woman, also drained. My mother was asleep. Her collapsed face was serene. Our energies had saved her, this time.

"Granny," the nurse muttered. "Poor, poor Granny." A tear ran down her stark black cheek. "She is so brave."

Later, sitting alone in the living room, I had some hard thoughts.

The strains of Beethoven's "Ode to Joy" swelled from the T.V. as the evening's program ended. The chorus rose over a still of the Zimbabwe Ruins.

> *Rise, O voices of Rhodesia,*
> *God, may we Thy bounty share,*
> *Give us strength to face all danger and*
> *    where challenge is, to dare.*

The image changed as the anthem soared. The statue of Cecil Rhodes replaced the Ruins, pointing north to our hinterland.

*Guide us, Lord, to wise decision*
*ever of Thy grace aware,*
*Oh, let our hearts beat bravely always,*
*for this land within Thy care.*

The Founder's photo faded. The sound went dead. I left the blank screen flickering to accompany my musings.

They were jerky: "Bomb Day" — solved nothing. Lightness gone, no "walking on water." Back to *mud*. "Simple unambiguous act" — complex, ambiguous consequences. Such as: I was now, in Nkunzi's view, a fully-paid-up *terr*; a member of the Zimbabwean *Chimurenga*.

Had I made a perfect circle from the coils of White Snake? A ring? A noose? *The serpent that bites its own tail!*

"World Snake" — symbol of Divinity. But "God is a fool!"

"A Question of Grace in Striving ... " I had striven too well. Yes, *Nyogamhlope* had bitten his own tail. White Snake had stung himself to death. My own personal *Chimurenga* was done.

I had to inform Nkunzi. Would he accept it? Would the Old Bull, Father of Zimbabwe, allow the White Snake to roll his tail-biting circle out of the game?

Or would he hand me over to the Special Branch, as a final act of white embarrassment? As if to say, "See, even your own colour can't be trusted!" The fact that I was only an Honorary White Man, a Rhodesian by virtue of my Grandfather's mistake with the boat so many years ago, would be irrelevant.

As irrelevant as survival ....

It was up to Nkunzi. My fate was in his hands. So be it.

I went to bed and slept like a baby.

Next morning my mother was almost chirpy. Her survival for one more day brought a glint to her eye.

"Granny's asking for soft-boiled eggs!" Josephine exclaimed. "And she wants me to do her hair!"

"Vanity is the surest sign of life," I said. "Make her pretty, Josephine."

I went in to see the old woman after she had been

groomed. She'd refused to let me see her in a "mess". She was sitting up holding a hand mirror to her face. Her cheeks were pink with health, her eyes were dancing, her hair was brushed back in a neat wave. She smelled of rosewater.

"Paul," she said clearly, from a throat that had not been able to shape a single word for many hours. "Paul." She grinned with glee at her own cleverness in uttering that magic syllable.

I sat on the edge of the bed and took her hand. "You look pretty," I murmured. "A pretty old thing."

Her grin grew. "Not dead yet," she stated. "No."

"How are you?"

"Fine." She stopped smiling. "Dad?"

"Okay. Off at work."

"You being kind?" she asked, searching my face.

"Yes."

"Good."

Josephine was hovering in the background. "Not too much talk, Granny," she warned.

"Bully," the old woman humphed.

"Hey, she saved your life," I protested.

"And you."

I blinked. "You remember?"

"Not dead yet," she said crossly, and gestured me away.

"Granny is amazing," Josephine whispered to me in the passage. "I have been with many terminal cases, but she is — " The nurse threw up her hands in wonder.

"A stubborn old fox," I said.


That afternoon I drove my father's car into town to meet Georgina at the Mug and Jug. I was a little early for the rendezvous, so I wandered about window-gazing for a while.

I was looking in a jeweller's window when I saw the silver snake. "Mona!" I grunted, in instant identification.

The slim little serpent had diamond-chip eyes and a body of segmented silver. Its forked tongue was gold. It hung by the tail from a silver chain.

It was Mona.

The jeweller wanted a lot for the snake, but I paid up. He

claimed it was "Ancient Persian". I asked him to deliver it to Mona's house and wrote an accompanying note: "A silver serpent from the deadliest snake to the snakiest lover in town."

I hoped she would accept the peace offering.

The Mug and Jug went in for African curios and barrel tables, a kind of tribal chic. There were few customers at three, between the lunch hour and teatime. I chose a seat in a corner by the window, my back to the wall. A black waitress with an Afro wig decorated with pink bows took my order.

The coffee was pungent if a little raw; a local blend. I sipped it and gazed at the decor. Strings of bean beads hung on the walls between crudely cut masks in charred pine. The counter was stacked with postcards featuring lions, zebras and crocodiles. The Afrikaner manageress had a pink and surly face made sour by having to deal with *munt* waitresses.

Georgina entered. Her face was framed by a paisely headscarf tied under her chin. She wore a rather formal dark linen suit with wide lapels. She saw me at once and came over.

"Mr. Kahn."

"Mrs. Halesworth."

She sat down. There were pink splotches on her cheek and chin, as if her face were smeared with strawberry ice cream. As I watched, she deliberately untied the headscarf. Her head was cropped close. In patches the hair had been burnt off, scorching the scalp.

She stared at me as I registered this atrocity. Her green eyes were stony. "Thanks for the flame lilies," she said. "That was — thoughtful."

My hand holding the coffee cup gave an abrupt jerk, like a Parkinsonian spasm. The liquid squirted over the flowered table cloth.

Georgina smiled. "Am I so ugly?"

"Yes!"

She laughed outright. "You owe me a camera, sir."

"And you owe me a contrition, ma'am," I shot back.

"Eh? Oh yes. For bitching at you in my article. Well, we lost that chance, didn't we? You blew it." Her gaze sharpened. "Death and destruction seem to follow you around, Mr. Kahn."

The waitress came to take Georgina's order. I asked for another cup of coffee as the black girl mopped the mess on our cloth.

A silence followed. Georgina fussed with her crop, trying to get it to lie evenly over the gaps. I polluted my temple with yet another cigarette.

"Are you a Bulawayo girl?" I asked, to make conversation.

"Born and bred," she nodded. "Head Prefect at Eveline, captain of field hockey, *victrix ludorum* in the school games. Yes, I am utterly local. I've never lived anywhere else, apart from three years at Rhodes University, down south." She gave an even more emphatic nod. "Between the Zambesi and the Limpopo — that's where I live and where I'll die."

"Bravo."

Her eyes sharpened. "The bomb at Tshabalala, the fire at the Telecom Centre — you were present both times. Curious, no?"

"How do you know I was at the Telecom Centre?" I demanded.

"I have my spies."

"My cousin, Barney Silverman, is in charge there."

"Was. He's being transferred, to Gwelo."

"But that's the sticks!"

"Sure. Maybe, in future, he'll be a little more choosy in his cousins?"

"Poor old Barn. He loves this town."

She jutted her chin. "Many people do."

"I'm also Bulawayo born and bred," I countered sharply.

"Yes. I know. I've been researching you. You were a King Scout!"

"Indeed. I led the Bulawayo Fourth Troop. We won the Royal Cup at the Kimberley Jamboree in 'fifty."

She cocked her head. The shorn hair gave her a birdy air. "What makes you tick?"

"Georgina," I said abruptly, "what's all this about?"

"I think that you are a highly ambiguous character," she said evenly.

"Aren't we all?"

"We're fighting for our survival, here," she said, very much the Head Girl. "We intend to survive!"

"Who, exactly, is this 'we'?"

"Us." She gestured round the cafe, including the street, the city and the entire territory. "Civilization."

"Not a hope," I said bluntly. "Civilization has had it — here as elsewhere."

"Oh no." She was deeply shocked. "Look, I'm not talking about being white or black, I'm talking about standards. This conflict now, that's temporary. A lot of Africans are with us. Our army is eighty per cent black. In fact, a lot of quiet contacts are happening, under the uproar. I could tell you — " She broke off on the verge of indiscretion. "My husband is a very influential figure behind the scenes."

"Not another Grey Eminence, please!"

Her eyes flashed fire. "You know, Mr. Kahn, I suspect you're a puritan. A man who finds ordinary life, ordinary folk too corrupt or boring for his refined idealism. In short, a hater. Even a murderer." She leant forward abruptly, shoving her pink blotches at me. "You are the type of Raskolnikov in *Crime and Punishment*. You would murder for metaphysical reasons."

"You, er, flatter me — " I stammered.

"Ha." She sat back triumphantly. "I think I'll have another cappuccino, please."

I beckoned the waitress. After she had taken the order, I lit yet another cigarette.

"You smoke too much," she said. "Sign of a weak character."

"Can't say the same for you, can I?"

"No. I am strong. Clear and unambiguous. There are people like that left in the world, Mr. Kahn."

"Only in Rhodesia."

"Perhaps. If so, we must fight to preserve it, wouldn't you say?"

"Absolutely."

She frowned at me. "You really did save my life. Shaun told me. If you hadn't reacted so fast I might have been trapped too long in the burning wreck."

"Shaun is too kind."

"I love him," she said simply. "That's why it hurt to rubbish your project."

"Yet you did so."

"You got under my skin. What about that camera?"

"Give me the details, and I'll write to a friend in London."

"I have them with me." She opened her leather bag and pushed a folded paper towards me. Then she rose. "Goodbye, Mr. Kahn."

"Aren't you waiting for your cappuccino?"

"I have to meet my husband. There's his car." She stuck out her hand. "Take care. *Hamba gahle.*"

"You, too. I hope you get your tresses back."

"I'm sure I shall," she said grimly, and marched out.

Through the cafe window I watched her cross the pavement to a grey Rover sedan. The car door opened and a man got out to greet her.

I froze. It was Mona's "Grey Eminence"!

Yes, it was the same lank pinstriped figure with the cap of grey hair I had seen getting out of Mona's Datsun down by the riverbank under the willows.

Georgina's husband, Tom Halesworth, the Member of Parliament, Ian Smith's "string-puller," was Mona's *éminence grise!*

# 18

# METHODS MAKETH MAN

A drained cup of coffee is a grimy thing. There are no leaves to tell your fortune, only dregs. I sat staring into mine for quite a while as my head buzzed with questions.

Main Question: Had Tom Halesworth set up my meeting with his wife as a warning of some kind? If so, what exactly was the warning?

That the authorities were on to me, but had no proof of my guilt as yet? But, under the emergency regulations now in force, they needed no proof to arrest a terr on suspicion alone and hold him without trial forever. Perhaps they wanted to avoid the embarrassment of having to admit the existence of a white traitor. If they arrested me it would soon come out in public. A European has connections. He could not be made to vanish into the Special Branch limbo quite as totally as an African.

But there was something that didn't quite add up here. The method of warning was odd. It was too personal, almost friendly. Unless Halesworth, that "Grey Eminence," was going easy on me because his wife was convinced I had saved her life?

The sunshine blinded me as I came out of the cafe. I did not see the yellow taxi waiting at the curb until the back door swung open and a voice hissed, "Mr. Kahn! Get in!" Then I recognized the old Vauxhall and its apache-capped midget driver. They had driven Nkabi and me to that first meeting with Nkunzi in the Matopos Hills.

"Mr. Kahn! Get in!"

As soon as I complied, the taxi swung out into the street. There was a young African on the back seat beside me. He wore a yellow tweed hacking jacket and crisp beige linen pants. In the dim interior his oxblood loafers glowed with high polish.

"What's up?" I asked. But the young man was craned round to peer out of the Vauxhall's narrow back window.

"Car following!" he exclaimed. "Lose it!"

The driver hunched his shoulders and began to weave the taxi's lean snout through the thin afternoon traffic. I looked out the back window and saw a white Citroen DS behind us at a distance of about thirty yards.

"Specials?" I muttered.

"Specials," my companion confirmed. "They always drive white Citroens."

The Citroen closed in. I could see two pale faces with crewcuts staring at us through the windscreen, eyes slitted against the lowering sun.

The taxi turned right at Eleventh Avenue. We drove past the concrete cooling towers of the power station. After several twists and turns, we were out in the bush, running alongside a railway embankment.

"Lose them!" snapped Yellow Hacking Jacket.

The driver ducked his head. "Fast car, sir," he mumbled.

My companion burst out in a spate of furious Ndebele. The driver shouted back. They screamed at one another as we sped along beside the main rail line to South Africa.

"Turn!"

The command was so peremptory, the driver swerved at once. The old Vauxhall rode up the steep gravel embankment and bounced onto the rails. Its wheels spun on the timber sleepers, then slid down the far side, spurting granite chips. The pursuing Citroen vanished for a moment as we clattered into the scrub, careening wildly, missing trees by inches. A cloud of dust rose up in our wake like a beacon.

"Holy Mary!" the man beside me shouted, clutching at the seat. He jerked his head round. "Here they come!"

I turned to see the Citroen flying over the raised tracks like a lean white eagle. It landed with a thump in the dust. Its rear swerved, turning full circle. Then it came at us, charging through the bush like a rhino.

Yellow Hacking Jacket was mumbling a prayer. He

crossed himself several times in quick succession. His eyes were frantic as the Citroen began to close in.

The driver discovered inspiration. He zipped the old car over the erratic terrain, sped through bushes, flipped round tree trunks, spun over boulders at sixty miles an hour. The ancient Vauxhall seemed to know we needed every last trick it had left. Its motor throbbed like a racing heart, putting an increasing gap between us and our hunter.

The Citroen was clumsier. It plowed down bushes, smashed into rocks, scraped a roadway through the dust. It had more power but less fleetness. Its driver was less inspired by fright than ours.

"Losing them!" my companion yelled gleefully. "Losing!"

"Shooting?" the driver screamed.

"Losing, man, losing!"

The Citroen dipped into a ditch we had avoided and vanished. It did not reappear.

"Lost!" shouted Yellow Hacking Jacket triumphantly.

All at once we were out of the bush among a tangle of rail lines in the shunting yards. The taxi wove through the tracks, cutting between parked engines, ignoring the yells of the railwaymen.

Then we were out into the light industrial area, not far from my father's factory. I had a glimpse of the Bulawayo Beauty Furniture Manufacturing Company Proprietary Limited as we sped along the Mafeking Road.

"*Zhii,*" my companion hissed in relief as the Vauxhall's pace eased. He took out a red-and-blue-spotted hankie and mopped his brow. "That was close, sir."

"Close," I agreed. My hand was shaking as I lit a cigarette. "But it seems they have our number, anyway."

"Oh," he shrugged, in command of himself again, "they know us well, those Specials. It's an old game. They chase us, we dodge." He frowned. "But why did they want to catch us today?"

"For me, perhaps?"

He scowled. "Perhaps."

"Then they know me."

"No. I don't think so. I think they saw a white man

getting into our car and they wanted to find out who he is."

"Perhaps. Where are we going?"

Yellow Hacking Jacket did not answer. He was too busy brushing down his smart outfit. He finished off his impromptu toilet by dusting his oxbloods with his hankie.

The taxi began to weave through the backroad ravines and bare-bouldered hills of the Matopos. We were in the Tribal Trust Lands, according to an occasional signpost. I saw a kraal in the distance, its mud-walled huts dusty as the earth from which they were made.

We rode up along the edge of a vast slope of grey granite. Above us puffy clouds were tinged yellow by the sinking sun. The Mercedes was parked at the peak of the rise, an immaculate black crow on the high horizon. Its dusky wings were free of dirt in this dusty land.

The Vauxhall stopped nose-to-nose with the Mercedes. Yellow Hacking Jacket got out and beckoned me to follow. A back door opened in the Mercedes and he pushed me into the limousine's dark womb.

I landed almost on Nkunzi's lap. The Leader grabbed my hand and squashed it between his broad plates of flesh. His face close to mine was a big black boulder.

*"Sakabona, Nyogamhlope!"* he said hoarsely. "Welcome!"

I edged back, pulling my squeezed hand free. "Afternoon, sir."

"How are you, my friend?"

"Surviving."

He chuckled. "That is much, in these times."

"Indeed."

As I got my breath back, I stole a quick look at Nkunzi's outfit. He wore a grey gaberdine shooting jacket with a black leather butt patch on the right shoulder. His double-knotted striped tie looked Old Etonian.

His sponge-rubber eyes were intent upon me. "So," he said, "we've given those chaps something to ponder, eh, White Snake?"

"I hope so."

My mind was racing now. Why had he summoned me? How would I tell him I wanted out? But The Bull seemed perfectly at ease. He was in no hurry. The Mercedes perched at the top of the world seemed to inhabit a space all its own.

We were alone. Yellow Hacking Jacket and the taxi driver had vanished. Nkunzi's own chauffeur, and any guards he might have brought along, were nowhere to be seen.

"Have a Montecristo?" he said, offering a leather cigar case.

"Thanks." I took the long cigar and sniffed it. "Real Cuban?"

"Compliments of Fidel Castro," he said gravely, snipping his Montecristo with a gold cutter.

I severed the tip of my cigar with his cutter. He flicked a fat silver lighter. We lit up. In a moment the limousine's interior was blue and rich with good cigar fumes.

"I love a good smoke," the big man said, rolling the tobacco tube round on his lips.

*"Viva la Revoluciòn,"* I murmured appreciatively.

*"Patria o muerte,"* he echoed. "Country or death."

"So the Cubans are in Matabeleland?"

He winked. "Can't you smell?"

"Nothing quite like the aroma of revolution, is there?" I said, falling into his jovially urbane manner.

"You're a good soldier," he said, abruptly severe. "The best."

I took a deep breath. "Sir — " I began.

He cut me off with a gesture. "But your service is done. You must vanish."

"Pardon?"

"Don't be upset. You've done your job. Now it's over. We've been tipped off that the authorities suspect you. We want no complications."

"Ah. Who tipped you off?"

"We have our connections. Call it the Methodist Mafia."

"You mean, a white?" I blurted.

"God binds all men of goodwill," Nkunzi said solemnly.

I stared at him. Could this be the hand of the "Grey Eminence" yet again?

"You've done your job," Nkunzi repeated. "Your arrest would be counter-productive. Surely, it would embarrass the government, but it would also embarrass certain very important allies in official circles." He tapped his nose shrewdly. "A word to the wise, eh?"

"I see. No more White Snake." Perversely, I was disappointed. Being *Nyogamhlope* had given me an identity. Now I was just me again, plain old Paul Kahn with all his ambiguities intact.

"In a sense," Nkunzi went on, "your actions were too perfect. You are *too* professional, Mr. Kahn. It's foreign to our style," he added, with an apologetic shrug. "We don't kill so efficiently as the white man."

"Oh."

Nkunzi leaned back in his corner. His big face was obscured behind a screen of blue smoke through which his cigar tip glowed like a red taillight.

"The European is the most efficient killer ever known," he murmured. "Look at the Nazis. Look at the H-bomb. Look at the last world war. Yes, the white man forfeited whatever moral authority he might have had when he began to slaughter his brothers by the millions in the 1940s. It was a barbarity on a scale no black man could even imagine. Mechanized war, then the gas ovens, then the atom bomb — murders by the million."

He punched a hole in the screen of smoke with his fist. "We saw that. It was the beginning of Africa's liberation. The European revealed himself as a naked fratricide. His magic was blown."

Nkunzi sat forward suddenly. I could feel the heat of his body beside me.

"A black man's bloodlust is hot and strong! But passing. We cannot plan mass murder, over years. We haven't the wit for it, or the stomach, or the heart. We are not efficient killers."

"Idi Amin seems to be doing okay," I murmured.

"Amin is a buffoon," he said curtly. "But he touches an African nerve. He embarrasses us, but we understand him. He needs to reverse the long humiliation of our race."

"So my efficiency embarrassed you?" I asked.

"Ah," Nkunzi sighed, and retreated back into his corner. Beyond this dark German womb Africa was all too bright. "We are grateful," he muttered, "but we are — uncomfortable. Anyway, you've made our point. We can hit the white man where he lives. Point taken. No need to rub it in."

"I don't think you quite grasp the intensity of Ian Smith's pigheadedness," I argued. " 'Never in my lifetime', he said at the Ministers' funeral."

Nkunzi chuckled. "That's an improvement over 'Never in a thousand years' which was his slogan a while ago."

"The Simple Farmer is a very stubborn man."

"He can't be that stupid. Surely he must know by now that, if he continues to refuse to compromise with us, he'll soon have to deal with the angry children who call me 'Uncle Tom'? The man must have begun to think?"

"Thinking is an un-Rhodesian activity, sir. This is Rip-van-Winkleland, after all."

"I am not as cynical as you are," Nkunzi said curtly. "I have faith in God and man."

"Well," I murmured, "maybe the Methodist Mafia is more powerful than I know."

"It always is. Faith is always more energetic than doubt."

"Ah, yes; but doubt is always more dogged than faith."

He scowled at me through the smoke. "I pity you, Paul Kahn. You have only yourself. That is not enough."

I changed the subject. It was getting late. The sun was below us now, a great orange ball dropping towards the dust.

"Maybe Ian Smith is doing you a favour? Nationhood is forged in struggle. It's not only power that grows out of the barrel of a gun. Identity blooms there, too."

Nkunzi was lost in his own thoughts. His opaque eyes were inward.

"What is the destiny of a truly African Africa?" he asked. "Once the obscenity of White Supremacy is removed, what have we here? Can there ever be a true Africanness in a land corrupted by the White Snake's deathliness? Hell, the European's technology itself is a form of desperation! Yet the black man needs these techniques, to feed himself, to grow. Can we take the white's amazing cleverness without his emptiness? The methods themselves are charged with ethic. They require a very particular type of soul to operate them successfully." He nodded grimly. "Yes, 'Methods Maketh Man.' 'The medium is the message.' A very great dilemma for our kind."

"For every kind."

He grunted. In that darkening, deep-buttoned chamber, marooned in the blank bush, we sat and mused, each one wrapped in his own black thoughts.

"Our people are changing," he said suddenly. "We are becoming urban. In a city it is a man's job that gives status. He breaks free from the entangling yet noble bonds of kinship and peer-group. Our youngsters relish this liberty. It breaks the old shell, cracks the egg of tradition. It's a man's talents that matter now, not whoever his father was. For Africa, it is already too late."

"Poor old Africa ... "

"Behind us lie the old traditions," Nkunzi growled on, "that the white man has tried so hard to convince us are 'primitive'. Certainly, they are unsuited to the modern world. Certainly they were more subtle than anything the modern world has to offer." He tossed his cigar butt out the window in a spasm of anger. "Those rituals transformed our fears into hopes. Damnitall, have you whites any idea how subtle our societies are?" he demanded. "You can't even grasp the distinction between the *nganga* and the *isangoma* — the 'witchdoctor' and the 'sorcerer'. What you call 'witchcraft' is, for us, a metaphor for Nature, an intimacy with Mlimu, the Creator. Sorcery is mere superstition. It cannot draw down the powers of Heaven as 'witchcraft' may. It is narrow, envious and mean. It is spells to injure an enemy or capture a lover. But all that is too subtle for a white mind!"

"What happens with this 'white mind'?" I asked gently.

His eyes focused on me sharply. "You must vanish."

"Into thin air?"

He grinned. "Are you that clever, *Nyogamhlope?*"

"I doubt it, *Induna,*" I smiled back.

"But you must vanish — and at once."

"My mother is very ill. She is dying."

"I'm sorry to hear that."

"My father needs me now."

"You should have thought of all this before you came to us," he said sternly. "Your life is no longer personal. You are a soldier. You must go when ordered. Imagine if the Specials get you! They would be merciless with a white traitor, and they are real brutes. Besides,'' he added, voice gentling, ''I had to leave my own mother, when they 'restricted' me. She died alone, without comfort.''

''I'm sorry. But yes, you're right. I'm no longer simply my own man, if I ever was.''

''Ah, but you are your own man, more than ever,'' Nkunzi said. ''You've jumped off the safe white raft into the great black sea. You've cut the cord of your tribe. You are completely alone.''

I grunted at this. It was like a fist in the gut. The cigar stub was burning my fingers. I tossed it out into the bush.

''We could start a fire with our Montecristos,'' Nkunzi smiled. He pulled something from his jacket pocket and laid it on my lap. It was a small black pistol.

''What's this for?''

''Can you shoot?''

''Yes. But I haven't used a gun in years. Why?''

''Just in case.'' His voice was flat, but the meaning was clear. I must not fall into the hands of the Specials.

''It'll take me a day or two to organize my vanishing. Will the weekend do?''

''Certainly. Saturday November the tenth is the eighth anniversary of U.D.I. — Rhodesia's illegal declaration of independence. Mr. Smith and his crew will be at the Liberty Ball, chiming the cracked midnight bell, while our White Snake slides away into the bush. Perfect!''

I slipped the small pistol into my pocket. ''Okay. That's it, then.''

Nkunzi put out his big hand. I took it. We shook solemnly.

''When Zimbabwe is ours, you may return, as a private citizen and an architect. You understand that we will never want to acknowledge your contribution to our *Chimurenga?* It must be a black struggle, entirely.''

''Of course. And it is. My *Chimurenga* was my own affair.''

''Naturally. *Hamba gahle, Nyogamhlope.* Take care. And remember always, Methods Maketh Man.'' The Old Bull's ironic chuckle followed me from the limousine as I departed.

## 19

# HIS OWN MAN

The silver snake was in the package Leonie handed me as I came in through the door of my father's house. Mona had returned it promptly. Her note was short and sweet, added as a footnote to mine: "Go bite yourself!"

There was also an official letter bearing the imprint of the Rhodesian Department of Defence. Inside was a standard notice requesting me to report for military service at the local recruitment centre within ten days, or face summary arrest and possible imprisonment.

"They've called me up," I told Leonie.

"So?" she shrugged. "Every male between the ages of seventeen and fifty-five is liable."

"But I've a British passport!"

"You were born here. You've come back to stay, you say. The army may do you good. You've never done anything in your life you didn't choose."

"True. But this has come too late. I have to leave."

"Leave? Oh no! Not when we need you? When Dad needs you, and Mom? You can't leave now!"

"I must. And soon. By the weekend, at the latest."

"Do you mind telling me why?"

I thought fast. I had not had time to decide what excuses I would make to my family for my abrupt departure. "Work," I said. "My office in London phoned me late last night. There's a crisis in a big project we're handling, in Venezuela. I have to get the plane from Jo'burg to London, then fly on to Caracas."

Leonie's narrowed eyes were disbelieving, but she shrugged resignedly. "We can never quite rely on you, can we, Paul? You're very much your own man, brother. Always have been, always will be. No point in trying to change you, is there?"

"Seems not." I put out my hand, but she ignored it. "Leonie, I'm sorry. What can I do?"

"What you've always done," she said curtly, and moved towards the front door. "Poor Dad," she said as she went out.

I felt like shit. "You're very much your own man .... You are your own man," Nkunzi had said. "You've cut the cord of your tribe .... You are completely alone."

Everyone, it seemed, was convinced of my-own-manness. Except me. I had yet to grasp it. But, standing there alone in my father's hallway, I sensed this understanding was upon me. I would know it soon.

The phone jangled suddenly. I answered.

It was Shaun. His voice was terse. "Paul. I must see you. Urgent personal matter."

"Yours or mine?" I queried, equally clipped.

"Both," he said. "You'll come to my ranch. Saturday morning. Pick you up at ten."

It was an order.

"Look, I have to fly out on Saturday. To Jo'burg and London. Urgent personal matter of my own."

"You can't," he said curtly. "They won't let you."

"Pardon? Who won't let — ?"

"Special Branch."

"Oh."

I tried to take this in, but it would not penetrate.

"My ranch is on the Botswana border," Shaun said.

"Ah."

"Saturday morning. Ten o'clock," Shaun repeated, and rang off.

I put down the receiver. Things were happening fast. "My ranch is on the Botswana border" ... "The Special Branch won't let you" ... "Report within ten days ... or face summary arrest and possible imprisonment."

My father came out of the bathroom fastening his belt. "Had a good opening," he announced. "My tummy's happy."

"Dad, I have to leave Rhodesia."

It was blunt, but I could think of no gentler way of telling him.

He blinked, but did not seem overly surprised. "When?"

"Saturday morning. I have to go to Jo'burg, then London. Shaun Connaughton is driving me down south. It's to do with work."

I could see from his expression that he neither believed or disbelieved me. I was going — that was the point.

"Mom will miss you. Me too."

"I'm sorry." It came out very lame.

"You're your own man. I never thought Bulawayo would hold you for long. It's been wonderful having you."

"Dad — " My throat was choked. "Wonderful having you." How adroitly he rearranged facts to make a pretty picture!

"I mean that," he said, understanding me well. "Your mother may not be alive when you return — if you return. She's dying, you know."

"Yes."

"She's so brave."

"Yes. Dad — I'm sorry. Truly."

"So am I," he said. "Let's have supper. I'm peckish."

We were about to go through to the kitchen when the doorbell rang. My father frowned. "Who's that calling? At this time of night?"

It was barely seven o'clock, but that was close to the old man's bedtime, as his family and friends all knew.

I opened the front door. Two uniformed police officers stood there; a captain and a constable.

"Mr. Kahn," the captain said. "Remember me? Captain Williamson, of the Special Branch, and this is Constable Fourie. May we come in?"

I stood back to let the policemen enter. When my father saw the uniforms his eyes dilated in shock and he instinctively protected his stomach.

"My father," I introduced. "Captain Williamson, and Constable — ?"

"Fourie."

The Afrikaner constable looked familiar. Then I remembered: this man had arrested Tenja.

"Ah," I said, "Fourie, L.S., Number 2491."

The policeman bared his teeth in a grin. "Mr. Kahn. We meet again."

"Indeed. Sit down, gentlemen."

I showed them through to the living room. My father took a step backwards. "I'll leave you to it," he mumbled, and hurried out.

The captain did not sit down at once. He wandered round the living room, sniffing out the scene. He paused at the display of my accomplishments on the mantlepiece — the photos and the framed diplomas.

"Parkview Junior Tennis Champion, eh?" he murmured. "And a King Scout, to boot." He turned to me. "You were a true Rhodesian, once, Mr. Kahn." His thorny Adam's apple jerked with derision.

"Still am," I retorted. "Please sit down."

The policemen sat — Williamson at his ease, Fourie on the edge of his seat. The constable took out the inevitable black police notebook from his top tunic pocket.

"So, you still consider yourself a loyal Rhodesian?" the captain murmured, almost dreamily. "That is interesting. Very."

"Have you come to talk about Tshabalala?" I reached into my jacket pocket for cigarettes and got a shock. The gun! It's small L-shape was nestled down behind the pack of smokes. If I took out the cigarettes, its bulge would show plainly through the thin cotton pocket. I decided not to smoke.

"Smoke, if you wish," Williamson said courteously, acting the host in my house.

"No, thanks."

"Dreadful habit," the captain agreed. "Mr. Kahn, perhaps you wouldn't mind telling us where you travelled to in a Vauxhall taxi, licence number — ?"

"B5437," the constable supplied, "at approximately four-fourty this afternoon?"

"To the Matopos," I said at once. It was as well to tell some of the truth, at least.

"I see." The policeman nodded, pleased at my frankness. "For what purpose, may I ask."

"Pleasure."

"I beg your pardon?"

"I went to see the grave of Cecil Rhodes."

The captain stared at me. His Adam's apple made jagged jumps. "Do you often visit The Founder's tomb?" he asked evenly.

"Not often."

"Why today, may I ask?"

I shrugged. "I needed a bit of air. It seemed like a good idea."

"Your companion was an African?"

"Yes."

"Mind giving us his name?"

I hesitated. Fourie's pen was poised over his pad. The captain noticed my caution. "His name?" he repeated firmly.

"Maxwell Shongololo." It was an inspiration. *Shongololo* means "millipede" in Ndebele. "S-H-O-N-G-O-L-O-L-O," I spelled it out. The captain blinked. Fourie, the Afrikaner, solemnly wrote it down.

"Mm," Williamson humphed. "Is this, er, Maxwell Shongololo a good friend of yours?"

"Oh, I've known him for years," I rattled on blithely. "He's the son of an old family servant. I knew him as a boy. He heard I was in town and contacted me. We had a chat about old times."

Fourie was scribbling busily. His ballpen squeaked like a mouse. Under his hard-peaked cap his country boy's face was earnest. He bit his lip with his straight white teeth as he strove for absolute accuracy.

"What would you say, sir," the captain said, "if I told you this man was known to us under a different identity? If I told you he was an active member of the ZAPU military organization? In short, a terrorist."

"You can't be serious!" I exclaimed.

"Come, Mr. Kahn, why do you think the taxi you were travelling in went to such lengths to avoid pursuit?"

"The driver was terrified of getting a speeding ticket," I invented promptly. "Seems he's committed several traffic offences. He was afraid of losing his licence."

Williamson laughed outright. "Are you trying to tell me he was so scared of a speeding ticket he all but ruined his own taxi, and wrecked a police Citroen into the bargain?!"

"The Citroen was wrecked, eh?"

"A write-off," the captain said sourly. "Mr. Kahn — "

"That's all I can tell you," I retorted, to cut the comedy short.

What, exactly, did this policeman know? Was he playing games with me? Had he really only come here because I had been seen getting into the yellow taxi?

My mind was racing. I was dying for a smoke. My mouth was hot with nicotine lust. It was torture.

Williamson was watching me. His blue-grey eyes were intent upon my face. He said quietly: "Mr. Kahn, your father is a well-known, well-liked, and very loyal Rhodesian. I'm sure you would not like to cause him any distress."

He rose suddenly. The constable was taken by surprise. He dropped his pen and had to fumble for it, then scurry after his superior towards the front door.

I saw the policemen out. On the threshold, Williamson paused. "You will do us the courtesy of not leaving the town without informing us, sir," he said.

"I'm going to a friend's ranch for the weekend."

"Who is the friend?"

"Shaun Connaughton. He has a ranch near Plumtree."

"Ah. Yes. Excelsior Ranch, on the Botswana border."

"Correct."

"Major Connaughton is a fine man," the captain conceded. "A loyal Rhodesian and an excellent officer."

"And a good architect," I added.

The throat-thorn jerked at me. "Indeed. We'll be in touch. Goodnight."

"*Totsiens*," Fourie added, narrowing his Boer eyes at me.

"*Totsiens*," I echoed. "*Au revoir.*"

The policemen went down the driveway and got into a white Citroen DS. It vanished into the night like a squat pale toad as I sucked at my long-lusted-for smoke. Then, transferring the pistol to my back trouser pocket, I went in to comfort my father. He was sitting at the kitchen table, hunched over a half-eaten "doorstep" sandwich of cold beef and lettuce. His face looked sick.

"Policemen — in my house?" he wailed.

"Nothing serious." Standing over him, I stroked his

silver head. Tenderness flushed me. He was so worried! Worried for himself, worried for me, worried about everything.

"Nothing serious," I repeated.

His head stiffened under my soothing hand. He did not believe me. I had brought the police into his house. "Tricky Joe" Kahn had an atavistic fear of men in uniform. The descendant of ghetto Jews, he was terrified of the "cossacks." In his whole life he had never even exceeded a speed limit.

"I'm leaving, Dad."

"Yes!" It was a gasp of relief as much as anguish.

"Saturday morning."

"Yes."

I left him alone with his thoughts.

*"Baruch atah adenai Elohenu melech ha'olam ... "*

Leonie mumbled her way through the Friday evening prayer for blessing the Sabbath lights. Her hands wavered over the candles. Her eyes were shut tight. At the conclusion of the incantation she touched her fingertips to her lids, then immediately yelled for Ray.

The houseboy ran in with the food trolley. The children screamed at one another, tussling for favourite seats next to Grandpa. My father forked up a chunk of soupmeat and smeared it with horseradish sauce. David bellowed for silence and was ignored. Beside me, Snuggums buried her muzzle in a dish of boiled beef. The bitch had been allowed to sit at the table for the whole meal in honour of my departure.

"Hey, kids!" Leonie shouted, cutting through the uproar. "This is your Uncle Paul's last night. Can't you behave yourselves, just for once?"

Louie stopped taunting his sister. His grey eyes turned to me. They were clouded. "Are you really leaving, Uncle Paul?"

"I have to, Nephew Louie."

" 'Nephew Louie'!" Eric exploded. "Oh, Uncle, you say such funny things!"

"Don't be stupid," Lawlene snapped. "What's funny about that?"

Eric was confused. My gnomic retort had always been funny before. He chomped on his drumstick.

Louie's gaze wavered over my face. It was charged with a baffled accusation. Why was I deserting him? It was bad of me.

Leonie intervened, sensitive to her son's distress. "Paul has to leave, Lou. He has work to do. Besides, he is his own man. Understand?"

The boy did not want to understand. There was no comfort in it. He chewed his chicken grumpily.

My father spoke up. "Your Uncle Paul is a very important man. Many people need him. We can't be selfish."

Louie shrugged. We finished our meal in relative silence.

I made my farewells in the driveway. David, Eric, and Louie shook my hand. Lawlene and Leonie hugged me. Snuggums licked my shoes.

"Remember us," Leonie said, as she released me from her large embrace. "Eh, brother?"

"Oh, sis, how could I forget you?" I smiled.

"Easily," Leonie retorted, and turned her face away from my last kiss.

My father and I got into the Toyota. As we were driving away, I had a last view of the Mandel family bunched together under the porch light. The lamp was reflected like a moon in the dark blue glistening of the pool.

# 20

# GO BITE YOURSELF

**M**y father slept late the next morning. This was unusual, but I understood it. He wanted to diminish the time spent on our last breakfast. I packed quietly, tiptoeing about so as not to wake him from his uneasy dreams. It did not take long; I always travelled light. One medium-sized bag was all I ever needed.

The outfit I chose for travelling was the one I had worn on Bomb Day: white denim slacks, the oversized safari jacket, a paisely Indian scarf and the electronic necklace. I slipped the small black pistol, a Walther 6.35 mm, into one of the capacious tunic pockets.

My mother was asleep when I went in to see her. Josephine sat upright on the bedside chair gripping the old woman's hand. She blinked at me wearily, as if to acknowledge that we had lost the struggle for the invalid's survival.

In the past few days my mother had taken little nourishment. She had not spoken a word. Her breathing was choked and shallow. Her temples were hollowing out. And now I was removing my will and my strength from the fight. Josephine's face was stark with resignation. Nurses always lose, her black eyes seemed to say; it's in the nature of things. But she would never learn to like it.

There was a letter for me in the early morning post. I read it as I had my toast and coffee. It was from the South African Housing Ministry. They replied to my rejection of their offer of a consultancy by upping the ante. The Minister guaranteed a fat fee and a free hand if I would "do us the courtesy of giving our Department the benefit of your wide experience in the field of mass housing." Their appreciation would be "boundless".

Their problems were "of the utmost urgency," the Minister wrote. I had been "more than highly recommended both by local experts and by Mr. Theodore Theophilus." Would I please respond as soon as possible, "bearing in mind the gravity of the matter."

I sipped my coffee and reread the letter several times. Of course, I must again reject the offer. Yet, as I stared at the typed sheet of heavy embossed paper, I felt a prickle of pure design lust, a tremor of excitement at the prospect of working, of imagining lucid solutions to complex problems, of moving awkward shapes around in my head till they began to lock in a jigsaw of meaning and order. I felt rather as a monk must feel at the surge of a diabolical randiness after a long night of self-denial.

This was what I was made for — to dream up mud Jerusalems. The urge was all there, real as an ache in the loins. I stuffed the letter in my tunic pocket, beside the pistol, and tried to put it out of my mind. This was not the moment to think about it too much.

My father came into the kitchen just after nine. He looked haggard. The spaniel folds over his eyes were so droopy he seemed like a sleepwalker.

We drank our coffee in silence. Susan, the housegirl, refilled our cups regularly, without having to be asked. Her loose cotton print could not obscure the voluptuousness of her young black body. She oozed life and sex and youth. Our white dramas were remote to her. They happened on another planet.

My father began to speak suddenly, articulating scraps of the complexities in his tousled head.

"My father was a cruel man!" he burst out. He blinked, bemused by his own ferocity. "He treated me badly," he mumbled. "I never loved him." He hunched his neck apologetically. "He was of the Old School, you see. Fathers, then, didn't try to love or be loved. That was for mothers."

I kept silent. He had to get this out. My role was to listen.

"Until I married, at thirty, I gave him all my wages. He handed me back half-a-crown a week, for pocket money. Out of which fortune I was supposed to stand my two sisters, your Aunties, to the bioscope. But he was never loving. Never — "

My father rubbed his eyes. His pajamas smelled of sleep.

"You have to understand, Grandpa Kahn remembered pogroms. He told me once — on a rare occasion he actually talked to me — how his whole family had hidden in his Grandfather's flour bins while the Ukranians were slaughtering Jews. 'I came out white as a ghost,' he said. There was Jewish blood on the cobbles. Russia was a cruel world, for our kind." He raised his head and looked me in the eye for the first time that morning. "My father was a cruel man. He didn't try to love or be loved."

I reached out and touched his cheek. "I'm very fond of you, Dad."

He let me stroke his grizzled face without recoiling. His brown pupils, ringed with yellow, were sad as a dog's.

Shaun's horn hooted in the driveway promptly at ten. I carried my bag to the front door, signalled that I would be out in a moment, and went back in to say my goodbyes.

My mother was still comatose. I bent over to kiss her brow. It was hot and dry. It smelled of death.

"Bye, Brave Soldier," I murmured. There was no response. Not even her eyelids flickered as I drew away.

"Did she say anything?" my father asked urgently as I came out of the sickroom

"Nothing."

"She's so brave."

"Yes."

He accompanied me to the front door. We embraced awkwardly. He patted my back as if he were burping me. "Keep well, my boy."

"You, too, Dad."

"Write."

"Yes."

I picked up my bag and walked away. As I got into the Citroen I looked round and saw that the front door was shut.

Shaun merely grunted in answer to my greeting. He put the white car in reverse and we backed out of my father's driveway.

There was another white Citroen parked across the road, under a jacaranda tree. It had been there some time, judging from the sprinkle of light purple blossoms on its bonnet. In passing I caught a glimpse of Constable Fourie's tense pale face through the windscreen.

The police car followed us out of town for a few miles, then turned off. Presumably, the Specials were then satisfied that we really were on our way to Shaun's ranch.

Shaun drove fast. The Citroen's speedometer edged over the eighty-mile-an-hour mark, a dangerous speed on the narrow tarmac of the Mafeking Road. But there was little traffic, apart from a few Africans on cycles. The strip was clear.

In the car the silence was intense. Shaun said nothing; neither did I. I wondered how he had suddenly come to know that I was suspected of treachery. Had his friend, the colonel in charge of the Central Police Station, tipped him off? Had Captain Williamson? Or the "Grey Eminence" via Georgina?

Certainly, from the grim thrust of his jaw, there was no doubt. A part of him had always suspected me of something tricky. I was too clever; I was a Jew; I was never quite Rhodesian — now it had all been confirmed. I was even more treacherous than he ever could have imagined.

This was painful, I could see. It was anguishing. After all, he loved me. I was, he had thought, "ripe for redemption." He must feel very foolish. He must feel sick.

I felt for him, but there was really nothing I could say. Silence was the only soother. He had to work out his own pain.

We hurtled towards Botswana. Just before Plumtree, we turned off along the dirt track to Excelsior Ranch. The tin-roofed shack came up out of the desolate bush.

Wantenaar, Shaun's foreman, was on the veranda. Jannie, the nightape, peeped out of his shirt at his navel.

The Boer ignored me, as if he intuited at once that I was in disgrace. But the little galago cheeped in welcome and extended a tiny humanoid hand.

"Hi, Jannie," I murmured, putting out a finger to the big-eyed beast. Quick as a flash, the nightape sank its needle canines in my knuckle. "Ouch!" I shrieked.

My pain made the Afrikaner grin. "Jannie hates strangers," he said cheerfully. He looked at my punctured knuckle. "Better smear ointment," he said, still smirking. "Could turn septic. The beast has a dirty mouth."

We went indoors. In the bright light of day, the shack's one room looked even rougher than by night. Shaun dumped his bag on the pine table and took out a bottle of Irish whisky.

"Here," he said, gesturing curtly, "this'll cleanse it." He unscrewed the cap and poured liquor over my hand.

It stung. I winced. Wantenaar laughed. "Hurts, hey? You might even get tetanus," he promised.

"Get the first-aid kit," Shaun barked. The foreman brought the battered medical tin and Shaun took out a disposable hypodermic, yanked up my jacket sleeve, and jabbed the needle into my forearm. "Piss off, Joel," he said. The foreman jerked down his soiled wide bush hat and left.

We had a lunch of bread, bully beef and whisky. Outside the sun was high in the sky, baking the veld, but the shack's interior was cool. The tin roof cracked as it expanded in the heat.

"You saved my life, at Tshabalala," Shaun said suddenly. "I owe you one." His eyes had lost their clear green glow. They were dark with rage.

"Okay."

"Tomorrow we'll slip you over the border, into Botswana. It's across the Maitengwe River, at the bottom of my property. The ditch is dry this year. No rains here. Then you're on your own."

"Where's the nearest border town?" I asked, keeping my voice as flat and hard as his.

"No town, just a kraal, ten miles due south. There's a police post there. Tell them you're a Freedom Fighter. They'll love you."

"Fine."

"I'll fit you out with a canteen and some sandwiches. And a knife, but no gun."

"Fine."

He rose. A crack of sunlight from the door split his cheek. "I've got work to do, with the cattle. Amuse yourself." He strode out.

There was a general store a few miles back down the road I had noticed as we drove by. I decided to walk there to buy a few extra provisions for tomorrow's trudge into Botswana.

My injured knuckle gave off a dull ache as I walked along the dusty road. The punctures looked clean, a ring of neat little holes round the bump at the base of my right forefinger. The finger was stiffening a little. I waggled it, to keep it supple. It was my trigger finger.

To distract my thoughts, I pressed the knob of the breastplate of my electronic necklace. The radio crackled. The reception was bad at this distance from the African station in Bulawayo, but a tinny whistling came through. It was not rings-on-the-fingers and bells-on-the-toes, but it was music of a kind in the wide and empty bush.

The general store stood back from the main road. An ancient hand-operated gas pump guarded its battered veranda. A crowd of young blacks in tattered khakis squatted there, chattering as they passed round roll-ups of cheap tobacco in newspaper.

They fell silent as I mounted the rickety steps. A dozen pairs of dark eyes watched my shoes cross the creaking boards. Soon as I had passed by, their voices broke out like birds in an interrupted dawn chorus.

The interior of the shop was dark, dusty and musty. The plank shelves were jammed with tin cans of every label. Open sacks of meal, flour, sugar and kaffir rusks made an obstacle course between door and counter.

The Hindu shopkeeper was tiny in his spotless white dhoti. He bowed to me as if I were royalty. "What can I be doing for you, sir?"

"I'd like some Elastoplast, some plain chocolate, five packs of Gold Leaf, and a bottle of iodine, please."

The little man ran about collecting my items like a squirrel. I also bought a cheap rucksack to repack my clothes into for the walk across the border, and a khaki bush hat to protect my head from the sun. I felt a little like a Boy Scout preparing for a trek. This thought reminded me I would need a compass, which the shopkeeper found somewhere under his cluttered counter.

I stuck a bandaid on my knuckle, which was throbbing. The Hindu noticed me wince, and clucked sympathetically. He brought me some balm in a gaudy orange packet with Hindi lettering. "Put in hot water, sir. Then stick in finger, so. In the morning, lovely!" I thanked him.

On the spur of the moment, I bought half-a-dozen tins of canned fruit. I gave these to the young Africans on the veranda. They could not believe their good luck. Then the pocket blades flashed and thick syrup gurgled down dusty throats through yelps of joy.

The walk back seemed longer. The afternoon heat was so harsh I had to take shelter in patches of acacia shade. Sweat darkened my T-shirt and stuck my pants to my thighs. My throat was dry as dust, but fortunately I had also picked up a few oranges from the store. Their sweet juice was ambrosia in my gullet.

I shared one shadow with three kaffir cows and a dozing herdboy who wore nothing but a faded drawstring tobacco bag on his loins. The cattle's ribs stuck out through mangy hides like the skeletons of shipwrecks. The cows' eyes, and the boy's, were pussed with flybites. Other flies crawled over the sleeping herdboy's swollen lips. I left a slab of melting chocolate in the sand beside him before I walked on.

Back in the shack I brewed myself some tea on the primus and repacked my gear. Most of my clothes fitted in the rucksack. Those that did not, I abandoned.

I wrapped the chocolate bars in tinfoil to keep them from melting further. I put the compass and two packs of cigarettes in the pockets of my safari jacket. They balanced the weight of the pistol, which I took out and checked. There were six rounds in the clip. The gun was well greased, the safety worked smoothly. I hoped I would never have to use it, but it was just as well to be sure of one's weapon.

At twilight a gentle dusky breeze began to air the shack. The flies stirred and started to bite. I bathed my knuckle in the Hindu balm, as instructed. The ache seeped out of my bones into the soothing potion.

Shaun came in around six. He went to the sink without a word and washed his face in cold water, then towelled it roughly. He poured himself a slug of whisky and drank it at a gulp. His eyes seemed lighter. The afternoon spent with his Brahmins had eased his tension. I lay on the bunk and smoked. It was almost companionable.

A delicious aroma of roasting meat seeped into the shack. I salivated with hunger, and went outside to investigate. Wantenaar was squatting beside a fire. Two skinned bushrabbits were skewered over the flames, glossy with fat. He grunted as I came up. "Food. Better than bully beef. For the boss."

I squatted down beside him and offered a Gold Leaf. Sweet potatoes were packed round the edge of the coals. I had never felt so ravenous.

It was dark, now. The sky and the bush were black. The fire's low flame was the only light in the world. Shaun had not yet bothered to turn on the pressure lamps in the shack. He was too engrossed in boozing.

"Where's Jannie?" I asked.

"In his cage, in my *pondok'*," the Boer said, jerking a thumb into the darkness. "He hates fire."

"Jannie's a great hater," I smiled.

The foreman cracked a grin of pure pleasure. "*Ja*. He loves to hate, that *ou*." He nodded, as if this were a profound insight. "He jus' loves to hate, you know?"

"I know."

The Boer squinted at me. He was without his hat and his brow was dead white above the brim line, dark red below. "Yeah. You look like you do." He rose. "The rabbits are cooked. Let's skoff."

The roasted rabbit was scrumptious. Its firm, juicy meat tasted of all the herbs and grass the animal had consumed till Wantenaar's shotgun had ended its roaming. Even Shaun ate heartily. His cheeks were lean and sculptured in the blue glow of the pressure lamps. He never looked at me once. His eyes were blinkered.

We wiped our plates clean with bread. "*Ag*, man," Wantenaar said, leaning back and patting his stomach, "that was good, hey?" He winked at me. "Better than bully beef, any day."

Shaun filled our glasses with whisky and we got down to an evening of serious drinking. It was silent. The three of us sat round the table and watched the level of whisky drop steadily in the bottle as if it were an hourglass.

Shaun had his elbows on the table. His profile jutted like a prow. As the hours passed it grew sharper and sharper, slicing through an unseen sea.

Wantenaar lolled in his chair. His sun-darkened face seemed to end at the hat-line, just above his brows, as if the top of his head had been cut off. His stillness was serene; contained yet watchful.

I leant back in my seat, legs crossed, at an angle to the pine table facing Shaun. I, too, was watchful.

The blankness of the dark bush surrounding us was absolute. The occasional shriek of animals hunting or hunted only emphasized its desolation. Silence within; silence without. Our three-man tableau was eternal.

*"Why?"*

The shriek ripped the stillness. My blood froze.

It was Shaun.

His face was aimed at me. His eyes were black bullets. I did not flinch. I did not answer. He needed no reply, not from me.

But the gut cry seemed to have released him. His neck eased a fraction. His jaw drooped. "What do they call you?" he muttered. "Your terr mates."

*"Nyogamhlope."*

"White Snake?" He blinked at me. "White Snake!" He released a rip of laughter. "Ho! Go bite yourself!" He punched my necklace; static exploded the silence.

"I have." I switched it off.

"Ha."

He refilled his tumbler. The bottle was almost dry. The silence resumed.

Wantenaar leant forward some time later and clicked on the small portable radio on the table. "Independence Bell," he grunted. "Salisbury. Midnight."

The voice of the master of ceremonies burst through the static: "And now for the crowning moment of this brilliant occasion! Our Prime Minister, the Honourable Ian Smith, will toll the Liberty Bell . . . . he's grasping the rope, beaming with pride . . . he tugs — wait for it! Another heave — "

*Bong! Bong! Bong!*

The cheering was tumultuous. A thousand throats sang

an ecstatic "Ode to Joy": "Rise, O voices of Rhodesia — "

"Eight years of independence!" the M.C. shouted above the uproar. "Eight years of freedom!"

Shaun snapped off the radio. He rose abruptly. "Let's hunt," he said.

"Hunt?" Wantenaar protested. "It's after midnight, man! And there are leopards out there. Some of the *munts* have lost cattle — "

"Hunt," Shaun repeated. He was looking at me.

I stood up. I owed him this, whatever it was. My knees were uncertain, my head was awash with booze, but I was beyond fatigue. This was a night for hunting.

Wantenaar looked on with a derisive grin as we pulled on sweaters and boots. I wore my safari jacket over the sweater.

"Take that bloody silly thing off your neck," Shaun barked, jabbing at my necklace radio.

"No," I retorted. "It's mine."

"Have it your own way. Here, you carry the game bag."

He tossed me an army knapsack rusty with dried blood. He strapped a hunting torch to his forehead like a third eye. He worked the bolt of a .303 rifle.

"Hey, boss, you're not taking that old lion gun?" Wantenaar said. "Blow the head off a springbok, one of those shells!"

Shaun ignored the Boer. He filled the pockets of his windcheater with rounds. The ammunition bulged there like stones.

He strode towards the door. "Let's hunt, *Nyogamhlope*," he said curtly, and stepped out into the dark.

It was, by contrast, pitch-black in the bush. My boots stumbled over stumps, my head was confused by the darkness and the whisky. I followed Shaun blindly.

Gradually, my eyes adjusted, my mind cleared. The chill air refreshed me. It was a splash of cold water in my face.

The veld became luminous under a glitter of stars polished by a high wind. It was a nightscape of ashes.

We trudged on for miles. I kept direction by the Southern Cross, that heavenly crucifix. We were heading south-west, towards Botswana.

Occasionally a nightbird screamed; owl or hawk. A rabbit shrieked as sharp claws punctured fur and flesh. There was a whistle of great wings overhead as a dark shape swooped. I felt the brush of its wind on my cheek.

Shaun marched forward lightly. His back was hunched in a hunter's crouch, ready for action in a split second. The heavy rifle was balanced in his right hand like a club.

On and on. I saw several pairs of eyes in the black bush that could have been springbok or kudu. Shaun, it seemed, was not interested in deer. He was searching for bigger game. But leopards hid in trees, and there weren't many in this desolation, only stunted acacias too small for a big predator's body. And lions were a rarity in Matabeleland.

All at once I realized I was alone. Shaun had vanished.

Between one blink and another, that solid shape ahead of me had melted into the blackness.

I stopped dead. My nape prickled. "Shaun?" I hissed.

The answer was a bullet. It zinged by my ear like a hornet.

"Shit!" I cursed, and flung myself to the earth.

Not a fraction too soon. The second shot passed a few feet over my buried skull, just where my belly had been. The .303 projectile punched a hole in the night.

I dug myself deeper into the dirt, tasting dust. My saliva was clotted with it. It was mud in my mouth.

A light clicked on. The beam of the hunting lamp swept the bush in an arc over my head. Out of my one unburied eye I saw it probe towards me greedily.

*"Nyogamhlope?"*

Shaun's whisper came out of the night. It was searching, almost tender; a lover's coo. I was the hunted and he the hunter. We had a bond of blood.

Very stealthily, I eased the Walther from my pocket. It felt tiny in my fist — a toy. I knew it had little accuracy or stopping power over more than twenty yards or so. Ten yards would be safer. I primed the pistol gingerly and lay still as a corpse.

Shaun chuckled indulgently in the dark. I could place him by the beam from his head lamp. "White Snake? Lying low, eh? I'll get you, never fear, little serpent."

He began to walk towards me. The beam approached. He did not know I was armed. This White Snake was toothless, so far as he knew.

I would have to stop him. It was him or me. Perhaps I could get him through the shoulder, disable his shooting arm? But that was a long shot, in the dark. If necessary, I would have to kill.

He was out for the kill. His voice was harsh with mockery as he sang out: *"Nyogamhlope?* Let's have you, brother. Let's see the white of your snaky eyes."

Shaun was coming on. He was no more than thirty yards off, I guessed. I eased my cheek up slightly and slid my elbows under my shoulders. Resting evenly, I gripped the automatic with both fists and sighted along the weapon's snout.

I took aim at a point about a foot and a half below the Cyclops eye of the head lamp, where I estimated his breastbone would be. It was too risky to shoot for the shoulder. The shot might fly wide, and then he'd have me. He was a skilled and experienced bush fighter, used to zapping guerrillas who sprang up out of the grass. He would not give me time for a second shot.

The beam would soon pick me out against the black bush in my white safari jacket. I snuggled into the dirt, trying to get as much cover as possible. The earth was warm, still giving back stored sun heat. Its embrace was musty and sexual.

Suddenly, there was a crackle under my chest. Static blared from my breastplate radio.

The oncoming light stopped dead. I heard Shaun's amazed curse over the buzzing beneath me. I could almost feel the snout of his rifle sniffing me out.

I took aim. Just then, the beam flicked out. I blinked as I fired.

His grunt was a very small explosion of air under the radio's racket. I reached under my chest and fumbled for the breastplate knob. The radio clicked off.

A silence. My eyes began to pick out his shape standing a dozen yards distant. It seemed statuesque and still.

"Shaun?" I hissed. "You okay?"

The rifle dropped from his hands. It landed in the dust

with a soft thud. Then, very slowly, he bent forward, clutching his middle.

"My tummy — " he mumbled, and sagged to his knees.

I scrambled up out of the earth and ran to him. "Shaun — "

He raised his bowed head as I stumbled up to him. His eyes were green and innocent. "You had a gun?" he murmured.

It was a reproach. Once again, I had not played fair.

I touched his tousled head. "Where are you hurt, mate? In the gut?"

"Yeah," he grunted. "Gut shot. You bastard."

"Can you walk? Or shall I go back to the shack to get help?"

For answer, he fell flat on his face in the dust. I knelt down beside him. He was out cold. I put down my pistol and eased him over on his side and unzipped his windcheater to examine his wound.

His khaki shirt was black with blood. The blood had mingled with the dust to make a sticky mud. The wound would soon turn septic if it wasn't cleaned, but I had no means to do that. All I could do was stuff my wadded handkerchief between his shirt and his skin. I made a pillow for his head out of the folded game bag.

"Shaun," I whispered, hoping he would hear. "You stay put. I'll fetch the car. When you hear me coming, turn on your head lamp to guide me. Keep your rifle handy, just in case."

I put the .303 near his outstretched hand. He did not move.

Where, exactly, was I? The small compass was in my pocket. I tried to get a fix from the stars. It was very hazy, but it was the best I could do. It was a long time since I had been a King Scout.

Shaun was bleeding badly. I had to get help soon. I turned away and began to walk north-east, reversing the direction from which we had come. The Southern Cross was my guide through the night.

*Zinggg!*

The bullet brushed my thigh. It tugged at my slacks like sharp teeth.

*Zinggg!*

The second shot would have killed me if I hadn't swerved. I swivelled and saw Shaun up on one elbow taking aim. His cheek was married to the rifle butt. The gun was the tongue of a striking cobra.

The pistol was in my fist. I had picked it up out of the dirt as I had walked away. It jerked up and fired.

*Phuttt.*

It was a soft pop after the rifle's roar. Shaun fell over into the dust.

I straightened. Shaun's body was lifeless. It was a carcass.

I turned away from the corpse and walked south, following the sword of the Southern Cross towards Botswana. In my mouth was the taste of mud.